THE MAN AT THE TABLE

By Richard Scott

Winter Island Press
Salem, Massachusetts

The Man at the Table

Copyright © 2024 by Richard Scott

All rights reserved. No part of this book may be reproduced or transmitted in any form or by any means, graphic, electronic or mechanical, including photocopying, recording, scanning or by any other information storage and retrieval system, without permission in writing from the author: rtscott22@gmail.com.

ISBN 9798875805738

This is a work of fiction. Names and incidents are a product of the author's imagination. Any resemblance to actual events or people, living or dead, is also a product of the author's imagination.

Ms Doris Rogers
103 Brooksby Village Dr Unit 116
Peabody, MA 01960-1464

Special thanks to Kim Scott and Judy Palmer for reading my manuscript and providing me with many helpful suggestions.

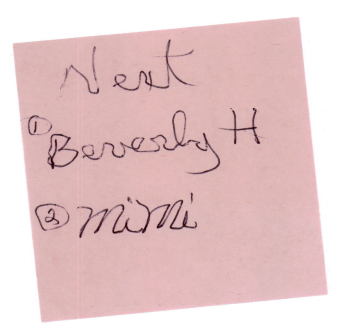

If you like
The Man at the Table
You might also like the following novels by Richard Scott.
(Available in Kindle and Paperback from Amazon.)

Time Travel Trilogy
Mission in Time
The Second Mission
The Third Mission

Tony Dantry Thrillers
The Reluctant Assassin
The Eager Assassin
The Assassin Chip
Assassin on Main Street
Revenge of the Rising Sun
2024   (A political novel)

Other books by Richard Scott
Salem, the Novel
Jefferson and the Barbary Pirates
Murder on Third Avenue
The Rail Trail Murders

Children's Book
Magic Bird

THE MAN AT THE TABLE

Prologue

Buchenwald Concentration Camp 1944

It is February and the camp is numbingly cold. Only the prisoners who were brought to camp in the winter had coats of any kind. Those coats are now ragged as they wear them day and night. There is no heat in the barracks or anywhere else during their day.

This morning, like every other morning in the camp, the prisoners are awakened at 4 AM. It is still dark, and the day promises to be a repeat of yesterday. Gray, damp and cold. There is nothing to look forward to except gnawing hunger, grim discomfort and the possibility of abuse. In the back of the minds of the prisoners there is always a grain of faint hope. Hope for survival. Optimists hope that somehow this will all come to an end soon. Either the war will end, or the Allies will liberate them. Pessimists just pray it will end one way or the other. For many, death would be better than more years of this misery. The worst of the miserable discomfort is seeing your loved ones suffer. As the days and months go on the number of pessimists grows.

Gisela and Helga's parents struggle to get up. The two sisters are already awake. Gisela is 11 years old. Her sister Helga is 13. The girls love each other dearly but are totally different. Gisela has always avoided discord and contention. She usually goes along with suggestions made by other people. Helga, however, is headstrong. She has a mind of her own and everyone in the family knows it. All four members of this tight family quickly search for their shoes. Without their shoes they can't work. This sometimes means death.

Each family member then has to make their straw-mattress bed with its one ratty blanket in a perfect military manner. This is almost impossible to do with the shapeless piles of straw they're using as mattresses. Occasionally, if the guard feels like it, he uses an almost certain poor performance as an excuse to beat a prisoner. Today, fortunately, their beds are approved. Once beds are made, Gisela and her family must run to morning roll.

After roll call they have to take their mess-tin with them to the mess line. A guard gives them some bread and tasteless coffee. No sugar or milk. Occasionally they get some margarine and a thin slice of sausage. The bread is the only food they get until the next day. When the guard pours their coffee, he sometimes pushes the prisoner so that the coffee spills. If the guard is so inclined, he then punishes the prisoner for wasting coffee.

Prisoners quickly learn that protesting only brings beatings. They also learn to obey the least little command or risk death. Gisela and her parents constantly fear that Helga's tendency to speak up when things don't go her way will get her into serious trouble in the camp.

After Gisela gets her cup of weak coffee, Helga holds up her cup. The guard pours some coffee into her cup. He then hits into her elbow, spilling most of the coffee to the ground. With a sinister grin the guard smacks her on the face with the back of his hand. The force of the blow is so hard that it knocks her to the ground. As she struggles to get up he says, "*ungeschickte Hündin*." Clumsy bitch.

Eyes blazing, Helga is about say something, but Gisela puts a hand on her shoulder and with her other hand puts a finger to her lips and says *shhh*. Heidi swallows the retort she was going to make, but she will not forget this. She knows that she probably should if she wants to avoid abuse in the future, but she has never in her young life been submissive. She is not going to start now. Still, she knows that life in the camp is difficult enough without enduring beatings. She continues to fume as the guard just grins maliciously.

Less than an hour later, when the four of them have reported to their workstation, a young German soldier approaches holding a pile of uniforms in his outstretched arms. He says, *"Ende des tages fertig."* Finish by the end of the day.

The girls' father is a tailor. Because of this skill the guards treat him better than the other prisoners. He is needed to keep the German uniforms from falling apart. He will not be killed as long as he is of value to the camp. At this point in the war most soldiers and many prison camp guards are not getting replacement uniforms. They have to make do with what they've been wearing for months or even years. A tailor in the camp helps preserve these uniforms a little longer. Gisela and Helga's father told the guards that he needed the help of his entire family just to keep up with the staggering number of uniforms that needed repairs. Because of this the family has been spared so far.

A half hour into their workday the same guard who'd poured their coffee approaches their workbench. With a contemptuous smile on his face he makes a beeline for Helga with a uniform jacket in his left hand. In his right hand he holds a button. He barks, "Sew this on, *hebräische Hündin.* Hebrew bitch. Do it now!"

"Sew it on yourself, Nazi pig."

At this Helga's family is aghast. Her father said, "Apologize, Helga. That was rude."

"He was rude before when he made me spill my coffee."

The guard's face is now a flaming red. Two of his fellow guards have witnessed the scene. He cannot afford to be seen taking verbal abuse from a prisoner, let alone a girl. "Get down on your knees and beg for mercy, bitch."

"That'll never happen, Nazi pig." With this the guard pulls out his Luger and points it at her, saying. "I'll give you one last chance. Get down on your knees and beg for mercy. Her sister Gisela is frantic, tears streaming down her face.

Helga, trembling with anger, blurts out, "Apologize for this morning and I will do as you say."

Glancing behind him toward his comrades the guard then faces her and says, "Apologize to a Jewish bitch. That'll never happen." With that he pulls the trigger. A red splotch appears on Helga's gray threadbare dress. She stands there with a look of amazement. Then her stricken body slowly crumples to the ground. Gisela runs screaming to her fallen sister. Her mother stands screaming. The guard snarls, "Take her away and then get back to work. You have 15 minutes, or you will join her."

1

Present day

Dinner time at Liberty Village was always the highlight of Jean Fullbright's day. It was one of the reasons Jean and her husband Frank decided to come to Liberty Village three years ago. It wasn't just the food. No, it was the sociability of the dinner time. The food was okay, sometimes quite good, but it certainly wasn't gourmet. Dinner time was just a great way to meet new people and a wonderful way to get together with your friends. As senior living communities went, Liberty Village was bigger than most. It had several restaurants and plenty of clubs and activities you could get involved in. Tonight the Fullbrights were seated at a round table for six. They knew two of the people at the table and had just met the other two.

One of the new people at the table, Marc Candelari, said, "I hate to cast a pall over the table, but I just heard something pretty shocking." When he had everyone's attention, he continued. "The rumor is that two men who recently moved into Liberty were guards in one of the Nazi death camps.

Buchenwald. Just a rumor, but if it's true it's damned upsetting."

Frank Fullbright said, "Even if it's not true it's damned upsetting that someone would spread such gossip. I don't suppose this rumor says who these former guards are?"

"Of course not," said Candelari. "The person who told me heard it from another person. I didn't get their name so, as I said, it's a rumor. Sometimes, though, gossip is based on facts. I just don't know if this is."

"Did this person who told you say anything more about the alleged prison guards? Like their appearance. Height, size? Their age has to put them in the mid-to-late 90s."

"Supposedly both guys are above average in height and seem fairly healthy for their age. Moved in in the last few months."

"More important than that, did your contact tell you how someone here at Liberty Village learned that these new residents were former camp guards? I mean, that's not something that new residents would volunteer freely. That's the last thing they'd want known."

"No idea. As I said, this is just a rumor. Maybe there's nothing to it."

"Well," said Jean Fullbright, "It's a helluva rumor.

Across the dining room, at a table for four, Arthur Jankowsky took a large sip from his glass of Merlot and said, "There's a story going around that there are two residents here who were former guards at one of the Nazi death camps.

Marlene Larsen drew in a quick breath upon hearing this. "This has to be nothing more than a rumor. I can't believe men like that would move here."

"Why not?" asked Jankowsky. "They have to live somewhere."

"How would such gossip start? If it's just a rumor, it's one irresponsible rumor. You don't even suggest something like that unless you're fairly certain of what you're talking about."

"If there's anything to it," said Jankowsky, "it has to be that someone here saw these men and recognized them. Someone who was a prisoner remembered these guys."

Larsen then said, "This someone is calling two Liberty Village residents death camp guards and hasn't seen these guards in almost 80 years. How can they be so sure they're the same guys? The guards obviously were young men. Anyone here who could have been a guard has to be in his 90s. I don't think this rumor should go beyond this table. It's irresponsible to spread such talk. They could ruin the lives of two fellow residents."

"If they're just rumors," said Jankowsky. "But what if it's true? What if we do have two former death camp guards on campus? Do we just ignore it? Don't we need to get to the bottom of this?"

"Maybe you do," said Larsen. "Not me, though. I'm not getting involved in this."

2

Madison just got home from her job at the hospital for a short time when her phone rang. Her work as a nurse had gotten more stressful in recent years, but she still loved it. The call was from her husband, Liam. She could see that on the screen of her cell phone before she even picked it up. Just knowing it was from him made her smile.

"Hi Hon, what's up?"

"I made those reservations. Two months from now we'll be in sunny Italy. Our kids are settled, we can afford it and we're finally doing what we've wanted to do for years."

"How long?"

"How long what?" he asked.

"How long will we be gone?

"Two weeks. You okay with that?"

"I am if I can get the time off. Oh, hell. I'll make it work. This is wonderful. When are you coming home so we can discuss it and celebrate?"

3

He'd spent the last 75-plus years creating a new self. It hadn't been easy, but as he thought back over the years, he'd done a damned good job of it. No, it really hadn't been easy at all. This was his third adopted country, each time with a new name and a new identity. Each time he'd not only been accepted, he'd become a welcome member of his new community.

It had been an intellectual challenge. He knew to be accepted and thereby safe, he had to be likeable. He laughed inwardly as he thought about this. He knew that he was not inherently likeable. Yet he also knew that he was a lot smarter than most people. He could play the part when he needed to. It was a skill like any other skill. It was kind of fun turning it on when he needed it. People ate that stuff up.

He'd had to do it if he was going to survive. The Nazi hunters had been relentless after the war. They couldn't just leave things alone. It was wartime and people did things in wartime they wouldn't do in peacetime. Some of his fellow guards claimed they had no choice but to be tough in the camp. They didn't enjoy it, but if they didn't do their job, then *they* would have suffered. After all, someone had to deal with these pitiful vermin. He, personally, hadn't been bothered by the work. It was kind of interesting seeing how the inhabitants of the camp reacted under adverse conditions. It was like being in a laboratory where you studied the behavior of lab animals.

The only difference was that this was a lab where you studied human behavior. Admittedly, most of them were inferior humans, but still it was interesting. As you would in a laboratory, you observed and you learned.

Probably his best performances since leaving Europe had to do with proclaiming his heartfelt concern for these sad creatures. Yes, it was hypocritical, but it brought him acceptance. Especially in the early years after narrowly escaping Buchenwald Camp when the Americans were closing in. He remembered vividly how he'd just gotten away in time. When word made it to the camp that the U.S. troops were advancing on the camp, he and a few buddies had decided they'd get out of the camp before it was too late. They weren't sure where they would go, but they would figure it out as they went along. Better than dealing with the Yank troops. He and two other guards eventually made it to Argentina first and then to Uruguay where they were able to carve out new lives. From Uruguay they found a way to make it to the United States. He and another guard made it here to Liberty Village with their wives. They'd both agreed this was about as safe a place for them as they could hope for.

4

It was a second marriage for Bill and Gisela Miller. They'd been married for 12 wonderful years now. Gisela's first husband, Horst had passed away almost 15 years ago, though she still thought about him a lot. It had been a good marriage. Especially since they'd had so much in common back in Germany. But Bill was just as good a man in his own way. He never resented her feelings for Horst. He understood.

This was probably the first time the Millers had had a serious argument in the entire 12 years of their marriage. Gisela had told Bill that she'd seen a Liberty Village resident she was almost certain had been a guard at Buchenwald back in the forties. She'd only been eleven or so when she'd seen him in the camp, but this had to be the same man. Bill understood what she was going through. Her memories of the camp were horrendous. Gisela's belief that she'd seen a former guard was not what caused the flare-up between them. No, it was that she'd told one of her lady friends about her suspicions. Bill said she had no right to do that. She wasn't sure about this man and to suggest in their senior community that there was such a man living among them was reckless and irresponsible.

"How can you be sure this is the same man? That was a long time ago."

"There are certain things that don't change over the years," said his wife. "The eyes for one thing. And the way he walks. Kind of a loping stride. It's hard to describe, but I'll never forget it and this man has it."

"But you were just a kid. And he had to be in his twenties."

"Barely. He could have been in his late teens. He wasn't very old."

"Well, unless you check someone's DNA, how can you be sure?"

"How about his German accent?"

"I didn't see this guy or hear him, so I can't comment on that except to say that there are several people here who used to live in Germany. A German accent proves nothing." He let some time pass before adding, "I still say you acted impulsively by telling Olivia or whatever her name was about your suspicions. It will be all over Liberty Village in a few days."

"If I'm right about this guy, don't you think that's a good thing? Shouldn't people know what kind of man is living in their community?"

"Yeah, I suppose, but you don't know for sure that this is the guy."

"I'm pretty sure."

"Pretty sure is not good enough if you're going to accuse a man of being a prison guard in a Nazi death camp. You have to be absolutely certain."

"How do I do that?"

You get the help of an expert. Someone in law enforcement. That's a big step, though. I'm not sure you want to do that?"

"Like go to the local police? I wonder if they would look into it unless I could give them some proof?"

"There you go. Even you realize that your suspicions are based on nothing more than gut instinct and a fuzzy memory."

"Not so fuzzy, but I realize as we talk that the police probably won't pursue this without some solid evidence. C'mon, Bill, help me out. I need help here."

"Well, if you're serious, remember that Tony Dantry fellow we met last year. Ex-CIA and a hell of a nice guy. Probably has the resources to look into the man's background. He might be able to help you, but it probably won't be cheap. If you're really serious, I'll give him a call."

5

I answered on the second ring. The caller was fortunate. If the weather had been nicer Joanna and I would have been out on Long Island Sound on our aging 36-foot Chris Craft. It was mid-summer and most of the weather had been great allowing us to get out on the Sound two or three times a week. Not today, though. Today it was cloudy with a hint of rain.

Joanna and I live together. We have for a number of years. We're not married. We're not against marriage, but we've seen no need for it. She's my life partner. Life is great for us, so why change things?

We live on City Island, just off the coast of the Bronx. In many ways it's more like a New England coastal village than a part of New York City. It has a lot of advantages being part of New York City. We can go into Manhattan on a whim, yet the sea is instantly available to us. We can easily get to the real New England by water if we choose.

The caller said he was Bill Miller. I vaguely recalled the name. He could tell by the sound of my voice that I wasn't sure who he was so he reminded me that we'd met last year at the marina. He had a fairly new 32-foot Bayliner.

Then it came to me. "Yes, Bill. I remember. What's up?"

"My wife, Gisela, and I live in a retirement community called Liberty Village up in Putnam County. Not too far from Carmel."

"I know it. Worked on a case up there not too long ago."

"Really? What was that?"

"Let's not get into that now. Why don't you tell me what's on your mind?"   "We have a situation here that we were hoping you'd help us look into. With your background we thought you would know what to do. You probably have connections that would help in this situation."

"Well I suppose it depends on what your situation is. Just what is this situation that's troubling you?"

"We think there's a man here who was a guard in one of Hitler's death camps. Buchenwald, to be precise."

"Whoa! That's a serious accusation. How certain are you?"

"It's Gisela who remembers him, and she's fairly certain, but she has no proof, and we don't want to accuse somebody of this unless we're a hundred percent certain. We thought with your resources you might help us decide one way or the other. We'd pay you for your trouble, of course. I don't even know if this is something you'd want to get involved in. With your background it seemed like you might."

"What about the local police. Have you contacted them?"

"It's a very small force. I don't see them having the resources or the skills needed for something like this.

Besides, without any proof, what could they do?"

"There's the FBI. They certainly have the resources and the skills."

"Again, without a grain of proof other than my wife's memory I don't think they're going to want to get involved. Frankly, I was hoping to appeal to your curiosity and your interest in getting to the bottom of something like this. I also assumed that, if you did get involved, you wouldn't stir up things here and point the finger at this man unless you were certain he was guilty. Accusing an innocent man of this crime would be worse than letting the guilty party get off."

"I have to tell you, Bill, that this is one of the most unusual phone calls I've ever received. I'm going to have to think about it. Give me your phone number and I'll call you back in a day or two."

"I will hear from you, though?"

"Definitely. This is serious. I'm not ignoring it. I will call you."

Later that day, when Joanna returned from her job at Hunter College where she was chair of the history department, she asked me how my day went. I told her I had an interesting phone call. Said I'd fill her in over our pre-dinner drinks.

After I'd explained the call, Joanna scrunched her face in deep thought before she spoke. Finally, she said, "Are you sure you want to look into this. I can imagine all kinds of problems for you. I know you like a challenge, but if this goes wrong you could be in the middle of an awful mess."

"I didn't say I was definitely going to do it. I thought we should discuss it, but I can see you've already made up your mind."

"No, not at all. It's fascinating and if there really is such a man there, he should be found out. It's just that—"

"I know, I know. If innocent people are accused, that's terrible for the accused, the accuser and for Liberty Village, too." I grimaced as I visualized this, then said, "But Gisela Miller was in Buchenwald with her parents. She remembers how horrible it was. She remembers how cruel this guard was."

"But," said Joanna, "she's not a completely certain about these guys. By the way, don't you wonder how she survived Buchenwald?"

"Yes, I do. I suppose I should know if I'm going to look into this."

"Then you've made up your mind. You're going to get involved. You're not happy being retired. Fishing and going out on the sound are a little boring, right?"

"No. Besides, my life with you is pretty damned fabulous. But, I suppose, I do occasionally like to dip my feet into law enforcement. I suppose investigation is more accurate. I like solving things. I haven't done anything like this in quite a while. It's good for my brain. Keeps it young."

She grinned. She saw through me very accurately. She knew I loved this stuff."

6

The Miller's apartment was on the third floor of one of the Liberty Village buildings. There must have been nine or ten buildings—all connected by glass-enclosed bridges or links as they called them. It was a comfortable apartment decorated in a fairly contemporary style.

    As soon as they opened the door on my first knock, I got the feeling that they were relieved to see that I'd actually come. Bill Miller, slightly below average in height with receding gray hair was a bit stooped over, but he received me with a welcoming grin. Gisela was about average height for a woman. Her hair was gray, not unlike many of the women at Liberty, but stylish in that it was fairly short and tapered in the back. While she had to be at least in her late eighties or early nineties, she had good posture and appeared to be in good condition for her age.

    "Please come in, Mr. Dantry," said Gisela as she motioned me in with a welcoming motion of her left arm. After shaking hands, Gisela asked me if I wanted coffee or tea. I said coffee would be fine as I took a seat in a comfortable looking easy chair.

When all three of us were seated and had taken a sip of our coffee I said, "Sounds as if you have an interesting quandary you're wrestling with. Why don't you tell me about it?"

Bill Miller looked over at his wife. She nodded a go ahead and he began.

"About a week ago, when we were at dinner, I noticed Gisela staring at a nearby table. It's not like her to stare, and afterwards I asked her what that was all about. She said that a man at the next table reminded her of one of the guards at Buchenwald. She and her parents were prisoners there." I looked at Gisela and she nodded somberly. "Anyway, continued her husband, she said she was almost certain it was the same man—obviously much older."

At this point I had to jump in. "As you just said, this man was much older. After all these years how can you be so sure this is the same man?"

"His face, though much older, looks like a senior-citizen version of what it was back then. One eye blinks frequently when the other remains normal. It did that back in the camp. His voice is pretty much the same as it was then. And he does have a German accent."

Gisela was a nice woman. She didn't seem like the type of person who would let her imagination get the best of her, but I was still not convinced.

"I can see how everything you've mentioned could remind you of that prison guard from a long time ago. Still, I assume you do realize, this man you're talking about could just as easily be someone else?"

"Yes, of course. That's why my husband called you. We hoped you would help us find out if he really is the same man. If he's not, we don't want to accuse an innocent man. I hope you can help us, Mr. Dantry."

"Tony, please."

"Tony."

"Do you know the name of this man here at Liberty Village?"

"I think it's Heinrich Zweig. I don't think that was his name at the camp."

"What else do you know about him? When did he come to Liberty Village? Where did he live before he came here? What kind of work did he do when he was younger? Is he married?"

"I honestly don't know the answers to any of that," said Gisela. "As you can imagine, I'm very curious, but at the same time I feel very uncomfortable getting close to this man. Anything I know is what I've heard from someone else and the people I've spoken to who even think they know who he is don't seem to know much about him. He's fairly new here though." She drew in a deep breath and went on, "You must have ways of finding these things out?"

"I could just go to his apartment and ask him but—"

"No! No! I don't think you should do that."

"I was about to say that I don't think that's a very good idea. Not now anyway. Later, if I have evidence he is who you think he is or might be, I might do that, but not now."

"How will we get evidence?"

"I'll do a search of the Internet. Check social media, background checks for anyone with the name Heinrich Zweig. You must have something here at Liberty Village that lists the names and backgrounds of residents?"

"We have something," said Bill Miller, "that lists the names and Liberty Village addresses. Sometimes it shows interests and other things that relate to the resident. Here, I can show you right now." He picked up an iPad and brought up a site. In a minute, he said, "Here's what they have on Zweig. It shows his apartment location, and says he likes to read and likes art. That's about it, though. Oh, it shows there's a Mrs. Zweig. A Doreen Zweig."

"Okay," I said, "That's something. Not a lot, but it might be enough for me to get started. By the way, can you describe this Zweig fellow?"

"He's about six feet. He looked about that when he got up. Maybe 190 or so pounds. He's old—mid-90s or older. Obviously. Yet he seems fairly healthy and alert for his age. Doesn't need a walker to get around."

"Now," I began, "I have a rather delicate question to ask you Gisela."

"Anything if it will help. What is it?"

"You and your parents were held captive in a terrible death camp. Yet you survived. How did you manage that?"

"My father was a tailor and the Nazi's needed someone to keep their uniforms and other clothing from falling apart. They needed my father and he convinced them that he needed my mother and me because we helped him. My mother and I treated these guards with respect they didn't deserve, but those were desperate times. Anyway, they seemed to like us. My older sister didn't play along. She said there was no way she was going to even sew a button on a Nazi uniform. She treated them with contempt, and they killed her. This Zweig guy is the one who actually shot her.

"It was toward the end of the war. The American troops liberated Buchenwald April 11, 1945. If they hadn't, who knows what would have happened to the rest of us?"

I was appalled by this. I suppose I shouldn't have been. It wasn't the first time I'd heard about the evil that took place in the death camps. It was, however, the first time I'd heard it from an actual survivor. For a moment I was speechless. Eventually I said, "How old were you when all this happened, Gisela?"

"I was 11 when we were first taken there and 12 when the Americans freed us."

"And your memory is clearly quite vivid?"

"Yes. Of course."

"But you're not a hundred percent certain this is the man?"

"Naturally I can't be completely certain. A lot of years have gone by, and this man has obviously aged a lot in those years. Still, I'm better than 90 percent sure. What I don't have is proof. No proof. No evidence other than my memory."

I smiled. "Let's think about that memory. Did the guard have any distinguishing features or characteristics? Tattoos, blemishes, eye tics, bad breath, body odor, a limp?"

"You can't go by body odor. This wasn't the cleanest place on Earth. But as I think I mentioned before, he did blink a lot with his left eye. I remember thinking about that way back then."

"Okay, then did he do it when you saw him here?"

"Yes. That's one of the things that made me think of him. He was at a different table but even at that distance I noticed the blinking."

"How many times have you seen him here at Liberty Village?"

"Only twice."

"Have you told anyone here about your suspicions other than your husband?"

"I might have mentioned it to my friend, Olivia Perez."

On hearing this I forced myself to control myself. Still, I couldn't just say nothing. "I'm afraid that might have opened up a can of worms. By now it could be fairly widespread here at Liberty Village."

"Olivia's a good person."

"I'm sure she is, but something like this is hard for a person to keep quiet about. There's a good chance she's told more than one person. Pretty soon a lot of people are talking about the man here who was a prison guard at Buchenwald. By the way, when you told your friend did you mention the name Zweig?"

"No, I don't think so. Even then I realized how bad it would be to name someone if you weren't absolutely certain."

"That's good. I'll look into this. Not here at Liberty Village but using some of my resources and connections. See what's on the computer and what, if anything, is in any databases. Give me a week or so and I'll get back to you. If I have made any progress, I'll stay on it. If I haven't found anything I'll probably tell you that there's not much else I can do. Give me a week and I'll let you know either way."

"Before you go I need to tell you something else." She looked nervous as she said this.

"Something else I should know?"

"Yes. You'll think I'm crazy, but I can't let you go without telling you this." Her husband Bill drew in a deep breath as she said this.

"Yes. Go ahead. Anything you can tell me could help," I said.

"Just last night I think I may have seen another man who was a guard at Buchenwald." I slowly turned my head from side to side. I was beginning to wonder about this nice lady.

"Another one? You think there are two former camp guards here at Liberty Village?"

"I know, it sounds crazy but there's another man who also reminds me of one my guards back in Buchenwald. Bill has his doubts, but please hear me out. He's almost exactly the same height as Zweig. Same body type. He and Zweig or whatever his name was at the time were buddies at the camp. They hung around together. If I'm right about them they could still be buddies and could both have decided to come here to Liberty."

"What's this guy's name here at Liberty Village?"

"Max Schmidt."

I said, "Have you told anybody about your suspicions of Schmidt?"

"He and I have had a couple disagreements. He's not a very nice person. The only person I've spoken to this morning is Olivia. I did mention him to her,
but made her promise to keep it to herself. I even reminded her that she shouldn't mention the name Heinrich Zweig either." I rolled my eyes as she said this.

"Gisela, you just told me before that you hadn't given Zweig's name to Olivia. Now, this morning, you reminded her not to mention it. She didn't even know it until you told her this morning. Gisela, you've got to be more careful about this. Please don't tell anyone else about your suspicions about these two men. It could be dangerous."

"Dangerous! Why would it be dangerous?"

"These men, if they were prison guards, could very well be killers. You already said that Zweig, or whatever his name was, killed your sister. If they think you might reveal their identities to the authorities, who knows what they might do to keep you quiet. You should be careful who you let into your apartment."

7

Last night at dinner some of the men at his table were talking about the latest rumor. This immediately got his full attention. This was his third country and third identity. After all these years it was the first time anyone around him had even hinted at the possibility that a former camp guard was living nearby. There could only be one reason now. Somebody here at Liberty had to be a survivor of the camp. And that somebody had recognized him as their former guard. This was not good. Not good at all. What was even worse was the fact that he didn't know who that survivor was. He didn't remember most of the prisoners under him. He could see how some of them might have remembered him, though. He used to bark his orders to the prisoners. As he thought back he realized that he was considered one of the toughest, cruelest guards in his section of the camp. It was a reputation he took pride in. Still did.

As a guard he'd had all the advantages. He was armed, fed and supported by all the other guards. He had the support of his fellow guards as long as he adhered to the rules. One of the rules was that you shot prisoners who disobeyed you. There was no discussion. Certainly no trial. And definitely no second chance. If you, the guard, thought the prisoner deserved a second chance and you showed leniency, then *you* would be shot.

The survivor here at Liberty Village would know that, but probably wouldn't take it into consideration when judging him. He knew he couldn't expect kindness and forgiveness from the survivor. Maybe if this person was a religious zealot, he might hope for a little forgiveness, but he wasn't counting on it. After all, as he thought back to Buchenwald, he hadn't extended much kindness to his pitiful charges. Just the opposite. He smiled as he realized that he still missed the warm feeling he got when he saw them suffer. It was a feeling of power and superiority that he had not experienced in over 80 years.

Now, though, he had to focus. If this rumor continued to spread, sooner or later they'd be after him. Maybe his friend, Max, too. He'd eluded the Nazi hunters all these years. He certainly wasn't going to succumb now when he was so comfortable. If he had to take action, he would. Whatever action was necessary. Almost certainly the rumor would spread. Most likely sooner rather than later. He couldn't afford to wait long.

8

It was a beautiful morning—the time of day Gisela could be alone with her thoughts. She loved being outdoors and the trail past the little pond at Liberty Village was a lovely place to walk. The trail was just ahead. Sometimes she would see mallard ducks on the pond. At one end of the pond she could admire the lilies and lily pads. An occasional heron was always a possibility. Often a family of turtles occupied a rock that peeked through the surface of the mirror-like water. The little pond was a treasure trove of wildlife.

Today, as usual, she'd gone out early. It wasn't that she didn't like people. She was actually a people person, but at this time of day she enjoyed being by herself, walking at her own pace, alone with her thoughts. Sometimes she walked with her friend Jean Fullbright. She enjoyed that too, because they were close friends and walked at the same pace. She smiled. Her husband said she liked being up with the birds. He was happy to do his walking later in the day. Even though she adored her husband Bill, this was the one time of day she looked forward to. Everyone needed time for themselves, and this was her time.

Just as she neared the pond she noticed another person walking a stone's throw away. This was a rarity for this time in the morning. It was only six-thirty AM. As the person approached she could now see that it was a man hunched over with a hat pulled down over his eyes. She thought she detected a mustache, though the man was so stooped, it was hard to tell. If he stood up straight, he'd no doubt be a little over six feet tall.

The man offered a friendly nod and slowly made his way toward the pond path. He looked frail and was probably well into his nineties. A little unsteady, but getting along at his own slow pace. Good for him. She wasn't really looking for company though. Hopefully, he wouldn't want to walk with her, but would just continue on by himself. If he was out this early, he probably wanted to be by himself anyway.

She had now reached the pond trail and to her delight she spotted a majestic blue heron not far from the shoreline. What a strikingly regal bird it was. This was the kind of sight that made these early morning strolls so wonderful.

He noted that the Miller woman walked at a fairly good pace. She wasn't using a walker or even a cane. If he was going to catch up with her, he'd have to pick up his pace. He could do it, though it wasn't as easy now as it was just a few years ago. Age takes its toll. If he picked up the pace too quickly she'd no doubt wonder why. Still, if he was going to join her, it had to be soon.

He made that extra effort. Had to catch up with her while she was still on the pond trail—and not just anywhere on the pond trail. There were only a couple of spots that would work for him. She glanced over in his direction, but then turned her attention back to her walking. Good. She wasn't suspicious, so he could continue toward her without arousing any concern on her part. This was probably going to work.

As he got closer to the woman, he surveyed the ground around him. Neat as a pin. That was not good. He needed to find something, or this *wasn't* going to work. There! He found what he was looking for. It was perfect. In bending down for it he lost a few steps, so now he'd have to walk even faster. Faster than was comfortable, but it was either that, or not reach the Miller woman in time. He couldn't afford to miss her, so a couple more minutes of physical discomfort was worth it.

He was now about 15 feet from her. This time when she looked at him he could see that she was startled by his presence. He knew that she probably wanted to walk alone. Still, she made eye contact and said, "Good morning. Lovely day, isn't it?" She didn't recognize him. No doubt the hat and the mustache.

"It certainly is." He moved closer as he said this. Then he added, "Haven't seen you out here before."

"I'm surprised. I'm out here almost every day." He knew that, of course. He was just engaging in the kind of conversation he knew most people engaged in every day. Hopefully it would make him appear to be a fellow walker who was just being cordial. As long as she saw him that way, he could gradually move closer to her.

They were now less than 10 feet apart. He had to move in now. He glanced around quickly and saw no one, so this was the perfect time to act.

"If you're up as early as we are, there's no telling what you'll find. Look what I just found back there." He held up a paper bag that clearly contained something. As he said this he took several quick steps toward her holding the bag enticingly in front of him. Now he had aroused her interest. She waited for him to come closer and show what was in the bag. Now barely two feet separated them. To give himself an extra second he sneezed, knowing she would turn away briefly. As she did this he reached into the bag and pull out a rock the size of a softball. In one continuous motion he came down on her head with as much force as he could deliver. The cracking sound assured him that the rock had done the trick. The woman wasn't dead, but she was stunned. He went to her and put her arm over his shoulder. He then headed toward the silent, mirror-like pond. As he came within a few feet of the shoreline a frog jumped into the water from a sunken log creating a few ripples in the otherwise unbroken surface. He smiled, realizing that in a few seconds he would be creating many larger ripples.

His big concern now was that the land tapered sharply down toward the pond. It wasn't easy dragging the stunned old woman down this slope. At his age it wouldn't have been easy if the land were level, but this was precarious. The last thing he wanted to do was fall down this slope while trying to dispose of this woman. Fortunately, he was fairly steady on his feet for an old man and he was able to maneuver the woman down the slope without either of them falling. She was waking now so he had no time to spare. He gave her a forceful two-handed push toward the water, and she landed with a splash. She blurted out something that was unintelligible. Then she gasped and took in a mouthful of water, her arms flailing in panic. She struggled weakly and took in more water.

He wanted to get out of there before another walker came by, but he couldn't afford to leave until he was sure she was gone. She was still struggling, but not so vigorously now. *C'mon. Die! Damn you.* She was barely moving now. *Almost there. She seemed to be taking forever to die. Ah. Finally. She wasn't moving.* He waited another few seconds and then worked his way up the slope to the pond trail. When he reached the trail he looked back. Gisela Miller was floating face down—motionless. Good. He could be on his way now and breathe a bit more easily knowing he'd dealt with the problem. He'd always been good at problem solving.

9

After I returned from the Millers Joanna had greeted me with an all-knowing grin. "I see from your expression that you've agreed to take this case. Obviously I'm not surprised."

"It's conditional."

"Conditional?"

"It depends on whether I think I can find enough to build a case. If I can't, when I see them in a week it'll be *Sorry, but no can do.*"

"Right. Tony, we've gone through this scenario a dozen times. You always take the case."

"I want to take this one, but I do need to see what I can dig up from my usual sources. If I can't find anything, I'll have to back out. We'll see."

"Yeah, right. We'll see. "C'mon. I can see that you're already hooked. I admit it does sound interesting."

"You don't know the half of it. Now Gisela thinks she's seen a second former prison guard at Liberty Village."

"Sounds as if she's either onto something very big, or someone needs to investigate her mental health."

I grinned and said, "I'm going to go ahead on the assumption Gisela is of sound mind. If it turns out she isn't, then we'll deal with that if we have to."

I did some quick investigation and learned that 30 years earlier Heinrich Zweig had immigrated to the United State from Uruguay. Ten years before that he had emigrated from Argentina to Uruguay. He'd changed his name twice, so it wasn't easy to trace him. Both of those countries had welcomed Nazis fleeing Germany at and near the end of World War II. So far, I had no actual evidence that Zweig or Schmidt was a Nazi or Nazi sympathizer, but I had nothing that said they weren't. Based on the path Zweig had taken from Germany to America I'd guess he very possibly could have been a Nazi. I didn't have that much information on Schmidt yet, but I hoped to have it soon. I expected that in another day or two I'd have more information about both men. Maybe enough to help me decide whether to move forward on the case or walk away. Who was I kidding? As of now it looked as if I'd be moving forward on the case.

10

I was on my computer checking social media and other sources when our landline rang. I could see that it was a call from the Millers. Apparently they were impatient to hear something from me. I guess I could understand, but I couldn't imagine what they expected me to have so early on in my investigations.

"Yes?"

"Tony, it's Bill Miller."

There was tension in his voice. I was surprised that he was calling so early on in my investigations. "Yes, Bill. You don't sound happy. What's troubling you?"

"It's Gisela. She's dead. Oh good Lord, I don't know what to do."

"Oh my God, Bill! What happened?"

There was silence for a moment. I heard the poor man struggling to catch his breath. Finally, he said, "There's a pond here on the grounds. She somehow fell into it early this morning. She likes to walk. Usually walks along the pond on her circuit around the campus. On one side of the sidewalk the incline down to the pond is quite steep. She must have gotten too close and lost her balance. Though that's not like her. She doesn't make that kind of mistake."

"Do you have children, Bill?"

"We have a son who lives in Chicago."

"If you already haven't, I'm sure you'll want to get in touch with him."

"I'm definitely going to call him. That's not going to be an easy call."

"You just said Gisela must have gotten too close and lost her balance. Are you sure it was an accident? Did she often lose her balance?"

"No, she never loses her balance. Gisela is an accomplished hiker. She's hiked all over the Alps and the United States. She had excellent balance. As far as I know she's never fallen."

"Still, she might not have been as sure of her balance as she has been in the past."

"I suppose it's possible, but the more I think about it the more it seems unlikely."

I couldn't disagree with him. "I think you should call the local police."

"I think it might be too soon. All we have is supposition. I doubt if this small local police force can afford to get involved in something so iffy."

"I still think you should at least call them. Let's get their take on it. If you're not satisfied with what they come up with, I'll be glad to look into it."

Bill reluctantly called the local police. A detective came over and talked with him. Together they went to the pond where the detective spent a short time. After about 45 minutes the detective said that as far as he was concerned there was no evidence of a crime. He admitted that he could see how Bill was suspicious, but the bottom line was that this was a senior-living facility. Unfortunately, people died here fairly frequently—often from falls and unsteadiness. There was no reason to believe otherwise in this situation, despite Bill's suspicions.

The next day Bill called me and said, "Tony, if you're still willing to investigate a little more, I'd appreciate it." He seemed on the verge of tears as he spoke.

"Okay, Bill. I'll come out there. Be there in an hour and a half."

When I arrived, Bill seemed a bit more composed. He even offered me coffee, which I accepted because it gave him something to do.

When we were seated in his living room Bill told me that he was fairly certain that the detective believed he was a bit paranoid.

"Okay," I said. "At least you tried. Let's see what I can do. Do you know if anyone saw Gisela yesterday morning?"

"She sometimes walks with her friend Jean Fullbright. I don't know if she did today."

"Why don't you and I talk to her. You can say I'm an old friend who happened to be here today. You just want to know if Jean was anywhere near when Gisela went into the pond."

As Bill was about to respond his phone rang. He picked it up on the first ring. "Yes?" As Miller listened to the caller his face grew grim. Finally he responded, "My God, Jean, I can't believe it. I was just going to get in touch with you about this. Do you mind if I come over in a few minutes? I have a friend with me who wants to help. I'll explain when we get there."

When Miller was off the phone he turned to me with a stunned expression on his face. "She thinks she saw someone near Gisela at the pond yesterday morning. When Gisela disappeared from view that person just continued on his way as if nothing had happened."

"Did your friend say anything else?"

"She was distraught."

"Then we should see her right away, while all of this is fresh in her memory. I'll let you lead the way, Bill."

It was only a five-minute walk to the Fullbright apartment. Jean and her husband, Frank, met us and invited us to sit down.

Frank was the first to speak. He addressed me.

"I hope this doesn't sound rude, but Bill said you wanted to help. I'm not sure I get it. And help with what. What's your connection here?"

"You're not being rude. I understand. I'm an old acquaintance of the Millers and happen to be retired CIA. I got a call yesterday morning from Bill telling me what had happened to Gisela. He thought it was strange that she would fall into the pond since she was fit for her age and had walked in many more precarious settings. I suggested he call the police. They were here and found no evidence of a crime, so Bill asked me over today to get my opinion. I was at the Miller's apartment when you called." As I spoke, Fullbright nodded his head in silent understanding.

"Well," said Jean Fullbright, it was strange. Often Gisela and I walk together. Yesterday I was late and saw her up near the pond in the distance. I walked a little faster and figured I'd catch up to her soon. Then I saw someone coming toward her. It was a man. He looked familiar. I knew I'd seen him before, but I couldn't place him. At my age you forget things. Anyway, he seemed to have something in his hand that he had raised—as if he was going to throw it. Later it occurred to me that maybe he was going to hit her with it. Just as the man was about to reach her with his arm in the air, a car passed between us. When it was gone, so was Gisela. I'm sure that's when she went into the pond. I was frantic. I started running toward the pond as fast as I could go, thinking that the man who was much closer to her would have already gone to help her. But he hadn't. He just kept walking on his way. Obviously he didn't know I'd seen him. When I got to the pond I saw Gisela floating face down. I immediately called security and 911. As I got to the edge of the pond I wanted to go in and help her, but I don't swim and she was too far out to reach. Security came within minutes. A police car and a fire truck pulled up a few minutes later. The police asked a few questions. The firemen did too. After about a half hour they concluded it was a tragic accident and left."

"Sounds to me," I said, "like this man deliberately pushed her in."

"Good Lord," said Jean, "Why would he do that?"

"That's a good question," I said. "As far you know did Gisela have any enemies? I should rephrase that. Did she have any arguments with anybody?"

"No. She wasn't that kind of person. She wasn't confrontative."

"I agree," said Miller. "But she did sus—"

I wasn't sure we should be getting into this with the Fullbrights. "Bill, are you sure you want to bring this up?"

Miller thought for a moment or two, then said, "Yes. What the hell. The cat will be out of the bag soon anyway, one way or the other. If we beat around the bush, we'll never get to the bottom of this. First of all you folks know that Gisela was a prisoner at Buchenwald?"

"Yes, she told me that a long time ago," said Jean.

"Well recently she thought she saw a resident here who was one of her camp guards way back then." Jean nodded as if this was not news.

Frank then said, "A resident?"

"Yes," said Miller. "He was eating at another table."

"Yes," said Jean. "Gisela told me about him. He might have been the man I saw at the pond. She was fairly sure he was her camp guard. Even though today he'd be well over 90 years old. She said he still had mannerisms that reminded her of the guard those many years ago."

Bill Miller was shocked. "She never told me that she told you about this. She wasn't going to tell people because if she was wrong, she could destroy the man's life."

"Well, anyway," asked Frank. "Did she confront him?"

"Oh God no," said Miller, "but she did make one mistake. She told a friend. Now I learn that she told you, Jean, too. I have a pretty good idea that that's how a rumor got started."

"Well, Bill, it wasn't me," said Jean emphatically.

"Who was this man?" inquired Frank.

"I probably shouldn't say," said Miller."

I said, "I think we should know the name of the man she thought was the camp guard. If this wasn't an accident, it needs to be investigated."

Miller pursed his lips and finally said, "Heinrich Zweig. This should not be spread around if we're not absolutely certain he was a camp guard. And we're not. So please keep it to yourselves."

Jean looked startled. "I think that was him."

"Who are you talking about?" asked her husband.

"The man I saw at the pond. I think it may have been Heinrich Zweig, but I'm not sure."

"Then I gather," said Frank, "this Zweig fellow heard about Gisela's suspicions and decided to stop her before she could identify him to the authorities?"

I said, "The thought has crossed our minds. We have no proof of that, but Gisela's death does seem very suspicious. It would seem suspicious anyway because of how this mysterious man just walked away from the pond knowing she was almost certainly going to drown if he didn't help. Face it, we're almost certain this resident she suspected of being a former prison-camp guard pushed her. What is the likelihood of a perfect stranger pushing her to her death, when this suspect is our most likely candidate?"

"Yes, I see that," said Frank. "You're not going to just let this drop, I gather?"

"No, I'm going to look into it. By the way, while I'm here I probably should ask you this."

"Ask us what?"

"I know you said Gisela was not confrontative, but do you know if she ever found herself in a confrontative situation? Maybe not something of her own making, but something started by someone else?"

"Now that you mention it," Said Jean, "I remember a few weeks ago she told me about this guy who lives in her building with a terrible temper. He plays bridge and Gisela played bridge. I don't have to tell you that, Bill. She was a good player. Won all the time. Or it seemed like it. She told me this guy actually accused her of cheating. Can you believe that. A more honest person never lived than Gisela Miller. Bill, you remember when this happened don't you?"

"I sure do. This is the guy, Tony, that Gisela told you might be another guard from Buchenwald. Definitely not a nice guy. Blames everyone else for his troubles. I like most people, but this guy is hard to like. Then, to make things worse, last week Gisela got in her car and was going to the supermarket, and dinged his car. She apologized profusely. Knowing what a hothead this guy was, she went overboard with her apologies. She told me later that she thinks he's so paranoid that he thought her apology was done sarcastically. That she was mocking him. He told her she'd regret it."

I said, "Do you think, Bill, that he could have been so emotional that he would resort to violence?"

"Jesus, Tony. It never occurred to me, but this guy has a reputation for flaring up at the least little thing. I think he's unbalanced. And now as I think about it, Gisela had suspicions about him from the start."

"Is this a guy named Schmidt? I think she gave me that name when we were talking."

"Yes. Max Schmidt," said Miller. "Now that I think about it Schmidt and Zweig do look a lot alike. Especially from the distance. They're both in their 90s and both about the same height.

I said, "Right now we still have no actual proof that any crime was committed by either of these guys. Jean, you didn't actually see the man push Gisela into the pond. I know, you're pretty sure it must have been him, but you can't tell the police you saw it happen. And we don't know who the man was. Sounds like it could be either one of these guys. But it might not be either of them. When we have something more tangible we'll have to get the authorities involved. We should be able to get their attention then."

"Does that mean I'd have to testify in court?" asked Jean.

"If this ends up in court, yes. By the way a medical examiner's going to have to rule on this death. If they call it murder, we'll have the police here anyway."

It also meant that I had to contact my old friend Marco Polo, the special agent in charge of the FBI New York field office. I know the name is interesting. That's a story in itself, but not for now. I needed to contact Polo to see if my InfraGard credentials were still valid. InfraGard authorizes qualified people to represent law enforcement and to share information with the FBI in order to prevent hostile acts against the United States. I assumed murders by a former camp guard at Buchenwald qualified as hostile acts.

11

Marco Polo's office was on the 23rd floor at 26 Federal Plaza in lower Manhattan. I told the attractive young blonde behind the reception desk that I had an appointment with Special Agent Polo. She called his office and said to me that someone would be out to get me in a minute. It seemed that on those rare occasions I came to the FBI office at 26 Federal Plaza the woman behind the desk was always an attractive blonde. Coincidence, or was that a job requirement when Marco hired these women?

When I first met him several years ago he'd told me he'd been named after the famous explorer. People still were surprised when they heard his name.

A couple minutes later I was guided into Polo's corner office. What a magnificent view of lower Manhattan.

Marco smiled. "Been a while, Tony. Everything good with you?"

"Yep. Life is good. Joanna and I are still together, and still not married. We're happy with the status quo. How about you?"

"Life is good, but crime takes no holiday. What can I do you for, my friend. I can't give you much time. We're up to our eyeballs here."

"There's this situation up in Putnam County. Place called Liberty Village. You may recall we had a serial killer there a couple years ago. Well now we may have a Nazi camp guard from Buchenwald. Maybe two of them."

"Holy shit, Tony. At the same place? What's going on up there?"

"It's really a nice place. This is just a coincidence, I'm sure." Then I cleared my throat and added, "As if that weren't enough, I think a murder was just committed up there, too."

"Yeah, sounds like a nice place. You THINK a murder was committed. Listen, my friend, even if it was a murder, you know we don't investigate most murders." I did know that. Unless a murder occurred on federal property or against a president or federal judge, the FBI didn't get involved. If a local police department requested behavioral analysis or FBI lab assistance, then they would step in. Otherwise, they left homicide investigations to the local police.

"Yes, Marco, I know that."

"Then you must be here to renew your InfraGard credentials."

I grinned as I said, "I can see why you head up the field office. Yes, is mine still active?"

"I doubt it, but I can take care of that. So you think you can outsmart the local cops?"

"Not necessarily. It's just that the medical examiner hasn't ruled on the death yet, but it looks pretty suspicious, so I want to look into it myself—at the request of the victim's spouse. The ME did say that there was a contusion on the head as if the victim had either been hit with a blunt object or suffered it during the fall. As you know, I'm happy to work with law enforcement when they get involved. It's a lot easier for me if I have credentials."

"I assume you think this death is connected to the presence of one or both of these former camp guards?"

"As of now it looks like it. However, so far nobody has proven these guys really were guards at a Nazi death camp. Even if we can't prove they were guards at Buchenwald, the death itself looks fishy to me. Bottom line, I need the InfraGard credentials."

12

He hadn't taken a life since his days in the camp. No, that wasn't true. There was that guy 29 years ago who confronted him saying he was going to expose him as one of the guards at Buchenwald. It was in Florida when he'd first come to the U.S. from Punta del Este in Uruguay. He didn't want to take the guy out because there was always risk when you offed someone, but there was really no alternative. The risk was greater if he did nothing. It was that guy or himself. Too bad. The guy was an okay guy. Left him with no choice though. He'd strangled the guy in a dark parking lot. No witnesses. Pretty clean actually.

Gisela Miller was a similar situation. From what he could tell, she was a nice person. Had a lot of friends and didn't go looking for trouble. Still, when she started telling people she'd seen a former camp guard at one of the dinner tables he could see that that was going to be trouble. Ultimately, she was probably no threat. After all, how could she prove that a man in his 90s was the young guy who'd given her a hard time in the camp. He knew he didn't look like the same guy. Yes, he might have some of the same mannerisms, but lots of people probably had similar mannerisms. He probably could have survived her accusations, but he didn't need the aggravation.

Even if she couldn't prove anything, just the accusation would leave a stain on him that would ruin his life. Life was good right now and at his age there probably wasn't a lot more of it left. He intended to preserve whatever good years he still had. That meant doing whatever had to be done. Today it had to be the Miller woman. Who knew what it would be tomorrow? Hopefully Gisela Miller was the last threat to his security. Eliminating people, even elderly people, wasn't as easy as it was in the camp. Face it, he was not as strong or as scary as he was back in the camp.

But if you had the element of surprise on your side, you could still get the job done if you had to. He'd just proven that.

13

It was risky, but he had to know. He had to test the waters. Tonight at dinner he'd see how widespread the rumor was.

It was a round table for six. There were two women and three men besides himself. Max Schmidt knew both women and all three of the men. Usually this group was talkative and generally quite pleasant. Almost every night when he was with these five people or at least some of the folks in this group there were lots of laughs. So far tonight there was no exception. The mood at the table was light. Seemed like as good a time as any to see how rampant the rumor was.

"So has anybody heard the rumor about the World War II Nazi prison guard?"

"You mean about the one who supposedly lives here at Liberty Village?" The speaker was bald-headed Joe Avila, who ate more than he should and looked it.

"I find it hard to believe," said Malcolm, the retired dentist from Manhattan. Most of those guys have already been caught or are dead.'"

"I'm not so sure about that," said Lydia, a retired high school history teacher. Every once in a while you read about another one being caught. Liberty Village would be a perfect place for one of these guys to hide as he approaches the end of his miserable life. I don't know who's claiming they know this man, but it certainly could be possible."

Joe then said, "Does anyone here at the table know who started this rumor? Or more importantly, who it's about?" He scanned the table, and no one responded. "Then so far it is just a rumor. Wow, not a very nice rumor if it's just made up by somebody with nothing better to do with their time."

"Yes," said Lydia, "if someone just threw it out there without any basis in fact, that's almost criminal. Why would anyone do such a thing?"

"Unless it really is based on fact." Max couldn't resist throwing this out. Damn, why would he poke a hornet's nest when it had already settled down? He really was different. He'd always lived on the edge and even now in his dotage he still took unnecessary chances. What the hell was wrong with him? This was not just some verbal game. His life was at stake here. Why take such ridiculous chances? He should shut up and enjoy the rest of his meal.

Then Joe Avila, the one with the big mouth, turned to him and said, "It's guys like you, Max and your friend Zweig, that they'll come lookin' for. German accents. In your 90s. I'm not saying I suspect you or him, but you get the idea."

How should he react? Should he blow up or agree? As risky as it was, he probably should agree.

"No, I understand what you're saying. On the surface I suppose I do fit the profile."

"But you're not—"

"No, Lydia, I'm not and never was a guard of any kind. Neither was Heinrich Zweig."

"What did you do during the war?" pressed Joe.

"I was a foot soldier—like a lot of my countrymen. Infantry. Didn't have much choice."

"So you were a Nazi soldier?" Joe wasn't going to let up.

"Most German soldiers were not Nazis, Joe. Most were regular working men pressed into service by the military. I was not a Nazi."

"That's not the way I heard it," continued Joe. You weren't all Nazis, but a lot were."

This guy was getting annoying. "Well I told you *I* wasn't."

Joe was relentless. "Didn't you tell us once that you came to the States from some place in South America?"

"Yes, Joe. That doesn't make me a Nazi."

"No, but I know a lot of Nazis went to South America after the war to avoid being accused of war crimes."

"A lot of German soldiers went there to avoid being accused of being Nazis. It was easier than being brought up on charges and having to defend yourself. Once you're accused, a little of the stain clings to you even when you're completely innocent."

"If you're completely innocent—"

"C'mon, Joe. Lighten up," yelled Lydia. "This is a dinner table, not the Nuremberg Trials."

The others at the table voiced their agreement. Schmidt was thankful for Lydia's intervention, but could see that Joe was a threat. A threat to his and Heinrich's very existence. Something had to be done with Joe. And soon.

Joe then said, "What I meant was if you're innocent, why would you need to go to South America?"

"All right, Joe," snapped Lydia. "That's enough.

14

Madison yelled up the stairs to her husband. She knew he was glued to his computer. "You coming down soon? The show starts in 15 minutes."

Liam yelled, "Be down in five."

Less than five minutes later he came into the kitchen and kissed her. Not a peck on the cheek but a passionate kiss on the lips. They'd been married 31 years and the excitement had never gone away. It wasn't by accident or just dumb luck either. From the very beginning they'd vowed that they wouldn't get stuck in a marriage where they took each other for granted. They sensed at the time that they'd both have to work at keeping the excitement of their love alive and vital. And they had. It wasn't perfect. Not many marriages are, but they'd both done everything they could to keep the fun in their relationship. She loved to laugh, and he loved to see her laugh. He loved it when she was in the room, and she looked forward to being with him. It was a romance that kept on giving.

It was an unlikely romance from the start. They were the offspring of two German soldiers who were probably Nazis, though the fathers had never admitted it to their kids. Over the years, though, it had become fairly clear that their dads were not just infantrymen who had no choice but to do their duty in the German army. No, it gradually became clear that their dads had enjoyed the work that they'd done at one of Hitler's concentration camps. Just admitting that to themselves had been a bitter pill to swallow. Learning about it hadn't happened overnight. There were things that were said in anger. Things that were said when bragging. Things their mothers had said in frustration or anger. There were comments they weren't supposed to hear about their dads' satisfaction that so many Jews had been eliminated and comments about how unsatisfied they were that the job hadn't been finished. No, there was no doubt in the minds of Madison or Liam that their fathers had both been proud of their work at the camp. From what they'd heard the camp was very likely Buchenwald.

Tonight, though, Madison wasn't laughing. After they kissed, she turned serious. "I have to tell you something."

"I don't like the sound of this."

"My mother called a few minutes ago. She said my dad is under suspicion up there at Liberty Village."

"I thought things were going well up there. Our parents were finally living in a place where they could ride out their remaining years in peace. Not that our dads deserve it, but our moms certainly do."

"Don't be so hard on your dad, Liam. I know he must have done some bad things, but as far as we know he's lived a good life since the war. On the other hand, my dad almost certainly did some bad stuff and probably enjoyed it. Just the way he treats my mom."

"Face it, we don't really know exactly what our dads did other than that they were almost certainly camp guards at Buchenwald. And it's no secret what went on in those camps. If our dads worked there, they must have done some bad stuff. We just don't know how bad."

Madison agreed, "We have a pretty good idea just based on what we've heard them and our moms say over the years. There is no doubt they did bad stuff and probably enjoyed it. That's the worst part of it."

"I wish I could disagree but you yourself know what your father was like when you were growing up. He's a mean son-of-a-bitch. I'm sorry, Madison, but you know that's true. You've as much as said it yourself."

"But we're getting off the subject," said Madison. "Apparently someone up there at Liberty Village claims that our dads were their guards at Buchenwald when they were held prisoners there. After all these years that person could be mistaken, but you and I know that it's unlikely. We know both of our fathers worked in a concentration camp so I'm assuming this mysterious person has it right. Even if they're wrong it focuses the wrong kind of attention on Heinrich and Max."

"How the hell are they going to continue living up there if everybody thinks they're war criminals. And at their age it's not going to be easy finding somewhere else to live. Let's just hope this is just a big mistake."

"How likely is that?"

"I'm afraid it's not likely at all," he said. "Somehow we're going to be dragged into this. How can we avoid it? Our trip to Italy is just a few weeks away."

"We've been able to avoid something like this ever since we got married. Thankfully both of our dads have kept a low profile. Until now that is. It's always been hanging out there, though. I suppose it was inevitable. My mom isn't asking for our help. Just letting us know what's happening so if things get worse, we won't be shocked."

He said, "I have a feeling things will get worse."

15

Eliminating people at Liberty Village required a lot more imagination than it had back in the camp. Back then you didn't have to hide it. Your colleagues didn't challenge you if you got rid of somebody.

Here, though, it was different. Obviously. He'd already taken care of Gisela Miller at the pond. That had been easy. He knew she liked to walk around the grounds. He'd just waited for her to get near the pond and one push and the job was done. Fortunately, she liked to walk early—six thirty—when hardly anyone else was around to see him push her. He hadn't known if she could swim, but in case she could, he'd taken care of that, thanks to that serial killer on campus a couple years earlier. The serial killer had struck his victims on the head with a grapefruit-sized rock. Brilliant! It hadn't taken him long to find a perfect rock for Gisela. One blow to the head, then a good push and she'd tumbled into the pond. Nice and clean. No witnesses because of the early hour. The rock went into the pond after her.

His friend Max Schmidt had called him and told him about the grilling he'd taken from a Joe Avila. He'd urged Max to deal with Avila, but his old friend had hesitated—said he no longer had the stomach for such things. Out of sheer frustration he'd told Schmidt he'd take care of it. Just keep his mouth shut.

So he now had to take care of this Avila person. But he couldn't do the same thing that he did with Gisela. Avila was apparently so obese he probably didn't do much walking for exercise. So not in the pond. This Avila pain in the ass would probably not go anywhere near the pond, so the method had to be different. Two deaths in the pond in a week or so would draw too much attention to the manner of dying. Deaths at Liberty Village were not that uncommon, but two in the pond would be. So the pond was out. This was going to take a little more imagination. He had to come up with something soon, too, as this guy was a loose cannon. Then it came to him.

Joe Avila's apartment was on the fifth floor. He lived alone. His wife had died a few years ago. It took Avila almost a minute to open the door after the knock.

When Joe realized who his visitor was he stared and said, "It's you. You're the friend of that Schmidt guy aren't you? What do you want?"

"I just want to talk. I heard you got off on the wrong foot at the dinner table recently."

"I'm not so sure we did. I have my thoughts, and Schmidt, he's not going to say anything other than what he did say. I guess I'd keep quiet, too, if I was in his shoes."

"What shoes are they, Joe?"

"I think I've said enough. You should probably leave."

He stepped a half step closer to Avila. "Look, I just want to clear the air, Joe." As he said this he inched a bit closer. Avila was clearly uncomfortable.

Joe said, "We're never going to be friends, so why don't you just leave now."

He held his hands in front of him palms up as if asking for understanding. Before Avila could back away, he struck him on the right side of the neck with a karate chop. It was something he had learned years ago when training in the SS. He didn't know then, but had learned more recently that a sharp karate punch with the side of the hand on the vagus nerve or the carotid artery would incapacitate a man. It could incapacitate a fit young man. A man in his 80s could be killed. Avila fell immediately to the floor and lay there motionless.

He bent down slowly. He was, after all, in his 90s. He felt for a pulse and found a very faint one. He then went into Avila's bedroom and found a bed pillow. He brought the pillow back to the motionless Avila and placed it on his face, holding it there until he could no longer hear any breath from the fallen resident. He again checked for a pulse and this time found none. He then returned the pillow to where he'd found it on the bed, making sure to eliminate any facial impression. He checked to be sure he'd left no evidence of his presence in the apartment. Then he went to the door and peered through the peep hole making certain no one was in the hall. At least not near the door.

He then opened the door a crack and peered left, then right. At the right end of the hall he noticed someone disappearing into the stairway exit. It was a good 100 feet away so he doubted that whoever it was would have noticed him. Even if they had they most likely wouldn't recognize him because he didn't live in this building. Okay. No problem. He went to his left anyway because that was where the elevators were. He made it to the elevators without seeing anyone else. He then took the elevator down to the first floor. Whew! A job well done, and again with no witnesses. He was getting pretty good at this. Hopefully, though, he wouldn't have to dispatch anybody else. It was somewhat stressful, and every time he did it he put himself at risk. Anyway, now the two people causing him the most agita were out of the way. Zweig wondered if his friend had been undergoing any more scrutiny lately. He'd have to ask.

16

I must be psychic because I had a bad feeling when the phone rang. It was Bill Miller with more bad news.

"Tony, another resident here was found dead in his apartment."

"I'm sorry to hear that, Bill, but why are you telling me? A lot of the residents there are in their 80s or even older. It can't be that unusual for a resident to pass."

"You're right. It isn't that unusual, but I think this one might not be a normal passing. It was a guy named Joe Avila. I didn't know him personally, but I knew him by reputation. He was kind of a loudmouth. Liked to voice his opinions, especially when he knew they would rankle. Even if he hurt someone's feelings, Joe liked to *tell it like it is,* as he put it."

"I have a feeling this is leading up to something, Bill."

"Yeah, it is. A friend of mine told me yesterday that he was at a table with Joe and some other folks. Apparently one of the men actually asked the people at the table if they'd heard anything about someone at Liberty Village who was a prison guard in the past. No, not a regular prison guard, but a camp guard at one of Hitler's concentration camps. Buchenwald I think."

"Okay. And?"

"And Joe went on to say Schmidt, the man who was asking, was exactly the kind of person they were looking for."

"He said that?"

"This is what I heard. Well you can imagine how the man reacted when Joe said that to him."

"I think I can. Whether a man is guilty or not, he wouldn't take kindly to someone who said that to him. What I also don't know is why, if the man actually looked like he could have been a concentration camp guard, he would have brought up the subject. By the way, did your friend say who this guy was? I naturally wonder if he was one of our suspects."

"No, he didn't know, but he said the guy was in his 90s, fairly tall and able to get around without a walker. Oh, he did have a German accent. Maybe being guilty he wanted to get a sense of how widespread the rumor was. Wanted to know if he was in serious jeopardy. Just a guess. I have no idea other than that."

I could see that Miller might be on to something. "Maybe. Then again, This man might be perfectly innocent and just curious."

"I don't know, Tony. Someone questions a strange guy with a German accent and the next day they turn up dead. It is awfully suspicious. You can't just ignore this."

"This isn't being ignored, Bill. I'm already looking into it. I now have FBI credentials so it'll be easier for me to talk to people. The bureau is looking into Zweig's background. They may be able to prove he was a camp guard. Now they'll look into Max Schmidt, too. Some might say he had a motive for killing Gisela. Not a very good motive, but in his mind it might have been. He has a German accent, too. Who knows, he might be the one we should look at. I'm going to personally look into both of them. The bureau is checking into both of their backgrounds.

That night I told Joanna what I planned to do the next day. She wasn't enthusiastic about it.

"Are you sure you should be accusing these two men of war crimes and maybe even murder? So far, as I understand it, you have no evidence against either of them. Just suspicions."

"I'm not going to accuse either one of them. I'm just going to tell them that I'm investigating two deaths and that their names have come up in my investigations. The sooner I can clear them, the sooner I can move on to other persons of interest."

"Yes, but the very fact that you're interviewing them implies that you think they're suspects."

"That's true. Unfortunately, that happens in a murder investigation. You can't rule out people without taking a look at them. And frankly, both of these guys are suspicious characters. They should be looked at."

"Of course. Why am I even questioning you on this? You've been doing this for a long time and you're pretty good at it."

"Well somebody has to do it, and if I can rule out anyone early on it'll be better than having cops all over Liberty Village. They'll be there soon enough anyway."

17

The next day I was facing the door to Max Schmidt's apartment. I'd waited till 9:30 AM out of respect for the breakfast hour. Retired people eat breakfast at different hours, and I figured 9:30 wouldn't be too early. I knocked three times. I heard shuffling within and in less than a minute or so a woman answered the door. She had been pushing a walker and was somewhat stooped. She looked to be in her late 80s or early 90s. It was hard to tell from her stooped posture using the walker, but she appeared to be about average in height for a woman and somewhat heavy. She greeted me with a warm smile as she said, "Yes? Do I know you?"

"I don't think so, Ma'am. Name's Tony Dantry. I work for the FBI. Is your husband in?"

"Yes he is. Why does the FBI need to see him?"

"We're interviewing several people here in our investigation."

"FBI investigation? What are you investigating?" She was old, but she was alert.

"Maybe you could get your husband so I don't have to repeat myself."

"I'm coming," said a voice from a different room.

A man about my height came into the room. I'm a little over six feet by the way. He appeared to be in his 90s, but clearly didn't need a walker.

"What's this all about? Couldn't help hearing you say you're with the FBI."

"I'm with FBI InfraGard. We're looking into one, maybe two suspicious deaths that have occurred here at Liberty Village. I'd like to ask you a few questions if you don't mind."

"I don't know of any suspicious deaths here. People pass away here fairly commonly but their deaths are not usually considered suspicious."

"Did you know a Gisela Miller?"

"Oh yeah, I knew her. Can't say I liked her, but that doesn't mean I'd kill her. Besides, I heard she fell in the pond. An accident. Terrible accident, but still an accident."

"Well there's reason to believe it may not have been an accident."

"You mean someone did that to her?"

"Maybe. I think it's entirely possible."

"Good grief. That's terrible. But even if that's true, why are you talking to me?"

"It's my understanding that you've had some run-ins with her in the past. Some that got pretty heated."

"Oh you mean with the car? No big deal. She got very defensive. Had no right to because it was her fault in the first place. She hit my car. I didn't hit hers."

"I guess there are two sides to every story. That's not the way she told it. Said you got all heated up and made a big deal over a little ding. Said she apologized but you didn't accept her apology."

"Well it was a lot more than a ding. I'll tell you that."

"Why don't we go out and look at your car. You can show me the damage she did."

"I had it repaired. There's nothing to see now. Cost me nearly a grand."

"Really? Where'd you have the work done?"

"What is this? The third degree? If you must know it was a place in Port Chester. Don't remember the name of it."

I wanted to see this guy squirm. "You could probably take me there, though?"

"I probably could, though I can't promise I could find it. Just picked this place at random."

"Of course. We're not going there now, but we may have to in the future." Schmidt was struggling now to control his temper. I let him stew for a minute, then said, "You had another run-in with Gisela Miller when you accused her of cheating at bridge. I'm sure you remember that?"

I was getting to Schmidt, and he didn't like it. I had the feeling he was not used to being accused. He was used to doing the accusing. He was considering his answer carefully. Finally, he said, "Look I admit we had some disagreements, and I didn't like the woman, but I don't go around killing people I disagree with. If I did there'd be a lot of dead people around here." That in itself said worlds about the man.

"Do you mind telling me where you were the morning Gisela Miller died in the pond?

"I was right here in the apartment. Heidi here will attest to that." He nodded toward his wife.

Heidi Schmidt nodded her assent vehemently, adding, "He rarely leaves the apartment until after lunch." Then she added, "He has a temper, but he's not violent. We've been married 66 years and he's never struck me. He's a good man. He'd never have pushed Gisela into the pond."

Max then asked, "You mentioned two suspicious deaths. What was the other one?"

"Man named Joseph Avila. He was found dead in his apartment. He had no known illness or condition that could have caused his death."

"I know this guy. All too well. The other night he as much as accused me of being a guard in a Nazi concentration camp."

"Why would he do that?"

"Said I looked like the type who would be a prison guard. I'm from Germany, speak with an accent and I'm old enough to have been one. Hell, you could say that about a half dozen men here at Liberty. Everybody at the table told him he was out of line. The guy talks first and thinks later. Frankly I'm not sorry to hear that he's dead, but I certainly didn't kill him. He pissed me off, but I'm no killer. I hope you don't—"

"We're not accusing anybody right now. We're just asking questions. We need to do that. Let me ask you this. How long have you lived in the United States?"

It was clear from the expression on his face that he was hoping I wouldn't ask him this.

"About 30 years."

"And where did you live before that?"

"Uruguay. I lived there for about 10 years."

"And where did you live before that?"

"Argentina." He was fuming now. "Look, I know where this is going. I was born in Germany. I served in the German army. I was not a guard in a concentration camp. Every German in America was not a camp guard. Your country has thousands of us and most of us are good American citizens."

"I'm not suggesting otherwise. You have to realize that these are the sort of questions we need to ask when investigating what possibly may be two murders here at Liberty Village. These questions have to be asked. I'm not asking you about Mr. Avila because I suspect you of causing his death. You asked about the second suspicious death, and it was Avila's. And you're right, it may turn out to be normal causes. I'm sorry I bothered you folks this morning. It was only because we have to ask questions as part of our investigation. Hopefully you won't hear from me again." I knew, though, that the police almost certainly would want to contact Schmidt when they started their investigations of Avila's death.

18

It was still morning when I left the Schmidt apartment. This seemed like as good a time as any to visit Heinrich Zweig.

The woman who opened the door appeared to be in her seventies. If she was Heinrich Zweig's wife she must have been at least 20 years his junior. She appeared fit and must have been a knockout when she was younger. When she saw me she said, "Hello. I don't think I know you." Though her English was perfect she had an accent that I identified as Hispanic.

"Name's Tony Dantry. I'm with the FBI. Is Mr. Zweig in?"

"Yes, he is. The FBI? What in the world does the FBI want to see my husband for?"

"If you'd call him, I'll explain. By the way, I assume you're Mrs. Zweig?"

"Yes, Doreen Zweig." She smiled and then called, "Heinrich?"

From a different room a deep voice said, "Yes. What is it?"

"A man from the FBI is here to see you. God knows why."

Heinrich Zweig entered the room and stood facing me. I sensed that he was sizing me up. For what I didn't know, but he made me slightly uncomfortable. He was almost certainly in his mid-90s, though he had no trouble getting around on his own. I'd seen men a lot younger in Liberty Village using walkers to help them get around.

I introduced myself again. "Name's Tony Dantry. I'm with FBI Infragard."

"What's Infragard?"

"The FBI authorizes certain qualified people to represent the bureau. In my case I'm former CIA."

"I see. So what does the FBI want to talk to me about?"

"Would you prefer that we talk alone?"

"I have no secrets from my wife. I'd like her to stay." When he said this I studied her face for any telltale giveaway signs. I saw nothing, but she might just have been very good at hiding her emotions.

"Fine. I'm here looking into at least one suspicious death here at Liberty Village."

"Does the FBI usually investigate suspicious deaths? Isn't that normally up to the local police?" This old guy was well informed. That in itself was a little suspicious. Still, I'd found that a lot of the folks here at Liberty Village were well informed about a lot of things.

"Usually it is up to them. Right now they're waiting for the medical examiner's report."

"Then what brought you here?"

"Bill Miller, Gisela Miller's husband knows me. He called me when he learned about his wife's passing. At first it was unofficial, but after I heard about the way she died the FBI and I made it an official investigation. We'll work with the local police when the time comes."

"I see. What's all this got to do with me?"

"Are you sure you want me to go on with Mrs. Zweig present?"

"Of course, though I don't even know this Gisela Miller. Can't imagine why you want to talk to me. But go ahead. Let's get this over with."

"As a child Mrs. Miller was a prisoner in the Nazi concentration camp Buchenwald. She and her parents and her sister were all captives there. She claimed before her death that one night at dinner here at Liberty she saw a man who was one of her prison guards. She claimed that man was you."

"That's ridiculous. I was never even in a Nazi prison camp. Where did she get such nonsense?"

"Where were you during the Second World War?"

"I was a soldier."

"For what country?"

"For Germany. I grew up in Germany and when Hitler came to power most young men had to serve in the army. We had no choice."

"And you never worked in a concentration camp?"

"Never."

"Have you always gone by the name Heinrich Zweig?"

Zweig's face went white for a second before he answered.

"No, before I came to America I lived in Argentina. In Argentina I changed my name because a lot of people who moved to Argentina from Germany were labelled Nazis and I didn't want to have to deal with that. Many Germans in Argentina were not Nazis."

"Yes, and many of those Germans did not change their names. By the way, what was your name before you changed it?"

"Jürgen Bauer."

"This was the name you were born with?"

"Ya er yes." I thought he hesitated for just a split second, but that could have been my imagination.

Zweig recovered his composure and said, "I am sorry to hear about this Miller woman. They say she fell into the pond. Some people here have trouble keeping their balance. I didn't know her, but that must have been what happened. That aside, though, how could she have accused me of being a camp guard? That must have been 75 or 80 years ago. Any camp guard this woman remembers is probably dead. Even if he's alive he wouldn't look the same after all these years. I'm sure you must see how ridiculous such an accusation has to be."

"I can see how you would think that. Still, some people have amazing memories. Sometimes they see some little thing that reminds them of someone from the past. Might have been the eyes, or a tic. Who knows? The point is, she apparently accused you of being this guard."

"She didn't accuse me of anything," he snapped. "I never even met this woman."

"No, she didn't accuse you to your face. She mentioned her suspicions to a friend who apparently mentioned it to someone else. One thing led to another and a rumor was floating around Liberty Village. Next thing we know she's dead.

You can see why we thought of you. If you became aware of this rumor, you might want to put a stop to it."

"That seems like a quantum leap. You don't even know if I was aware of the rumor."

"Let's not play games Mr. Zweig or whatever your name is. I know you were aware of the rumor."

"How the Hell could you know that?"

"Because at one dinner table recently your friend Max Schmidt engaged in an argument with a man named Joseph Avila who was saying that you or he could easily have been this prison guard everyone was talking about. The people at the table remember that argument vividly. Almost certainly Mr. Schmidt would have told you about this confrontation. The day after it took place, Mr. Avila was found dead."

"Now that is a quantum leap. Every time someone dies here you want to link it to me."

"All right, we both know that as of now we can't prove direct linkage. Right now it's only a suspicious coincidence. However, we do know that if there *is* direct linkage, we at the FBI or the local police will find it. If you can prove there is no direct linkage right now you can save us all a lot of trouble and yourself a lot of unnecessary grief."

"You know as well as I do that no one in my situation could prove his innocence of a coincidental occurrence. By the same token you've already admitted that you can't prove my guilt. That, of course, is because I am truly innocent of these sad deaths."

"You could prove your innocence by simply providing alibis for when these two deaths occurred."

"I don't go many places. I was probably right here in my apartment."

"I imagine Mrs. Zweig can confirm that?"

"Yes, yes of course," said Doreen Zweig. "He was right here in the apartment."

"When was that, Mrs. Zweig?" I probed.

"When did these two people die?"

"How can you confirm he was here when you don't know when the deaths occurred?"

"What I meant was he's here most of the time. Tell me what times you're talking about, and I'll tell you if he was here those times. I can tell you now he probably was."

I gave her the approximate time that Gisela Miller went into the pond.

The tension lines in her face relaxed a bit and she said, "He's usually home at that hour. Just starting his breakfast."

I then gave her the date that Gisela had died. "Was your husband home that day at that time of day?"

"I certainly think so."

"You don't seem sure. Why is that?"

She glanced at her husband before she said, "Because he gets up earlier than me. Often I'm asleep when he has his breakfast."

"Could he have gone out while you were sleeping?"

She looked over at Heinrich Zweig again before saying, "It's not like him to go out that early in the day. I doubt if he went anywhere."

"But you can't say for sure because you were sleeping?"

"Good Lord. What is this? If Heinrich says he was home, he was home. I trust my husband. He's a good man."

"But he's been accused by two people of being a prison guard in one of Hitler's concentration camps. What do you know about that?"

"I know nothing about that. The man I'm married to could never have done such a thing. Those were terrible people. My Heinrich is a wonderful man." At this she moved closer to her husband. He put his arm around her, and she got this secure look on her face. It was more the look of a daughter being comforted by her father than the look of a wife being comforted by her husband.

I could see that I wasn't going to learn much more now so I said, "Well folks, I'll be going. Thanks for your time. May need to ask you some more questions in the future."

19

In my head I went over my visits to my two suspects. I definitely couldn't eliminate either one of them based on the answers they'd given me. Yet I couldn't make a case against either one that would stick.

I needed some hard evidence or at least some historical background to make a good case against one or both of them. I hadn't heard anything from the FBI so far. I was hoping I'd hear something soon. Until then I was stymied.

I had two cases to make based on what these two men had been accused of. I knew enough to be fairly convinced that they were both former Nazi prison guards. Before coming to the United States both of them had lived in Argentina. That in itself was not proof that they were Nazi camp guards, but mighty suggestive.

Shortly after Gisela's passing I stopped in at the local police constabulary and spoken with a detective by the name of Colin Ryan. After explaining my role in the Liberty Village investigation as an FBI InfraGard agent, I asked him if the local police viewed Gisela Miller's death a homicide.

He said that the medical examiner found no evidence of a crime, though couldn't rule it out either. I then asked, "Are you aware of what happened before she died? Do you know anything about a man named Heinrich Zweig?"

Ryan said, "No. Never heard of this Zweig. I assume you think we should?"

"Absolutely." I then took the time to explain the suspicions Gisela had had about Zweig and Schmidt. I went on to explain how Jean Fullbright had witnessed the drowning of Gisela and how she was certain a man had pushed Gisela into the pond. I told Ryan that none of that would have been known to the medical examiner.

"So," said Ryan, "You think this is a homicide?"

"I do, though I can't prove anything."

"You're saying that one of these two guys, Zweig and what's-his-name, look suspicious?"

"Yes. The other one is Max Schmidt. They both have motive, but I can't place them at the scene of the crime. They have alibis, though I don't think they'll hold up."

"Why is that?"

"Both alibis are given by their wives, and I think these guys have their wives snowed or terrified. I'm not sure which. In the meantime I'm waiting for the FBI to give me whatever they come up with on these guy's backgrounds. Obviously I want to work with you people in any way I can."

"You're probably surprised to hear it from me, but I'm glad you're working this case and glad the FBI is involved. As I'm sure you can understand, we're a small force. I'm the only detective who's ever worked a homicide. Once you have something solid on these guys, I'll come out with a couple uniforms and make the arrests." He saw me roll my eyes and he quickly added, "I know, looks like I'm letting you do all the work and I'm grabbing the collar. We'll give you guys the credit, but as far as I know the FBI doesn't actually investigate homicides unless it's the president or some federal official. I assume you're investigating this homicide because it's related to two possible Nazi war criminals. If you can make the arrests, let me know and we'll back off. Besides, I have to talk with my chief before I can make a commitment one way or the other anyway."

I sure hoped it would go this smoothly with the locals. On my way home I tried not to think of the case. When a case was stalled, as this one was, I found that getting my mind off it somehow allowed my subconscious to work in the background. Sometimes I would come up with a breakthrough idea that helped move the case along and sometimes I would get a call that would move us forward. Right now I'd accept any idea if it helped me with this case. As it turned out, my help came from 26 Federal Plaza.

"Hello, Is this Tony Dantry?" It was an unfamiliar female voice.

"Yes. Who's this?"

"Agent Marisol Svensen. I'm an intelligence analyst with the FBI International Human Rights Unit. Used to be the War Crimes Unit. I have some information for you."

"Good. Let me have it."

"You inquired about a Heinrich Zweig and a Max Schmidt."

"Yes."

"I can confirm that both of them arrived in Argentina from Germany in 1945. They went together through Spain. At the time Spain was supportive of Germany and—"

"Yes. I know. The Franco regime was a fascist state that benefitted from military aid from Hitler. Officially Spain was neutral, but Francisco Franco and Adolf Hitler were politically aligned and did help each other. If Nazi war criminals could make it safely to Spain, they could easily get to Argentina which welcomed these guys."

"We traced Heinrich Zweig back to the earlier name you gave us: Jürgen Bauer. It was on a work assignment sheet recovered from Buchenwald. As for Max Schmidt, he was Klaus Wagner on the work assignment sheets. He used that name in Argentina and became Schmidt in Uruguay. So unless there are men at Liberty Village with the same names and the same ages as the two at Buchenwald, I'd say you have these guys nailed as war criminals. You can probably go ahead and make the arrests, though you might want a couple of special agents with you. Actually, I don't have the authority to tell you this. I know you're working with Special Agent Polo. Probably should talk to him."

I didn't want to arrest these guys until we could get them on murder charges too. Not a good idea to leave two murders unsolved. If they weren't the murderers, I had to find out who was. As of now I had my eyes on my two war crimes suspects, and now they were looking damned guilty. I thanked Marisol and told her I would be in touch with Polo. I didn't tell her when because I wanted to have another crack at both Zweig and Schmidt first. I intended to be back at Liberty Village in the morning.

20

I arrived at Liberty Village just a few minutes after 9 AM. I intended to drop in on Zweig first. I know, I'd already spoken with him and gotten virtually nothing. Now that I had proof that he was a guard at Buchenwald I wanted to see how he would explain it. I also figured that, since I would have him at a disadvantage, I might get him to confess to the two murders. Wishful thinking maybe, but worth a try.

After leaving my car in Visitor Parking it took me a good ten minutes to get to Zweig's apartment. Liberty Village is big. I'd guess it has over 1,000 residents. Maybe a lot more. It's made up of quite a few large buildings all connected by glass-enclosed climate-controlled links so you never have to leave the place in bad weather. It's actually quite impressive.

No one answered my knock on the door. I knocked again louder and still no answer. Okay. They're out. I'd come back later. I'll try the Schmidts in the meantime. As I started to walk to the elevator the door next to the Zweigs opened. A woman in her bathrobe said, "You looking for the Zweigs?"

"Yes."

"They left for vacation last night."

"Last night?"

"Well, right after dinner. Told me they'd be away for a week. Going to visit their daughter in Virginia."

"You wouldn't happen to know the name of their daughter?"

"No. I didn't know they had a daughter, but then again I didn't know them very well. Kept to themselves. Not very sociable."

"Did they mention what town in Virginia she lived in?"

"No. Just wanted me to know they'd be gone at least a week so that I wouldn't worry. Fat chance I'd worry about those two."

I thanked the woman and headed off for Schmidt's apartment. That Zweig and his wife went away when he knew he was under investigation sent up flags. Especially interesting that they left at night. Not many people set off on a trip at night. As far as I knew he didn't have a daughter. I texted Marisol Svensen and asked her to check on that.

Five minutes later I arrived at the door of Max Schmidt. I knocked and waited. Nothing. I could see a pattern here. I knocked again. This time louder. Still no one came to the door. So they were both on the run. Not surprising, though I couldn't imagine where they were going.

On a hunch I knocked on the door of their neighbor to the left. The name on the door said Wilson. Silence. Then I heard someone shuffling to the door. The door opened slowly revealing a frail woman pushing a walker.

"Yes? Do I know you?"

"I don't think so, ma'am. Name's Tony Dantry. Would you happen to know where your neighbors, the Schmidts, are?"

"Normally I wouldn't have any idea, but last night they came over to tell me they were going on vacation to Virginia for a week, maybe a little more. Not to worry. It was strange, because we're not friends and they're not very friendly. Why would they even think I'd care if they went on vacation?"

"That is strange. Well anyway thank you ma'am. Sorry to have bothered you."

Before I left the floor another hunch told me I should try the neighbor to the right of the Schmidt's apartment.

The name on the door said Guinty.

A man who was a bit hunched over answered the door. I guessed he was in his 80s. Like much of the population here at Liberty. Before he could speak I said, "Mr. Guinty, my name's Tony Dantry. Would you by any chance know where the Schmidts went?"

"Funny you should ask. Normally I'd have no idea where they were. Frankly, I wouldn't care one way or the other. He's not very friendly and she doesn't say boo unless he lets her."

"But—"

"But last night he came over and told us that they were going on vacation for at least a week. Said they were going to Virginia. Not to worry."

"I gather they would normally not bother to inform you when they went away for a few days or more?"

"No! We weren't close. Far from it. My wife and I thought it was strange that he would tell us. Most of the time they made it a point of avoiding us in the corridor or in the dining rooms if they could. If they couldn't avoid us he would just nod. She might say hello, but all we ever got from him was a nod or a grunt of recognition." Before I could say thanks, Guinty said, "Hope you're not a friend of his? Here I am shooting my mouth off when maybe you're his best friend."

"No. I'm not a friend. Thanks for the information."

"Hey, who are you then?"

"Just someone looking for information. Bye."

When I got back to my car I sat and thought about what I'd just learned. Obviously the Schmidts wanted the authorities—including me—to think they had gone to Virginia. Almost certainly they had headed in a different direction. Almost certainly the Schmidts didn't have a daughter in Virginia. Very likely both the Schmidts and the Zweigs went in the same direction, and it wasn't Virginia. Quite likely both suspects thought that telling their neighbors they would return in a week or so would keep law enforcement from pursuing them immediately, thereby giving them plenty of time to get away to someplace safe. They must be getting desperate because that wasn't going to fly. A ruse like that was no doubt a skill they had perfected over the years since leaving Germany. Both of these guys were escape artists. It must have worked in the past, but it wasn't going to work now.

If they didn't go to Virginia, where did they go?

21

I called Marisol Svenson at FBI headquarters in Manhattan to see if she had learned anything about the Zweigs having a daughter.

"I was just going to call you. As far as I can tell the Zweigs have no kids. There is no record of them having any offspring. That doesn't mean they don't have any. Just that we can't find a record of them."

"Kind of what I thought. Say, can you trace the location history of two phone numbers I give you?"

"I'll need a warrant, but yes. Give me the reason for the warrant."

"Two war-crime suspects on the run."

"That should do it."

I gave her the information she needed and she said she'd get back to me soon. In the meantime I decided I might as well go home. Good time to check on my boat. It was really just an excuse to get on the boat in the marina. Not really much to check up on, but I loved being on the boat and loved being at the marina. Later that afternoon when I was still sitting on the boat soaking up a few rays my phone rang and it was Marisol.

"Your guys are a couple hundred miles north of you now. They've just recently entered the Adirondack region. Just south of Lake George."

"Can you tell what road they're on and what direction they're heading?"

"Yes. They're heading north on New York Rte. 9. Got off the Adirondack Northway or Interstate 87 a few hours ago. Then got on Rte. 9. We contacted the New York State Police and asked them to check on these two cars. Make arrests if they found the suspects. Looks as if they changed cars. Somebody must have met them because their car engines were cold and they were not near a restaurant or gas station. A war criminal suspect disappeared near this spot about ten years ago. Another about seven years ago. Even after all these years these guys seem to be well organized. Sort of an Underground Railroad for old Nazis. Does seem as if there must be some kind of safe haven for these guys in the area around Lake George. Still, they could be on their way to Canada for all I know. If they're really clever this could be the meeting point, but the safe haven could be miles from here. Though I doubt it. I have a feeling it's not too far from where they left their cars. No matter where it is they must not be too concerned. Must feel it's pretty safe. If they drove all night they would have been farther north than this. For that reason and one other I'm betting they're not too far from where they left their two cars."

"Marisol, if the FBI has suspected there's a safe haven for Nazi war criminals somewhere near Lake George or farther north in the Adirondacks we must have narrowed the location down over the years. I can't believe the FBI would have just left this alone?"

"You'll remember I just said there were two reasons I think these guys are not far from where they left their cars. The second reason is that a local man was just found shot dead on Assembly Point. It's a peninsula into Lake George not too far from where the two cars were abandoned. The shooting is near a residential area which hardly ever has shootings or any criminal activity. Might not be connected to our Nazis, but then again it might be. You might want to make a run up there to look into it.

22

I was driving at about 70 in my Honda CRV Sport Hybrid on the Northway. I was now about 60 miles north of Albany in Upstate New York. I had just passed Glens Falls and was heading north. Lake George village, which is about 10 miles north of Glens Falls, was just ahead. Lake George is often called Queen of American Lakes because of its beautiful deep clean waters. The lake is surrounded by the foothills of the Adirondacks.

I stopped for lunch just south of the Village of Lake George, then headed northeast along Rte. 9L, also called the Ridge Road. I was heading toward Assembly Point where I hoped to find the two cars our Nazis had used to flee Liberty Village down in Putnam County. I had instructions from Troop G of the New York State Police. After lunch I called them to tell them where I was and we arranged to meet at the place where the two cars were. They gave me the GPS coordinates so I didn't expect any problem finding them

I'd had plenty of time to think on my drive northward. I could easily imagine some kind of refuge or sanctuary where fleeing former Nazis could go if things got too uncomfortable for them in the general society. Cottages and houses along the shore of a popular lake would make ideal safe houses for such fugitives. People who live along lakes are used to renters and

other part-time residents coming and going. New residents would not arouse suspicion—
at least not among neighbors a few doors away. The closest neighbors might be curious—unless they were not too close in actual proximity.

Some of the thinking I'd done while driving was about when I'd lived on Assembly point as a teenager. My parents had had a summer cottage there that they eventually winterized so that we were able to live there in the winter as well as during the warm summer months. My father's business was in Glens Falls so we were able to maintain two houses. It was great for me because I was able to swim, waterski, fish and go boating in the good weather and skate and go ice fishing in the winter. The lake was amazing. It had no seaweed or other growths. The bottom in most locations was white sand. The water was so clear that you could see the bottom even when the lake was eight or ten feet deep. It was so clean that the people on the lake used it as their source of drinking water. So Lake George, and especially the area around Assembly Point, were familiar to me. It was hard to imagine Nazis or ex-Nazis living there, but I suppose there was no reason why they couldn't if they were smart and kept a low profile. Our fugitives were smart. We knew that. And they'd kept a low profile since World War II, so they very well could be hanging out somewhere near here.

It wasn't hard to find the two cars. They were parked alongside Rte. 9L on the left side in a clearing. It was very close to Assembly Point. Next to the two abandoned cars was a state police car with two men sitting in the front seat. When I pulled over the two men got out of their car and stood waiting for me to approach.

23

Heinrich Zweig leaned back in his La-Z-Boy recliner resting his chin between his thumb and forefinger. He could relax for the moment, but he knew the law was after him and sooner or later they would find him. A few feet away, in a less comfortable chair, sat his friend Max Schmidt. Schmidt found it difficult to relax at a time like this. "How long can we stay here, Heinrich?"

"A few days. A week at the most."

"And then? I have always left the planning to you. Probably a mistake."

Zweig gave him a sharp look. "Have I ever led you astray? Look at you, my friend. You're in your 90s and you are still a free man."

"I'm sorry. You're right. What do we do next? If we are not staying here permanently, why not leave right away? Why wait a few days?"

"I like it here. Reminds me of my days as a youth at Schluchsee in the Black Forest. Lake George is actually a finer lake than Schluchsee. Bigger and deeper. You will see. If we move again, it will be farther north—into Canada. A much more remote location. Safer, but quite desolate. Safe, but nothing to do. We should stay here as long as we can. This is somewhat remote, but at least it is near civilization. Lake

George village is not a metropolis, but there are people and restaurants and things to do. Just to the south is Queensbury and Glens Falls. Our retreat in Canada is far from such places. Very safe, but very boring."

"You say this Assembly Point is more interesting. But are we safe here? They have probably already found our vehicles. How long will it take for them to find us?"

"Our cars are about two miles from here. There is nothing in or on them to connect them to this location. Robert and William assured us that these cottages have never drawn the wrong kind of attention in the past. They said years ago when these cottages were first used by people like us they did draw attention because the owners deliberately leaked it out that the men living here were homosexuals. In those days homosexuality was not so well accepted as it is now in this sick new American society—a society that seems to exalt people with defects—people the führer sent to the camps as socially aberrant. While spreading the rumor that the residents were gay made it awkward for them, it also diverted any questions about their true identities. Instead of investigating the residents as so-called war criminals, people tended to avoid them. Robert and William laugh when they tell this. They say we're going to have to get used to being pointed at or thought of as a gay couple, but it's a small price to pay for being safe."

Schmidt shook his head and said, Our wives are with us, so we probably won't be considered gay. As for these young men, I assume their real names are not Robert and William. They're much younger than us. My guess is they're in their thirties. I know you explained it once, but I was so nervous it didn't register. Why are these younger men helping us?"

"They're members of a white supremacist group here in New York state. Their hero is Adolf Hitler. They consider it an honor to be able to help us. These two guys actually live in New York City, but spend a lot of time in the Adirondack region because its remoteness makes it such a good area to carry out neo-Nazi activities and help World War II veterans such as ourselves. You can count on these young men to help us. To them, we're celebrities. They'll do almost anything for us."

"Then," said Schmidt, "ask them how we explain our wives living here with us if we're gay?"

Zweig forced a rare smile and said, "We've already talked about this. We can either say we're bisexual or they're our sisters. I've already decided that I'm bi, so you decide how you want to play it. Chances are we're not going to be asked anyway." They both remained deep in thought for over a minute until Zweig said, "Frankly, I think our biggest problem *is* going to be our wives. Doreen knows about my past, but for most of our marriage what I did in the war has been treated by us as ancient history. It hasn't had much impact on our marriage. At least not on mine. I've succeeded in convincing Doreen that I'm not that person anymore. I did what I did because I was forced to, or I would have paid the penalty. You and I know that the penalty part of that is true, but not the part where I said I was forced to be hard on the prisoners. We both know that I enjoyed it. I'm fairly sure you did, too."

Schmidt grinned. "Yes, I've never felt so important as I did back then in the camp." He drew in a deep breath and added, "I think Heidi knows more than she says. Like you, I've tried to behave like the man my wife thought she married. It's made our marriage fairly pleasant, but sometimes when I lose my temper I think it frightens her. I think she believes that she's seeing the real me—the me that misses the days in the camp when we did our part to eliminate those inferior beings."

Just then the door to the bedroom opened and the two women entered. Doreen Zweig said, "Well, gentlemen, now that we're settled here in the woods on the shores of beautiful Lake George, how do we entertain ourselves?"

Heinrich Zweig said, "The first thing we do is buy some groceries."

"I assume," said Heidi Schmidt, that old Ford outside is ours to use?"

"Yes it is," said Zweig. "We can buy the groceries today, but I agree, we need to figure out what kind of lifestyle we want up here in the north country. We obviously can't stay holed up here all day every day."

Heidi then said, "So your crimes in the camp have finally caught up with us."

Both men were startled at hearing this. In all their married years neither of their wives had ever confronted them or even expressed disapproval of their husbands' pasts.

Heinrich Zweig cleared his throat and said, "You both know that our work in the camp was forced upon us. We had no choice. Yes, it was unfortunate and most unpleasant, but if we didn't do it we would have ended up as prisoners ourselves or worse."

"Unfortunate! That's what you call it. I can't believe," said Heidi, "that you couldn't have opted for service in the regular army. You didn't have to do what you did." As she said this Doreen Zweig held Heidi by the elbow and looked her in the eyes shaking her head slowly from side to side. She was begging her to stop.

"Where is this coming from?" demanded Max. "You have never made an issue of the past before. I thought that was all behind us."

"You think, dear Max, that your past isn't always nagging at my mind. You have been a good husband, but I cannot erase what I can only imagine what you must have done in that camp. Now we must live like fugitives. We are fugitives. Here we are—you in your 90s—living like criminals on the run. I have no stomach for this. Are we going to spend the rest of our lives living in the middle of nowhere?"

"Give us some time," said her husband. "We will figure something out. Until we do, let's enjoy this place. The lake is beautiful. It's very peaceful here."

"It'll work out, Heidi," said Doreen. "Our men always take care of us. Just give them a little time. We're safe here and the lake is beautiful. We just got here after all."

As he caught the eye of Schmidt, Zweig frowned. This wasn't good. Not good at all.

Heidi then went for the door to the porch. "I need some air." As the door closed behind her Zweig shook his head in disgust.

He then said, "Let's make a list of what we need and a couple of us can go out and find the nearest store. He had just finished talking when they heard the sound of a car starting up. They looked out and were shocked to see the old Ford slowly driving away.

"Jesus, Max, we've got to do something about that woman of yours. She's going to give us away. Do you know where she's going?"

Schmidt appeared stunned. "No, I had no idea she was going to do that. Assuming it is her."

"Oh it's her," said Zweig. Ever the practical one, he added, "Let's just assume she needs to assert herself. Some women obviously do. But she'll be back. We have access to the money. Fortunately, we both withdrew our funds when those rumors back at Liberty Village began. Moved them to new accounts under new names."

"She still must have a credit card," said Doreen.

"Yes, but obviously it won't get her anywhere," said Zweig. "Max and I closed out those accounts when we moved the money."

"This is truly strange behavior for Heidi. We've never lived apart in all our married life. I don't know where she'd go. She doesn't know this area."

"She'll be back, Max. You know that. Come out on the porch with me. We need to plan. Doreen, give us a minute."

Seated on the porch the two men's eyes met expressing their frustration.

Zweig said, "Do we need this shit at this point in our lives, Max? Bad enough we had to deal with those two rumor mongers back in Liberty, but now your wife is suddenly developing a conscience after all these years."

Schmidt said, "We have to remember that we're different from most people. Most people, or at least many people have this exaggerated sense of right and wrong. My Heidi, she can't sleep if she thinks she's offended someone during the day. I tell her that's life. They'll get over it. Next time be nice and they'll be happy. To me a conscience is something I understand intellectually, but I don't really feel. I know, when you hurt someone you're supposed to feel bad, guilty. Like at Buchenwald when those Jews suffered I didn't feel a thing. Actually I felt we were doing our part to eliminate them. I was definitely a hypocrite back at Liberty Village pretending to think the things we did were so awful. I was pretty convincing, too."

Zweig grinned. "I'm sure you were a good actor, but you didn't see me in action. I had those people snowed, as the Americans like to say. Mix a little charm with a weak conscience and minimal empathy and you've got a very successful person."

Schmidt couldn't help but smile as he said, "Never heard it put that way but that's not bad."

"Okay," said Zweig, "now that we've patted ourselves on the back how are we going to deal with the situation we find ourselves in?"

"You mean being up here in the Adirondacks or my loose cannon wife?"

"Both, but we need to deal with your wife first. If she doesn't come back within an hour I'm going to call Robert or William and get us another car."

"Will they do that?"

"We may have to pay for it, but what choice do we have? But let's assume Heidi does come back soon. I don't think you can control her."

"What are you suggesting, Heinrich?"

"If she's a threat to our security, she may have to go."

"I hope it doesn't come to that."

"You don't really love her, do you. If you do, then I've misjudged you."

"Of course not, but she's been a part of my life for so long that I suppose I would miss her presence. Besides, she loves me and makes life easier for me in a number of ways.'

"Well, my friend, I'm afraid you may have to get used to living without those conveniences. She's a risk to us we can't afford to take. Let's just hope she comes back or the horse is already out of the barn."

24

I went over to the two men and introduced myself. Love those trooper hats, but these guys were not in uniform, so no trooper hats. They were New York State Police all right, but BCI (Bureau of Criminal Investigation) Division. One of them, Detective Gary Melillo, was a sandy blond of about six two. The other Detective, Mac Steele, appeared to be a fairly stocky five eleven with military cut brown hair.

I said, "Hope you guys haven't been waiting long."
"Little while," said Detective Steele. Not long. I understand you feds have something to bring to the table. What have you got?"

"I assume you know the men who drove these two cars are former Nazis. Can you be a former Nazi? I suppose once a Nazi, always a Nazi. They were guards at the Buchenwald concentration camp. They're not young. Obviously in their 90s, but as we can see, they still drive. Anyway, they're on the run. When we learned that there was a homicide not far from here, we couldn't help but wonder if there was a connection. These guys are killers. Already killed two people down in Putnam County. Can you bring me up to speed on this local homicide and anything about these cars?"

"Well," said Steele, "the victim was a friendly groundskeeper. Worked dozens of the houses and cottages in this area according to his family. Many of the properties he worked are on Assembly Point. He liked to get to know the tenants. Went out of his way to meet them. We're guessing he may have approached these Nazis, not knowing they were Nazis, but wanting to welcome them. We're also guessing his curiosity and tendency to be a talker made your guys nervous so they offed him. This is all speculation, but I wouldn't be surprised if it was true."

"Where was the body found?"

"About a half mile away from where we're standing—on the other side of 9L. Like it was tossed there out of a car."

"How was he killed?"

"Blunt force trauma to the head. Looks like he was hit with a rock or a piece of wood. More likely a rock because bits of gravel and sand were found in the gash on his head."

"Blunt force trauma, huh. That could definitely tie them to these guys. One of the victims down at Liberty Village may have been hit on the head with a rock before being pushed into a pond.

"Blunt-force trauma may be their comfort zone. As for this homicide, these guys are old. Wouldn't have been easy for a couple guys their age to move this body. And where would they get the car? They abandoned these two cars."

"Yes," said Steele, "but somebody obviously met them with another car. They've had help all along. May have had help moving the body."

"Can your lab determine where the gravel and sand came from? Maybe not exactly, but narrow it down for us?"

"We've got people working on it now. It's obviously from this general area. We've got people going up and down Assembly point taking samples to see if they can find a match. Hopefully we'll get lucky."

"Assuming these fugitives are hiding out on Assembly Point."

"Of course, but it's a good starting point. Has a lot of houses and cottages, and it's closest to where these cars are and where we found the body. And our groundskeeper did much of his work on the Point. These guys probably didn't want to go too far from where they changed cars. Must have been exhausted after their long trip north. Jesus, they're in their 90s. If it weren't for the homicide, we probably wouldn't have put as much manpower into this manhunt. These two men, if they are the ones who killed this poor groundskeeper, they probably overreacted. He was no threat, but when you're on the run, you fear everything. We'll get these guys, but it won't be easy."

I said, "Assembly Point isn't that big. Shouldn't be that hard to check it out."

"It's a little over a mile long with houses rimming the entire peninsula. Must be at least a thousand people. Maybe more. It's gonna take some time and maybe some luck. I don't think we can rely on just the soil samples. We'll do that, but we need to knock on doors, too."

25

They all heard it at once. The sound of gravel as a car was pulling in. Zweig went to the door and looked out. He turned and addressed Doreen and Max. "I told you she'd be back."

A minute later Heidi Schmidt was heard ascending the porch steps. As she entered the cottage Max went to her and held her hands.

"Where in God's name have you been?"

"I just felt stifled. I needed air. I drove around the peninsula. It's actually very nice. I think we can be quite comfortable here once we get to know the place, Max."

"You have had quite a personality change in the last half hour, Heidi," said Heinrich Zweig. "How do you account for it?"

"I don't know what you mean. I'm the same person I've always been."

"When you left here you were consumed by your knowledge of your husband's and my past during the war. All of a sudden this became all consuming. I wonder if it isn't because suddenly you lack the comforts Max provided for you all these intervening years. Now, when you're facing a bit of adversity, you turn on us. It was okay when you lived well.

Now that things are not going so well, you take the moral high ground."

"It's just that all of a sudden our lives have been turned topsy turvy. I'm not used to that. You boys have done that before and it's made you stronger and more accepting of change. I've never in my life had to make such quick, complete changes. I can see that changes haven't hurt you men, so I'm sure I can learn to adapt. Just give me a little time."

"That's a nice little speech, Heidi. I hope it's not just a speech. We have to be able to depend on you. No more impulsive moves like the one you just did with the car."

"Ya, mein Liebchen, said Max. Don't scare us again."

"Don't worry. It was just a momentary reaction to something I'm not used to. Give me a little time and I'll be fine."

Later, when the women were unpacking in the bedrooms, Heinrich took Max aside on the porch and in a low voice said, "I don't trust that woman of yours. She may have to join that overly-friendly groundskeeper. Or the Miller woman. We can't afford any loose ends."

"She seems to have come around. I think she'll be okay now that she got that out of her system. Once in a great while she loses her self-control, but she always self corrects. She knows herself. Knows she can sometimes give in to her emotions."

"That's what concerns me, my friend. I'm afraid her emotions take over too much. We've both seen how emotions can destroy people. I don't want it to be us."

"You don't want to give her one more chance?"

"If she gets emotional one more time it could be our undoing, Max. I'm afraid it has to be done today."

Sigh. "I suppose it must. May I leave it in your hands, Heinrich? I'd find it hard to do. After all—"

"Yes, yes. I understand. The problem is I'd rather Doreen not know that I did this. It's going to have to look like an accident. A real accident. Any ideas?"

"I suppose," said Max, "she could always fall into the lake. I know you did that with the Miller woman, but it is effective so why not again?" But why would she go near the lake with you? With me, yes, but you and she have never been friends and today she's not going to go anywhere with you. At least not voluntarily."

"Well, as you know only too well, the deed doesn't have to be done near the water. It can be done around here and then the body can be found in the lake. That's probably the best way to do it."

"I agree, but you said you'd prefer that Doreen not know you did it."

"Yes. That's not going to be easy unless— Of course. Why didn't I think of this until now?"

"Think of what?" demanded Max.

"Robert and William. They helped us get rid of the groundskeeper. Why not Heidi too?"

"I agree. It keeps us removed, yet we can depend on their discretion since they'll actually be the ones with blood on their hands."

"I'm going to give them a call right now. I need to go outside so the women don't hear me. If either of them ask who I'm talking to you can tell them it's Robert and William. They might need to come by today to explain some things and show us some things that will be helpful to us."

Max then said, "On second thought, Heinrich, maybe you better not call them. You're still going to have a problem even with their help. If they come here and Heidi disappears, Doreen is not going to be fooled. Back at Liberty Village, where we lived in different buildings, we might have been able to pull it off. Here, though where we live with each other, we're all aware of each other's movements. You're not going to fool Doreen for a minute."

"Then are you suggesting what I'm thinking you're suggesting, my friend?"

"I think I am. I never thought it would come to this, but if we don't, we'll be taking an awful risk."

"Still," said Heinrich, "we've lived with these potential risks ever since we married these women. Are they any greater risk now? I guess I've already answered that. I'm the one who said we needed to get rid of Heidi. She really is the greater risk here. I think Doreen is stable and accepts us for what we are. Obviously your Heidi has never fully accepted it, and now, when things have become a bit difficult, she's losing her composure. We can't take a chance on her."

"And if Heidi goes, Doreen will know we did it. I'm afraid that leaves no alternative than to eliminate both of them. If one remains, they become a huge risk. Can you accept that, Heinrich?"

"Yes. She's been good company over the years, but sometimes she's a bit tedious. I will miss her cooking, though. All I can do is fry an egg."

"Yes, Heidi's not a bad cook either. We're going to have to adjust to that. I suppose many people would find the thought of losing a spouse emotionally draining. They say some are even grief-stricken. Thank God we're not burdened with such thoughts. In my case my only concern is going to be the loss of the convenience of having someone to take care of everyday household chores. Now I'll have to do them. That'll be a pain."

"Okay," Said Zweig, "Good thing I didn't call the two boys. Now you and I need to work out a plan and a division of labor. It's probably going to be easier to do this if we each take one. If I have to do both, it could get messy and the other one might run if I don't get to her in time."

"Heinrich, I'm not comfortable with this."

"Killing our wives or you yourself doing one of them?"

"Both, but my doing one in particular."

"You can see why it's necessary. I'm not as quick as I once was. If one of these women slips away we'll have bigger troubles than we do now."

"Yes, yes, Heinrich. As you well know, I wasn't born yesterday. All right, I'll do my part. Just had to get that off my chest. You can count on me. What has to be done, has to be done. Now how do you propose we do this? Gun, rock, strangulation, poison?"

"Has to be a blow to the head. With a rock or piece of wood or something. We have to make it difficult for the medical examiner. Leave enough doubt that they could have died by accident. We don't need more law enforcement looking into this than necessary. And we need to dispose of the bodies some distance away this time. The groundskeeper was too close I'm afraid."

Just as Heinrich finished saying this the women came out onto the porch.

"We're hungry," said Doreen cheerfully. "How about you fellows? Shall we go into town and have lunch? Afterward we can shop for food so we don't always have to go out."

Heinrich wasn't comfortable exposing the four of them in the local community, which was Lake George village, but they did have to eat, so he grudgingly agreed. "Yes, let's do that. Good chance to get familiar with our new area. Lake George village is fairly small and it's less than 15 minutes away by car."

He realized that this was only putting off what had to be done, but he was hungry and knew he worked better on a full stomach. Going to lunch gave him more time to figure out how he'd do the deed. He knew now that he not only had to worry about a panicky Heidi, but his friend Max seemed a bit shaky too. Was he, Heinrich, the only one who had his wits about him? Was he the only one who could be depended upon to do what was necessary? These people and their damned consciences. These people and their damned feelings. These people and their damned uncontrollable emotions were going to land them all in trouble. Right after they returned from lunch and food shopping he had to take care of things once and for all. They agreed to be ready to leave in 15 minutes. Meanwhile the women retired to the bedroom and toilet where Heidi finally seemed calm and more like herself.

"What do you think, Doreen. Have I reassured your husband that I'm reliable?"

"I think so. I have to tell you though, I've lived with Heinrich much of my adult life and I still find him unpredictable. Just when I think I've got him figured out, he'll say or do something that surprises me. Still, he seems fairly calm now. When he thinks things are under control—his control," she said with a hint of a smile, "he seems to relax. Let's just enjoy this little trip into Lake George village. Maybe it'll get our minds away from our own troubles for a short time at least. He's usually most relaxed when he's in public. He's spent much of his life since the war trying not to draw attention to himself. It's really an overreaction, but I suppose I can understand it. Especially because of those early years when those Nazi hunters seemed to be everywhere. Now they're after us again. My God, can't they just let bygones be bygones. It was a long time ago. And it was war."

"I suppose I can see why they're so upset. If what they say is true, our guys were not so nice back in the day."

"My advice to you my dear is don't share that sentiment with Heinrich. He has no patience for people who won't let the past die. As far as he's concerned, that was a different time in his life. He's not that man now and people shouldn't be treating him as if he were. A lot of the Allied soldiers were not so nice, but nobody is going after them. Leave the past in the past. Especially when you're around Heinrich. He still has a mean streak in him. You don't want to arouse that. Believe me. Okay, we better join the men or they'll have a cow."

Heinrich asked Max to drive, which was fine with him. Gave him something to do while he knew his friend was working out the details of what they were going to do later that day.

26

I found myself a Holiday Inn in Lake George village. Figured I might be in the area a few days. After a relaxing lunch I drove back to Assembly Point and decided to give myself a refresher tour of the peninsula. I'd lived on the lake as a kid, but that was a long time ago. I wanted to have a better understanding of what the place looked like now and what the typical cottages and condos looked like. Was this more upscale than I remembered? Was it more blue collar? Was it a place that attracted tourists and offered tourist attractions? Or was it primarily a residential area as it had been in my youth?

I took 9L which was also known as Ridge Road. From the Ridge Road I took Assembly Point Road which led out onto the peninsula. It didn't take long to see that much of Assembly Point was upscale. Many cottages appeared to have been expanded into full-time homes or certainly fine second homes. The Point was definitely residential. There were also numerous luxury homes that looked like they had been built in the last 10 years or so.

While Lake George was a major tourist destination, it was clear that certain parts of the lake shore were residential. It was a big lake—32 miles long with 108 miles of shoreline—so there was plenty of room for tourists and residents without one group interfering with the other. I'm a salt-water kind of guy myself, but I could see how people could love this lake. I'd loved it when we lived there.

I'd been driving around Assembly Point about 20 minutes when my phone rang. It was BCI Detective Gary Melillo.

"Special Agent Dantry," I have something that might be helpful. As an InfraGard Agent, I was technically not an FBI special agent, but this was not the time to split hairs. Or at least I didn't think so.

"Yes, detective, what have you got?"

"Our lab has narrowed that sand and gravel down to an area on the Assembly Point peninsula about a half mile long. There's also another area about a quarter mile long. I can email you a map outlining these two areas. That's still a lot of ground to cover, but it does narrow things down quite a bit. And it does seem to put your murder somewhere on Assembly Point. Detective Steele and I can help you cover these areas. Gonna be a lot of legwork."

"I'd really appreciate that. I think I can get a field agent to help too. I look forward to getting that email."

When I got the email I saw that we still had a lot of ground to cover if we were going to find our guys, but it was definitely a lot better than having to scour the entire peninsula and neighboring coastal areas. Before I started, though, I had to work out how I was going to question people without scaring the Hell out of them. If I told people these were two killers who supervised mass killings in one of Hitler's concentration camps it could cause a mass hysterical reaction on the peninsula. Still, I had to let them know that these were dangerous men who were not to be trifled with.

Once the two BCI detectives arrived and a field agent from the Albany field office, there'd be four of us scouring the two areas on Assembly Point. Things should move faster then. In the meantime, I figured I might as well get started. I called on the first house I came to on the southern limit of the lower area shown on the map emailed to me. An attractive woman in her thirties answered after my first knock. She eyed me suspiciously. I got the impression she didn't receive many callers.

"Yes?"

"Name's Tony Dantry. I'm with the FBI." I flashed my ID. "I need to ask you a couple questions. Won't take long."

"FBI, huh. Can't imagine why the FBI is asking questions around here. Go ahead. Ask away." I noticed that she didn't ask me in.

"Have you seen any new people around here in the last 48 hours?"

"I just got here last night. My husband and I rent this place for the month. I had to go down to Albany yesterday. Before that I don't remember anyone new since we started renting, which was a week ago. There are new people all the time. A lot of these cottages are rented during the summer months. Who are you looking for? I hope it's not anybody too dangerous."

"A couple of elderly men and their wives. They're actually in their 90s. You're probably safe if you don't challenge them or provoke them. They're not looking for trouble, but they're on the run and might act out if they think you recognize them. If you see them please give me a call, day or night." I could see that I had her worried now, so I added, "If you see them just ignore them unless they ask for directions or something. If they don't think they're recognized, you'll be fine." I left my card and moved on to the next house.

This was a much larger house. Didn't look like a rental cottage.

A man in his 60s came to the door. "What can I do for you?"

I introduced myself and inquired, "Have you noticed any new people around here in the last day or two? Two quite elderly men in particular."

"Why do you ask?"

"They're fugitives. We think they may have committed a crime downstate. Have you seen them?"

"Most criminals are fairly young. What possible crime could some elderly men have committed?"

I was hoping to avoid specifics. "They may have committed one or more homicides. You shouldn't worry. If they did these crimes they had motive. We think they might be in this area just to avoid apprehension. I doubt if they're a threat here as long as they're not confronted. I suspect they'd rather go unnoticed, so if you do see them, act as if you haven't noticed them. If they ask for something like directions, just tell them and let them go on their way."

"You said they're elderly. About how old? Some people might say I'm elderly."

I smiled. "Real elderly. In their 90s. They might have two elderly women with them. Their wives. Do you think you might have seen anyone who fits this description?"

"No, but I don't get out that much. You might want to check with my neighbors. They're out and about a lot more than my wife and I are. Hmm, 90-year-old killers. That's a new one. How did they kill these people if you don't mind my asking? I mean at that advanced age it probably wasn't physical force. Did they use a gun?" He seemed more fascinated than worried.

"I'm sorry. We can't get into that. The only thing I can tell you is in their minds they had a reason for these homicides, so be careful but don't worry too much. If you don't confront them you're probably safe."

I interviewed a few more area residents and then about an hour later was joined by the two BCI detectives. The three of us then mapped out a plan so that we didn't overlap each other. I was still expecting a special agent from the FBI field office to join us.

After a few more hours of talking to local residents it was becoming evident that our fugitives were not coming in contact with many if any locals. Clearly they were avoiding contact. I could understand that. They were in enough trouble without going looking for it. Still, they couldn't stay holed up for long. They had to leave wherever they were staying. Had to eat. Either they were going to restaurants or diners or buying groceries. The nearest supermarket was in Lake George village. There was a small country store in nearby Cleverdale, which was a small hamlet on a neighboring peninsula.

27

They found a sandwich shop in the middle of the village. The place was about half full. It seemed to Heidi that they were being stared at as they entered. Heinrich and the others didn't seem to notice.

When their food was served Heinrich said, "Let's do our food shopping fast. The less we're exposed, the better."

Doreen appeared disappointed and said, "I don't feel that exposed here in the village. We look normal enough, so I don't see any need to worry, Heinrich. You and Max went all of your adult lives without being spotted as German World War II veterans. So it happened once down at Liberty Village. The likelihood of it happening again is slight. Why not at least enjoy this beautiful area. People spend a lot of money to come here on vacation. I know, we had a nice life at Liberty Village. But we're alive and relatively healthy. Let's make the best of this. Let's not over worry it."

Heinrich looked annoyed at this naiveté. "Look, Doreen, things are quite pleasant here in the north country at the moment, but both the FBI and the state police are looking for Max and me. They're not going to stop looking. It's a feather in their cap when they haul in what they like to call Nazi war criminals. We're not war criminals, but that's what they'll call us just because we happened to fight on the losing side in the War." Zweig did not mention the two murders he'd committed down at Liberty Village because he was fairly certain the two women were not aware of them. Oh, they knew about the homicides, but they probably didn't connect them to him. He smiled inwardly as he realized that as far as he knew, neither wife knew that their husbands had actually enjoyed their work as a camp guard. Neither wife knew that Heinrich had killed when he was a camp guard. The men had always told them they were soldiers—SS soldiers stationed as guards at Buchenwald, but still soldiers. Whether the women ever knew the truth was unclear because, as Heinrich had just recently learned, the women thought about a lot more than they ever expressed. All the more reason to get rid of them as soon as possible.

Their waitress came to their booth and offered them more coffee. As she poured refills, she asked, "You folks visitors or do you live around here? Haven't seen you before." This was more friendliness than Heinrich or Max wanted. Heinrich thought quickly and snapped, "We live over near Cleverdale. Lived there for years." The server nodded and said, "Well come see us more often then. That's not that far away."

"Yeah, right," muttered Heinrich irritably. "We'll do that."

Heidi looked puzzled. "Why did you tell them that, Heinrich?"

He looked at her as if she were an idiot. "Because, Heidi, if she thinks we've lived in the area for years, she won't tell law enforcement she saw the people they're looking for."

"But you probably shouldn't have snapped at her like that," said Doreen.

Heinrich pursed his lips, but said nothing. He knew she was right.

Then Heidi said, "Why would law enforcement come here to ask about us?"

He looked up at the ceiling, then finally said, "We don't know where they'll look. Maybe they won't come here, but they could. Oh never mind. We should get out of here."

28

The Ford Police Interceptor was cruising along Rte. 9 heading north. BCI detectives Gary Melillo and Mac Steele were discussing FBI InfraGard Agent Tony Dantry. When they first made contact with Dantry they assumed he would be like a lot of InfraGard agents who had gotten assignments to help investigate financial fraud cases. Many of these InfraGard agents were CPAs or attorneys. Only after getting back to their headquarters and doing a little research had Melillo and Steele learned that Dantry was a former CIA operative who had worked in risky operations in different parts of the world including Russia. They also learned that even in retirement he had helped solved major cases involving terrorists, Russian agents and sociopathic mass murderers.

Detective Gary Melillo said, "I guess we shouldn't take this Dantry guy lightly. Sounds as if he knows what he's doing. Just recently he caught a serial killer at this same senior living center where these two fugitives were living. Must be quite a place. Serial killers, Nazi war criminals."

Mac Steele said, "These kind of things could happen at any place like that. Just their luck that they had both in a short period of time. But you're right. This Dantry guy must know what he's doing. He seems to have zeroed in on Assembly

Point as where these fugitives have taken refuge. If he's wrong about that we're all going to be wasting a lot of time. Going door to door could take a lot of time unless we get lucky. We have to ask him why he's so sure these guys are holing out on the Point. He must have a good reason."

29

As they got back into their car Heidi Schmidt said, "Instead of heading directly back to the house, why don't we do a little exploring. Be nice to see some of the surrounding area. Heinrich drew in a deep breath and bit his lip. He couldn't afford to lose his temper at this point. Better to keep everyone calm until he and Max did their thing. If the women got antsy things could be difficult. As if the women, especially Heidi, hadn't already made things difficult enough that the men now had to dispose of them. A real shame, too. Doreen could be pleasant and she did make life a lot easier for him.

As for that bitch, Heidi, if it weren't for her, he and Max wouldn't have to dispose of both women. He wouldn't mind killing Heidi. Actually he was fairly sure he'd enjoy it, but he would have some misgivings about Doreen. She'd never given him any trouble. Always viewed his past life as just that—something that happened in the past out of the necessity of war. He knew she didn't like his past as a camp guard, but he also knew she was kind of in awe of men who had a darker side as she liked to put it. They were far more interesting than men who always toed the line. Men who never crossed the line were boring to her. She knew she was like those few women who were infatuated with bad boys, only she knew her guy was a little *'badder'* than most. Because she viewed him that way, she treated him almost as if he were a celebrity. He would definitely miss her.

If she wouldn't make a scene over the killing of that bitch Heidi, he would spare her. But he was afraid she wouldn't understand. Then again, she'd been so understanding all those years they'd been together. She'd even understood the time he'd had that late midlife fling with that woman he'd met at work.

As he thought back, even that woman had been understanding. When he got her pregnant, she never demanded he claim the child. He'd sent her some money to show his appreciation. She'd accepted it, but never asked for more. A remarkable woman. To this day he had no idea if it was a boy or a girl. He smiled at the thought of this. At the time he'd turned on the charm, and she'd found him so likeable that she didn't want to put him in an awkward position. She told him that. She'd gone on to tell him that he was such a good-looking man and had such good manners, that she was looking forward to raising his child by herself. Said the pregnancy was a gift.

Maybe Doreen would understand why Heidi Schmidt had to be eliminated. Maybe he should take the chance and let Doreen live.

30

I felt that we'd make progress soon now that we had four people scouring the neighborhood. The Albany FBI field office had sent up a woman special agent—
Special Agent Maria Lopez. Usually I wanted people to work in teams, but because we had so much area to cover I asked everyone to proceed on their own and report back to me every hour.

After two hours Special Agent Lopez called to say she had something.

"A woman and her husband said they were in a coffee shop in Lake George village and saw two very elderly couples who somehow looked out of place. She couldn't explain what she meant by that except that she did notice that the men had accents. German, she thought. She said, if they were tourists they didn't look very relaxed. They seemed tense. One of the men seemed irritable. The woman knows this is all her impression and she didn't think much of it until I came to the door and started asking about people who seemed quite similar to the ones in the restaurant."

I thought that if these two couples were the fugitives, they were obviously still in the area, but that didn't help me locate where they were living.

The next day the four of us law-enforcement people resumed scouring the neighborhood. While most of the interviews didn't take long, each of the four interviewers took some time after an interview to make notes about the residents, their address and what they'd said. So while a typical interview took less than ten minutes, all-told each stop took about 20.

A pattern was emerging. A number of people interviewed said they had heard rumors that somewhere either on Assembly point or in nearby Cleverdale there was some kind of retreat for Nazi war criminals. Everyone who had heard these rumors said that they may have just been rumors because they had never knowingly come across this retreat. They admitted that their failure to be aware of the place didn't mean that it didn't exist. If there was such a place, these people would be smart and would no doubt do a very good job of protecting it by making sure it appeared just like every other place in the area. That shouldn't be hard to do, said a number of people, because the only distinguishing feature of a Nazi war criminal was probably his age. Oh, maybe his German accent, too. Even age wasn't that indicative, since a lot of elderly people owned second homes on lake property.

My cell rang. It was Joanna. She didn't usually call me in the middle of the day unless it was something important. She was at work now at Hunter College and usually had her hands too full to make a casual phone call.

"Hi. Are you and your colleagues getting any closer to these Nazis and their wives?"

"Hi. Surprised you called in the middle of your day. No. Not yet. Though they were spotted in Lake George Village, so we're fairly certain they're in the area."

"Well you're spending time in what must be a lovely area. People tell me it's beautiful up there."

"It is pretty nice, though I haven't had much chance to enjoy it. Someday we can come up here together and go out on the lake. It's magnificent."

"Anyway, I called to let you know that the search for these guys is now on the New York TV news. So now everybody knows you're looking for Nazi war criminals."

"Oh God. Who let that out?"

"Maybe your FBI."

"I don't think they'd want to alert our fugitives that we knew where to look."

"Or the State Police? Or even someone at Liberty Village."

"Doesn't matter now. It's out. Probably won't make any difference. I'm sure these guys know that we're looking for them and I'm sure they know we know about their safe house being on Lake George."

"Be careful. I know these guys are old and rickety, but they don't seem to have any difficulty killing. They must be desperate now, so please don't underestimate them just because they're so old."

"Don't worry. These guys have killed all their lives, so we know they won't hesitate if it helps them escape capture. Hey what's with this concern that makes you break away from your work? I know you care, and you know I always watch my back."

"I was just thinking this morning that we've gotten so close that I sometimes just take our relationship for granted. I don't want that to happen. I don't take you for granted and I love you more than ever my love. I just want you to come back to me in one piece. I can't wait for that hug when you come in the door." I was smiling as I heard the love in her voice.

"Don't worry. I really am being careful. I don't take us for granted for one second, and I too can't wait for that hug."

31

Heinrich's thoughts took him back almost 80 years to his second year in the camp. He had chosen the role of concentration camp guard because it meant he didn't have go to war. Even as a teenager he'd realized that it was far less risky to guard prisoners than it was to expose himself to the perils of combat. In his first year in the camp the other guards had chided him for treating the detainees with some consideration. He wasn't exactly kind to the prisoners, but he didn't abuse them either. He was young and new at the work and remembered how his mother had told him to be nice to his sister. He hadn't treated his sister very well and his mother kept harping on it. It hadn't been easy being nice that first year in Buchenwald, but he'd tried not to give in to his natural tendencies. He'd always enjoyed seeing others suffer. There was even a word for it: *schadenfreude*. He even killed a cat once just for the pleasure of seeing it suffer a slow death. When he first worked in the camp he remembered being conflicted. He wanted to please his mother, but it wasn't easy. He got no satisfaction out of being nice. He liked seeing other creatures—whether they be cats, dogs, squirrels or humans—squirm.

After being mocked repeatedly by his fellow guards he finally gave up on the nice guy stuff and gave in to what came naturally. Not surprisingly he soon found himself enjoying teasing the prisoners. He got a big kick out of offering a prisoner an extra piece of bread and just as he was giving the bread to the poor soul he would drop it in the mud and pretend to accidentally step on it. As he did this he would accuse the prisoner of carelessness and make him stand at attention for an hour. If the prisoner failed to do this, he would take him to the whipping stool and give him 20 or 30 lashes.

Anyone who refused to go to the whipping stool would be shot for disobedience. Heinrich smiled as he recalled this. Unfortunately, only one detainee refused the whipping stool which was a great disappointment for Heinrich. Sadly it was only the second time he had the opportunity to kill a detainee in the time he worked at Buchenwald. The first was that silly girl—the sister of that Miller woman.

Still, it was great fun doing the whipping. He made a game of trying to make the lash land in the same place as often as possible. When he was successful at this he was able to bring a lot of blood to the surface and leave a much deeper cut on the detainee's back than when he whipped carelessly.

He also found that he got great pleasure out of abusing women. Once in a while he would approach a woman and accuse her of hiding something. The woman would of course deny it, but he would claim she was lying. He would then reach inside her prison uniform and grab her breast claiming he was looking for whatever contraband he decided to claim she was hiding.

He smiled as he recalled that in his second year working at the camp he'd gone from one of the most easy going guards to one of the most feared. He was fairly certain that Doreen had no idea just how much he was feared or why. He was pretty sure she thought his toughness came from rounding up detainees when they tried to escape. He imagined her seeing him yelling at prisoners, demanding that they return to their barracks, occasionally even hitting them if they were unruly. She seemed to view the camps as almost as unpleasant for the guards as it was for the detainees. As far as Doreen was concerned nobody enjoyed the camps. It was an unpleasant part of the war.

He was almost certain she didn't know that he actually enjoyed brutalizing the detainees. Little did she know that only recently he had the most fun since the war. Getting rid of Gisela Miller and that Joe Avila had awakened feelings that had lain dormant for years. Then eliminating the groundskeeper was also fun, though he didn't enjoy having to deal with disposing of the body. That was not something he looked forward to with the women either.

Unfortunately, one always had to pay a price for pleasure. Now that price was going to be a lot more stressful. And for two reasons. One reason was that both the FBI and the State Police were out looking for him and Max. The other reason was that he was a lot older now. Everything he did was harder. A lot harder. Now it didn't take much to make him tired. When he was younger he could go on forever without feeling the least bit tired. Now, when he killed, he wasn't always sure his actions were sufficient to do the job. And getting rid of the bodies took a lot more effort. Sometimes a lot more effort than he could come up with.

Well, he was going to have to come up with serious effort if he was going to eliminate the two women. It was going to be exhausting. He and Max were definitely going to need the help of the two white supremacists, Robert and William. They knew the area and they were a lot younger and stronger than he and Max were. Sometimes you had to depend on others, even when that presented a risk in itself. The two young guys seemed dedicated to helping them, but in all honesty, what did he and Max know about them? Not much, but he really had no choice. Getting old was terrible, though it was better than not getting old. Just had to learn new ways of doing things.

He knew that he was not like most people. He also knew that most people would disapprove of his behavior. He'd read enough to know that he was either a sociopath or a psychopath. These words didn't scare him. He knew that many if not most sociopaths and psychopaths were well above average in intelligence. Some were amazingly great achievers.

He'd known all his life that he was smarter than most people. He'd learned over the years that sociopaths had little or no empathy. That was not such a bad thing. It enabled him to get the best of people without worrying about it. Oh he might worry about getting caught or about other repercussions, but he wasn't plagued by psychological concerns.

He also knew that sociopaths had very little conscience. That one was interesting. He couldn't identify with the notion of conscience emotionally and it took him a long time to intellectually understand what it meant when people referred to a conscience, but he did understand now and that too had proven to be an advantage, not a problem. Most people avoided getting certain things done because they were plagued by conscience. Not him, if it needed doing, he did it. Oh, he'd avoid doing it if he thought people would think less of him, but usually he'd find a way to do the deed without people knowing he'd done it.

He'd learned over the years that half the time a sociopath had to pretend to be the way most people would expect people to behave. He smiled as he acknowledged what he'd known for much of his life: that sociopaths could use their intelligence to charm and manipulate people. He couldn't count the number of times he'd acted out roles to convince people of one thing or another. He'd always been good at reading people, and it took little effort to pretend he was what they expected him to be. Did the hypocrisy of his performances bother him? Absolutely not. The object of life was to further one's best interests. Whatever it took. If he could further his own self-interest without conflict, so much the better. If the other person didn't know he was being manipulated, that meant that person could be useful in the future. It also meant that that person might even sing his praises. It was a win situation for Heinrich, and the other person went happily along his merry way.

However, occasionally there came a situation that couldn't be solved by charm and manipulation. When a person stood in your way and wouldn't move, that person had to be removed. Sometimes with a sharp nudge. Occasionally with something more violent. If a person was putting you at risk, that person had to be removed. That was the situation he and Max now faced with their wives. Especially Max's wife Heidi. Then again, sometimes you just wanted to remove someone. If they were a pain in the ass or if they seemed sort of worthless as a human being. If they made your life unpleasant. But he believed this had to be done judiciously.

Of course some sociopaths were less pragmatic. They just killed people for the sheer pleasure of it. Admittedly he could understand that, for sometimes he had that urge too. But it was too risky for him to adopt as a lifestyle. Those folks who took to killing as an avocation, could often do it because they had the time and were good planners. He'd heard of the fellow at Liberty Village who killed people on the rail trail. Sort of as a challenge for that guy. Maybe he was more of a psychopath than a sociopath. But what did he, Heinrich Zweig, know? He could easily imagine getting pleasure from killing a certain way and in frequent spurts. It wasn't his way, but he could understand it and see how it could provide pleasure. Not his thing though. He'd always gotten more pleasure out of seeing his victims suffer than the actual killing, though often the killing was necessary.

32

Heinrich nodded his head at Heidi's suggestion that they drive around the area. Might not hurt to do a little exploring to get to know this new place. He was really thinking hopefully he'd find a good place to finish Heidi off. Not too close to their cottage. He still hadn't decided what to do about Doreen.

The irrepressible Heidi said, "Why don't we drive north toward Bolton Landing. That might be interesting."

Heinrich said, "It looks as if it might be quite commercial up that way. Why not go back toward Assembly Point and drive beyond that?" The last thing he needed was to explore an area with lots of businesses. He needed as desolate and isolated an area as he could find.

"Oh, but that means there's probably a lot of fun stuff. Not just trees and water. Let's at least see what's up that way."

"Heidi, I think you're forgetting why we're here in Lake George. We're not here to do sightseeing. We're not tourists. We're trying to avoid detection. Going where everyone else goes could draw attention to us."

"Maybe just the opposite, Heinrich. Nobody would expect us to go where everyone is going. They'd expect us to hide out in the middle of nowhere."

"She may have a point, Heinrich," said Max. "Maybe we'll be safer in the middle of crowds."

"Yes," agreed Doreen. "That does make sense, Heinrich."

Zweig couldn't disagree with the logic, but it was still annoying the way the conversation was taking them because it was leading him farther from his immediate goal of eliminating the annoying Heidi. "Okay, we'll head north toward this Bolton Landing. We'll get an idea of what's up that way, then we'll come back and check out what's on the other side of Assembly Point."

Max Schmidt expelled a sigh of relief. While he understood the need to eliminate his wife Heidi, he wasn't happy about doing it. At least this drive north put off that final moment a bit longer.

As they directed the old Ford northward Heinrich gave a running account of what they were passing. "Arcades, games, restaurants, motels, cabin resorts, boat rentals, more restaurants and motels. Oh here's a golf course. Here's a public beach. There's a miniature golf course."

"Oh," said Heidi. "Let's play."

"Yes, let's," said Doreen. This was out of character for Doreen, thought Heinrich. She was a smart woman, but not usually inclined to do fun things.

"I really don't think we should take the time to do that," said Heinrich. "Maybe another time."

"Oh come on, Heinrich," said Doreen. Let's just act on impulse. It's a nice day. Might be fun."

"Yeah, let's do it," chimed in Max. "Haven't done this in years. We're in no hurry, are we Heinrich?" Zweig gave him the evil eye, but said, "I suppose not. All right, let's get this over with."

"Don't sound so enthusiastic, my friend," said Max.

Zweig shook his head disgustedly, but said nothing.

When they had parked Doreen started toward the miniature course and said, "Let's find a ladies room first Heidi."

When they were near the ladies room Doreen grabbed Heidi and said quietly, but intensely, "I don't like what's going on here, Heidi."

Heidi had a blank look on her face. "I have no idea what you mean."

"Whenever Heinrich does something he shouldn't do he acts just like he's acting now.

"You mean he's serious about everything?"

"He's always serious for Christ's sake. It's more than that. He acts with a sense of urgency."

"Well he is being hunted by the FBI and the state police."

"He's been hunted before. Yes, that does tense him up, but there's something else. It's the way he acts just before he commits a new crime."

"I thought he stopped committing crimes when the war ended in 1945."

"If only that were true."

"I'm not sure I'm following you. Heinrich has committed other crimes since then?"

"I'm afraid so. He can always justify them. At least he can in his mind, but sometimes they're serious."

"Don't tell me he's killed someone since leaving Germany?"

"Look, Heidi, we don't have much time. They'll be looking for us. Listen to what I have to say."

"I'm listening."

"Don't make any noise when I tell you this, but I think Heinrich wants you dead."

Heidi went pale and struggled to catch her breath.

"Why would he want to do that?"

"I think he believes you're a security risk. You might somehow either intentionally or unintentionally talk too much about Heinrich and Max. In the wrong places."

"Did he tell you this?"

"No, but I've overheard him talking on the phone to Max. He said a lot to Max that shocked even me. The biggest shock was when he even bragged about how he got rid of Gisela Miller. Dear God, Heidi, do you believe this? He'll do anything!"

"Then Max wants me dead too? Oh Dear God, I can't believe this. Are you sure?"

"I'm afraid so. Look, we don't have much time. Who knows when they plan to do it. We can't get back in that car with them. We have to get out of here—and now."

"Where do we go? We don't know anybody here. I only have about fifty dollars with me."

"You must have a credit card?"

"Yes, but Max said we should not use our credit cards now. The FBI may be able to track us."

"Jesus, Heidi. Better the FBI finds you than our husbands."

"You're not worried about what Heinrich will do to *you*, are you Doreen?"

"When he's got his defenses up even I don't feel safe around him. Now that he's on the run again I'm afraid he'll do anything to avoid detection. If he kills you I have no doubt that I'll become his next security risk. Frankly, Heidi, I'll feel a lot safer and better if we get away from our guys. But we have to act now. We'll worry about money later. Heinrich and I have some joint accounts so we won't starve. I even have one account of my own that he doesn't know about."

"But what will we do?"

"We'll worry about that later. Let's just get away when we can. I noticed a couple of taxis near the entrance. Let's grab one of them."

Heidi was trembling—both from fear for her life and the insecurity of not knowing what to do and where to go. She had never made such an important decision in her long life. In fact, she had left all of the important decisions to Max who was only too happy to be in command of her life. All her married life Heidi had seen the fear in her husband's eye when the subject of Nazi war crimes came up. That fear was magnified ten times over when he felt he had to move to a new country or even a new community. Living at Liberty Village had brought a feeling of security. For once they weren't looking over their shoulders. But then the rumors came and she saw how tense it made her husband. No doubt the increased intensity came with his age. It wasn't as easy to run now as it was when he was younger.

Unfortunately he had tied his fortunes to Heinrich Zweig, a man she always felt was evil. She knew her Max had done some bad things, but she believed he'd had no choice. He was not a bad man. Not so with Heinrich. She was convinced Heinrich enjoyed doing the bad things he did.

Heidi drew on inner resources she never knew she had.

"Okay, Doreen. You lead the way. I'll follow you."

"Follow me and move as fast as you can."

Two minutes later they'd found their way back to the entrance to the miniature golf park. Just at that moment, one of the taxis drove away. A young couple was heading toward the remaining taxi. Doreen waved at the taxi driver to get his attention. She wasn't moving as fast as the young couple, but the taxi driver apparently took pity on the approaching elderly woman and held the door open for her. Doreen stood waiting for the hobbling Heidi. They then got into the taxi. Doreen couldn't wait for the car to pull out.

"Where to, ladies?" said the unshaven man of about 50.

"The Queensbury Hotel in Glens Falls." She had found it on Google.

"Nice place. If you don't mind my asking, how did you get here if that's where you're staying?"

"We came with some friends. They want to continue playing golf and doing some other things here. Our friends are younger. We're tired and want to get back to the hotel." The driver rolled his eyes, but said nothing.

As they drove south on Route 9 Heidi said, "What are we going to do when we get there? We don't even have a reservation."

"I checked their web site. They do have rooms available so we'll get something."

"But when we get a room. What next? What do we do then?"

33

"Lady," yelled the driver. "Your phone is ringing. Aren't you going to answer it?"

"No, I'm not," said Doreen when she saw it was from Heinrich.

"Then maybe you should end it."

"Yes. That's what I'm doing." It took her a moment to decide, but she quickly disconnected the call. The driver shook his head in disbelief.

Heidi bit her lip and said, "They must be frantic. I feel bad running off like this without giving them any warning."

"Jesus, Heidi, you're forgetting what they want to do to you. Yes, they're frantic, but not because they care for you, but because they fear you'll run to the cops." She kept her voice low so the driver couldn't hear what they were saying.

"Well what are we going to do, Doreen? We can't stay in a hotel very long. Where do we go from there?"

"I'm thinking. I'm thinking. Look, let's check into the hotel and get the lay of the land. We don't have to decide today."

"We're going to have to decide soon. We have no home. The men will be looking for us. At our age this is all so stressful. Good Lord, Doreen, what will we do?"

"I know it's stressful. It's awful, but at least we're safe. The men will be looking for us, but they have no idea where to look. And they can't go to the police. You think we're in a bind. Imagine their situation. They're wanted criminals who can't go to the police for help. They have to avoid the police."

The desk clerk at the hotel reacted normally until she said, "Do you have any luggage?"

Doreen had anticipated this and said, "The airline lost it. They said they'll send it along as soon as they find it."

"Oh, I'm so sorry. That must be so annoying."

"You don't know the half of it," said Doreen, who then turned to Heidi and said "we may have to buy some clothes here in town if our bags don't get here soon."

In their hotel room Doreen said, "As I see it we have two or three options. One, we can stay here for a while and eventually move to another town after we do some homework and find a nice place to live. Two, we can contact your son. Your son Liam is in real estate near Philadelphia, right? Maybe he could help us find a little place in that area. Or three, we can contact the police and help them find our lousy husbands. We don't have to decide now. Think about it."

"I suppose I should contact Liam," said Heidi. "He'll be delighted. He and his father never got along. Especially when Max spent time with Heinrich. Liam had no use for Heinrich."

"I'm sorry to say a lot of people felt that way. Heinrich charmed me a long time ago and you know how people thought 70 or so years ago. Once married you should stay married. It wasn't easy with Heinrich, but I worked at it and overlooked a lot more than I should have. I should have left him years ago. I often cringe at what I imagine he did back in the camp. I'm glad I don't know, but knowing him I'm sure he did some very bad things. Anyway, yes, why don't you contact Liam? When was the last time you spoke to him?"

"Just a couple of weeks ago. He calls me often."

"When you call him you're going to have to tell him that you've left Max and I've left Heinrich. Ask him if he has a place where he can put us up until we find something more permanent. Tell him I have money so we can afford to rent a modest place. Oh, and you have to tell him that Max and Heinrich are now fugitives. This is going to be quite a phone call. Maybe we should get a bite to eat before you call him."

34

"Max! Where the hell are the women? They've been in the ladies room too long. If they're lost, who knows what they'll tell people. And if they're not lost, what could have happened to them?

"Relax, Heinrich. They're old women. They move slowly. Besides, when they get talking—"

"That's what I'm afraid of. Their talking. Who knows what they'll say and to whom? We should never have stopped here."

"They'll turn up."

"They better," said Zweig, "or we have an even bigger problem on our hands than we thought we did. If some cop tries to help them, one thing could lead to another and—"

"I get it. I get it. Let's just keep our eyes open. They have to be here somewhere on the grounds. It's a big place, but we'll find them. Let's walk in different directions. I haven't seen any police, so let's not worry about that. As soon as one of us finds them call on your cell phone and we'll get them back in the car." Schmidt smacked himself on the forehead and said, "Doesn't Doreen have a cell phone? Why didn't we think? You should just call her. Of course Heidi doesn't have one. Doesn't believe in them. But call Doreen right now."

"Of course. What was I thinking? Obviously I wasn't. I'll call her right now." He found her number and punched it in.

35

Special Agent Lopez said she wanted to meet with me, so the two of us temporarily suspended our search of the area in order to have a brief talk.

When we met she said she'd gotten some information from her office in Albany that was interesting and might be useful.

"According to people in my office, this safe house here in Lake George is apparently a temporary launching platform for Nazi war criminals who've been identified by the United States and are not welcome in this country. It's also a haven for those Nazis who no longer feel safe here in the States for whatever reason. They can't be deported because most countries won't accept them, so they spend time here until they feel it's safe to fly to Europe, usually Germany, ironically, or Austria. It's a voluntary exodus from the States. The fugitives go voluntarily, give up their citizenship and the U.S. government agrees to continue paying them social security. They make their way across the border into Canada and fly out of Montreal to Europe."

I couldn't believe that the U.S. did this. If it did, they certainly kept it quiet. Understandably so. Why the government didn't prosecute these people was a question in itself. Probably because they didn't have enough evidence and clearly there weren't many witnesses still around.

I said, "Interesting. Very interesting. Even if it's true I can't believe our fugitives would fit this profile. They're accused of war crimes, but also homicides they allegedly perpetrated quite recently. No way the government would let them get away now. Or do you know something I don't?"

Special Agent Lopez said, "This is all new to me. I agree, I'd be shocked if the government let them off the hook for any of this."

"However, if there is any truth to this safe house being used as a launching platform, then we can't expect these people to be around Lake George very long."

"I agree," said Maria Lopez. "With the FBI, local police and state police on them they can't afford to hang around long. I can't see how they'll get across the border, though. Two very old men with two very old women all with German accents. I can't believe the border patrol will let them pass without a thorough interrogation."

"However," I said, "I doubt that the border patrol has been alerted. Why would they be if our fugitives are parked here at Lake George. There's no indication that these fugitives would head to Canada. As far as we know, the state police and the FBI have not alerted Canada."

"What I don't understand is why this safe house hasn't been identified by law enforcement if they've been using it for years. You'd think that by now some agency would have found it."

"Yes. Very strange. Maybe they keep changing it. These people are obviously smart if they've evaded capture since World War II."

As soon as I'd said this my phone rang. It was Gary Melillo the state police BCI agent. "Special Agent Dantry, I just got an interesting call from the Glens Falls Police. They said that they got a call from a cab driver who thought they should know that two elderly women he'd driven to the Queensbury Hotel had received a call in the cab that they refused to answer."

"Okay, I said. That's interesting, but why did the cab driver think it was important enough to call the police?"

"He said the woman seemed terrified. The call scared the hell out of her. The cab driver had never seen anything like it. Just thought it might be worth looking into because the two old ladies seemed nice, and it was awful to see how scared they seemed when their phone rang."

"Did the Glens Falls cops or did you folks go to the hotel and talk to these women?"

"Detective Steele and I went to the hotel to talk to them. They're registered under different names. Not Zweig or Schmidt. They're registered as Mrs. Kern and Mrs. Stone."

"So did they say why they were so scared in the back of that taxi?"

"They denied they were scared. Said the driver must have imagined it. I could tell that they were covering something up. One of the women was nervous as hell. The desk clerk said they arrived with no luggage. The women said that the airline had lost it and would send it on when they found it. I'm not sure I buy that. The strangest thing of all is that the taxi wasn't coming from the airport. It came down from Lake George. From a miniature golf course."

"How did the women explain that?"

"Something about being so excited when they got to the area that they wanted to go exploring Lake George before they even checked into their hotel. Oh, by the way, they didn't have a reservation at the Queensbury. Just walked in and took their chances. All very fishy. I'm pretty sure these are the women you're looking for. When we asked about husbands, they said both of their husbands passed away several years ago. If they are the wives of the two Nazi fugitives, they're doing a lousy job of protecting those husbands. Still, while they may be lying, as far as we know they haven't broken any laws. We're going to keep an eye on them and take another crack at them before they leave the hotel. Thought you might want to talk to them first."

"Yes, I do. Thanks. I'm going there now with Special Agent Lopez."

36

"They didn't believe a word we said," said Doreen Zweig. "Can't say I blame them. We weren't very convincing. Who would go play miniature golf before checking into a hotel? No luggage, no reservations at the hotel, and we *were* frightened when we got that call from Heinrich. God, I'm still frightened that he'll find us somehow."

"How are they going to find us?" asked Heidi with newly found courage. "They had no idea what direction we went or how we left. They might guess by taxi but they still won't know where the taxi took us."

"Unless they guess. If you were them, what would you guess?"

"Maybe," said Heidi, "some hotel or motel in Lake George Village or somewhere else on the lake. My goodness, it's a big lake. Must be hundreds of motels and hotels on it. Maybe even Glens Falls. Maybe Albany. Maybe even New York."

"Would the men think we planned this? We always leave decisions to them."

"Well, they obviously didn't believe we'd bolt like we did, so they could just as easily misjudge our destination. Most likely they'd figure we'd take a taxi. How else could we get out here so quickly. We wouldn't walk." As the discussion went on Heidi felt more empowered than she had in years. "It's kind of fun putting something over on the men, isn't it?"

"It would be if they were fun-loving guys. We have to take this seriously. I think you should call Liam now."

"I suppose I'd better. It's times like this I wish I had a cell phone. Could I use yours? No, I'll use the hotel phone."

"Fine, but give him my cell phone number so he can reach us wherever we are."

"Hi Liam. Believe it or not I'm in Lake George, New York, with Doreen." *Pause.* "Upstate New York. Near the Adirondacks." *Pause* "That's what I'm calling about. Them. It's definitely not a vacation. Anything but that. We have a problem. What I told you about not too long ago. Well it's gotten out of hand. The authorities were called in. They're now after your father and Heinrich. Yes, because of that old World War II business. They never let that go. And now there's something more recent." *Pause.* "I'll tell you about it when I see you. It's not for the phone. It's serious. Very serious. We had to leave our apartments to avoid law enforcement. Doreen and I are afraid of what the men might do next. We found a way to get away from them, but we don't know what to do now. We're hoping with your resources you could find a place for us to stay." *Pause.* "No, not around here. Near you. I know, Liam, I caught you off guard. We're desperate though. We can't stay here much longer. We don't even have a car. The men have the car." *Long pause.* "Tonight? You don't have to make it tonight,

Liam. That's a long drive to start out now. Tomorrow will be fine. Okay, if you're sure. I love you too. Bye. See you soon.

"He's driving up now?"

37

When he ended the call from his mother, Liam Schmidt returned to the couch where his wife, Madison Zweig Schmidt, was sitting anxiously concerned about the frown on her partner's face.

"What's the matter, Hon. You don't look happy."

"I'm not. My father and your father are on the lam. All four of our parents are in Lake George, New York, of all places. To make matters worse, our moms and dads are in different locations. Both the police and the FBI are after our dads. Our moms have no place to go."

38

At 10:30 PM the phone rang in the hotel room. It was the front desk saying a Liam Schmidt wanted to visit their room. Two minutes later there was a knock on the door.

"Mom." Liam hugged his mother. He was about the same height as his father, but stockier. The way Heidi remembered her husband when he was younger.

"I'm so glad you're here, Liam, but so sorry it has to be under these circumstances. You must be so tired after driving all the way here from Philly."

"I'm fine, Ma. I'm worried about you." He turned to his mother-in-law and said, "Oh, sorry, Mom. Hi."

Heidi asked, "Are you hungry? Should we get something?"

"No, Ma, I picked up something along the way. I'm good. Now what's this problem the two of you have?"

"Your father and I were fairly happy at Liberty Village. Wasn't perfect, but not bad at all." She glanced over at Doreen Zweig and continued. "I think you know that your father and Heinrich, worked together at Buchenwald."

"Yeah," snapped Liam, "They were both prison guards. Not something I'm proud of."

"Well, your father wasn't proud of it either. He's worked all his adult life trying to make amends for it. He's a good man now. You must know that. Hasn't he been a good father?"

"Yes, most of the time. But I can never get what he did out of my mind. Anyway, Mom, what's going on that brought me up here to Glens Falls? Must be pretty bad."

"It is I'm afraid. Very bad. It started recently when someone in one of the dining rooms claimed she saw a man at another table who reminded her of a guard at one of Hitler's concentration camps. Soon after, this woman was found dead in a pond on the grounds of Liberty Village—"

Before she could go on, Doreen said, "Maybe I should take it from here as I'm almost certain Heinrich, killed this woman. There was also a man at Liberty Village who accused Heinrich of being a camp guard. He died unexpectedly, too. I wouldn't be surprised if Heinrich did that, as well. Face it, Heidi, Max wasn't like Heinrich. Your husband had a conscience. Heinrich didn't. I don't think it bothered him to do what he did in the camp. I think he actually enjoyed it. I have no doubt he enjoyed killing that poor Miller woman. Probably the man, too. The Miller woman suffered because of him years ago. And now, years later, he victimizes her again."

"If you don't mind my asking," said Liam. "Why did you stay with him all these years if you knew how bad he was?"

"Like a lot of psychopaths," said Doreen, "he could be

charming and a lot of fun. But that's not why I stayed with him. I stayed because I feared for my life. People don't cross Heinrich Zweig, or they pay the consequences. I didn't dare leave him, though I thought about it a lot." She drew in a deep breath and went on. "Now I have no choice. I overheard him telling your father that he had to kill your mother because she was too big a risk. Too emotional. He then said, he'd probably have to kill me too."

"You actually heard him say that?"

"With my own two ears. And unlike a lot of us old folks, my hearing is good."

"And what did my father say?"

"I couldn't hear him. All I know is they still seem to be doing everything together. I know your father isn't vicious like Heinrich, but when he's around Heinrich—"

"Oh my God. I can't believe this. Have you called the police?"

Heidi said, "We're afraid to because they might accuse us of complicity or something. My God, Liam. We haven't encouraged Heinrich's behavior."

"Of course not, Mom, but now that you know Mr. Zweig and Dad are fleeing from the cops, you could be accused of withholding evidence or something. You should be helping the cops."

"We're just two old women who want to live a few peaceful years before we—"

"I know Ma, but unfortunately you can't hide from this. I can find a place for you to live down in the Philadelphia area, but I can't do it if you don't tell the cops what you know. Otherwise you're fugitives yourself and I'm helping you. If Mr. Zweig and Dad are guilty, they should be arrested. If they're innocent, they'll be all right."

"If they get off," said Doreen, "they'll come after us."

"If what you tell me is true, I don't see them getting off."

"It's my word against theirs."

"Their words are the words of Nazi war criminals. It won't take law enforcement long to decide who's telling the truth." Liam thought for a moment, then said, "Of course if we say nothing the four of us may have to pay some price for all this. I'm including Madison. After all, we knew the whereabouts of two former Nazi war criminals and failed to reveal it to law enforcement. So we would not be totally innocent, but given the circumstances I don't see us getting too much of a punishment. After all, we've feared for our lives when we even considered revealing what we knew. We have to do it, though. Your lives are in danger if Mr. Zweig and Dad aren't arrested."

"Must we do that, Liam. I was hoping you could just find us a nice little place we could live out our days peacefully."

"Jesus, Mom, you can't really believe you could live peacefully with Dad and Heinrich Zweig still out looking for you. Once they're apprehended you'll both be safe to return to Liberty Village. You both like that don't you?"

"Yes, but only if it's safe from Heinrich and Max."

"Of course. Mr. Zweig has already said he wants you dead and as far as we know Dad is going along with it. They have to be arrested or you'll never be safe. And the sooner, the better. I'm calling the police in the next few minutes."

39

Ten minutes later there was a sharp knock on their hotel room door. An eye peered through the peephole in the door. A man's voice said, "Yes? Who is it at this hour?"

I said, "Agent Dantry of the FBI with Special Agent Lopez. Sorry for the late call, but it's important."

I guessed that whoever it was that answered the knock didn't want to open the door, but I doubted that he was going to snub the FBI. The door opened slowly and I was facing a man probably in his late 50s or early 60s.

I then said, "We're looking for a Doreen Zweig and a Heidi Schmidt. Who are you?"

"I'm Liam Schmidt, Heidi's son. The women are here as you can see. What can we do for you?"

"We're actually looking for your father and Heinrich Zweig. Are they here?"

"No, they're not. Thank God."

"Why do you say that?"

"Look, Special Agent Dantry, I'm pretty sure I know why you're here. My father and Mr. Zweig have a record."

"Yes, they do. But why do you say *Thank God they're not here?* After all, one of them is your father."

"Heinrich just recently threatened my mother."

"Threatened?" said Special Agent Lopez. "What did he threaten to do?"

"He threatened to kill her. And my father apparently is going along with it."

"I'm very sorry to hear that," I said. "We're going to need more details on that soon, but right now can you tell us where the two men are?"

Doreen came forward and said, "I'm Doreen Zweig. The last Heidi and I saw them they were at this miniature golf park on Lake George. Just north of Lake George village. I don't know the name of it, but it was the first miniature golf we came to when driving north. Before we left our cottage I overhear my husband Heinrich on the phone with Max. My husband was saying he thought Heidi was too big a risk. She talks too much and might reveal too much about what the men have done. I don't have to tell you about that. I'm sure you already know or you wouldn't be here."

"We know what they've done in the past," I said, "and we think we know what they did recently down at Liberty Village. Is there more?"

"Isn't that enough?" snapped Doreen.

I pursed my lips, then said, "It certainly is. They have a car, I assume. Can you tell us what kind, what year and what color?"

"It's a Ford. A silver-gray Ford. Not new. A four-door sedan. License number begins WC 7. That's all I remember."

"That helps. Now can you tell us where they're staying?"

"It's in a place called Assembly Point. It's on the eastern side of the lake I think, though I'm not too good with geography."

"Do you think they would have gone back there from the miniature golf?" asked Lopez.

"Probably. Their stuff is there. Clothes and other things. Besides, they have nowhere else to go. They can't go back to Liberty Village and they don't know any other place in the area. Heinrich would want to go back to the cottage and think. I'm sure he's frantic now that he doesn't know where we are. He knows we don't have a car and we don't know the area. He must have guessed that we knew what his plans were."

"His plans to kill you?"

"Yes. He's evil, but he's not stupid. Why else would we leave them?"

"You might have gotten lost."

"But if we did we would have called them. But, we didn't call. They called us but we didn't answer, so they must know we wanted to get away. That has to put the fear of God in them because they don't know what we'll say. Well you two do. We'll tell you everything we know."

I was about to say something when Liam Schmidt said, "I hope that because my mother and Mrs. Zweig are being as helpful as they can, they won't face any charges? If you hadn't come here they were going to call the police anyway.

I allowed a hint of a smile to show on my face. "What kind of charges are you thinking of?"

Now Liam wished he hadn't brought up the subject. "Maybe aiding and abetting two fugitives. I assume they can't be prosecuted because they don't have to testify against their spouses. But I was hoping charges wouldn't be brought up at all because my mother and Mrs. Zweig suffered dearly at the hands of Mr. Zweig and my father."

"Suffered?" I asked. "How did they suffer?" I could only imagine what it had been being married to these two Nazis for all those years, but I wanted to hear it from them.

Liam said, "You tell it Mom. Or you, Doreen. Why don't you tell them why you couldn't report your husband during all those years."

Doreen, who was not shy, thought for a moment, then said, "I knew what Heinrich had done back in Buchenwald. Well, I didn't know exactly. He never told me much, though occasionally in a fit of rage something would slip out. He would tell me how he sometimes treated the prisoners. When detainees, as he called them, would give him a hard time—by that he meant they wouldn't do exactly as he demanded—he would bash them in the head with the butt of his rifle. When he was really annoyed he would have them whipped until their backs were bloody. He even bragged to me that once when someone repeatedly refused to do his bidding, and it was in front of two of his fellow guards, he shot the offender on the spot. I guess he did tell me quite a bit. It was enough to keep me from complaining or leaving him. It didn't take much for him to lose his temper. I wasn't going to test it. Otherwise he was a good provider, so I kept quiet and enjoyed time with my friends. But even then it wasn't easy to be with friends. He didn't trust me when I wasn't with him. I would often find him observing me from afar when I was with my friends."

"Couldn't you have just driven off in your car and gone to a place where he couldn't find you?"

She smiled. "It wasn't that easy. First of all, he didn't let me drive. He kept the car keys. I was never allowed to even get a license after we got married, not that that would have stopped me if I could have gotten the car keys. He rarely let me out of the house unless he came with me. I wanted to get a job and he didn't allow it. I'm sure he was afraid I'd get close to other people and say too much."

"Okay," I said. "I can't imagine why they'd prosecute you, but it's up to the prosecutor, not me. If you continue to be helpful to us, we'll put in a good word for you both."

"What do you want from us?"

"We want you to help us find them," I said. "The best way will be for the two of you to come with us as we look."

"When do you want to do this?" asked Heidi.

"Now," I said. "I know it's getting late, but if they did go back to the cottage, we can't be sure they'll stay there long. Almost certainly they'll figure we'll come looking."

"But where else would they go? Asked Doreen. They don't know anyplace else in this area."

"You didn't either, but you found the hotel. Desperate people do amazing things. Besides, they found the cottage. How did they find that?"

"Apparently," said Doreen, "there's this organization that helps former German soldiers find safe places to stay."

"You mean former Nazis?" I said.

"Yes, I suppose that's more accurate."

"Why couldn't they help your husbands find a new safe place?" said Lopez.

"I guess they could," said Doreen.

"Do you know these people?" I asked.

"I don't. Heinrich would never have shared that with me. I do know that there were two relatively young men who helped us settle in. They also helped us switch cars."

"What were their names?"

"Robert and William. That's what they called themselves. I didn't hear a surname. They were here to help us, but they were not from around here. I think they were from New York City, but I can't be sure. They sounded like white supremacists, too. Just the things they said. They were not nice young men I can assure you."

"Okay, let's go downstairs and we'll take two cars. I'll drive one and Special Agent Lopez the other. Mrs. Schmidt, why don't you go with her. Mrs. Zweig and Liam can come with me."

"Can't Liam come with us?" asked Heidi Schmidt.

I said, "I'm sorry, but I'd prefer to do it this way."

"But he's my son. I haven't seen him in quite a while."

"This shouldn't take long. After we finish you can catch up with your son." She shook her head in disbelief, but didn't pursue it. The two women and Liam were ready to go in just a few minutes. I drove the lead car with Maria Lopez and Heidi Schmidt following.

I headed toward Assembly Point. Amazing how after all these years it was still familiar. As we drove I said to Doreen Zweig, "I can't believe during your long married life there weren't times when you felt like breaking away from Heinrich. Knowing what you knew about his past."

"Many times, but I already explained to you why I didn't dare do anything about it. Actually I did try to leave him on two different occasions, but he nearly killed me when he caught me trying."

"What did he do?"

"He practically beat me to death." She glanced at Liam and added, "I told your mother about this. She was the only one I could talk to."

I then said, "Why did you marry this man?"

"When I met him he was a perfect gentleman and elegantly charming. I knew nothing about his ugly past. I've learned since then that sociopaths can be charming at times, and believe me, he's a sociopath."

"You never saw the other side of him before you got married?"

"Of course not. He told me he'd served as a German soldier in the war. I didn't think that was strange. I was from Germany and because I was German I would meet a lot of men who'd been in the German military. They weren't Nazis, though. Most of them had no choice but to serve. Heinrich, however, was proud of his service. He really believed he belonged to the superior race. He still believes that. God, whenever I think of it, it sickens me."

"Liam," I asked, "how much do you know about your father's past?"

"I knew he was a guard at Buchenwald. I've tried all my life to keep that from others. I've admitted to my friends that he was in the German army, but that was it. Never mentioned that he was a camp guard."

"I understand that, but how much do *you* know about his activities in the camp?"

"Nothing, really. Once or twice I confronted him, but his answer always was that he was assigned to camp guard duty and never liked it. Claims he didn't like to see people suffer— even Jews. Said he tried to go easy on the detainees as he called them, but couldn't go too easy or his fellow guards or superiors would be on his case."

"On his case? What would they do to him if he was easy on the detainees?"

"At the very least he would have been humiliated and disrespected by his fellow guards and the SS men at the camp. At worst, I don't know. But my father said that he and his fellow guards all believed the propaganda of the time that Jews were the enemy. They represented the 'international Jewish conspiracy.' They were the cause of World War I. They were responsible for the miserable condition Germany found itself in. Jews were the enemy and had to be eliminated."

We were now on Rte. 9L and approaching Assembly Point. I said, "Now we need you, Mrs. Zweig, to get us to the cottage. Is it far from here?"

"I don't think it's too far, though I'm not that familiar with the area. Just turn into Assembly Point Road and if I recognize anything I'll tell you."

A few short minutes into Assembly Point Road and Doreen said, "We're close. I recognize that house." She pointed to a trendy modern-looking one- story house that was more than just a cottage. To many people it would be a luxurious primary residence. "It's just a few houses beyond that. I noticed that the house she was pointing at was not on the water side of the road. If these people wanted to get to the water or the beach they would have to cross the road. Did they have mooring rights or beach rights? I didn't care that much, but it did make me wonder. Our Nazi safe house wasn't here for the water benefits obviously. Not that surprising. I drove on slowly, allowing her ample time to consider each structure as we moved along the road leading into the peninsula. After her initial comment, she didn't say anything else that was helpful.

40

Miniature golf park

Max was starting to shake, "Heinrich, I'm beginning to get worried. Where are the women? They're not here. Could they have taken one of those taxis?"

"Of course they did, you idiot. How else could they have left? They didn't walk."

"But where would they go?"

"Yes, where would they go, and who would they talk to when they got there? They don't know anyone around here. My guess is Doreen must have overheard me talking to you about what we planned to do. Doreen is behind this. The first thing she'd want to do would be to find a safe place to stay. At least for the immediate future."

"Do you think they would then call the cops?"

"If they think we'll go after them, they probably will," said Heinrich. "They can't feel safe knowing we're still out here."

"We're still out here, but we don't know where they are. What good does our freedom do us if we can't silence them?"

"If they go to the police the police will want to know where we're staying so we can't remain at Assembly Point. We have to go over there now and get our stuff before the authorities find out about the place."

"Yes, Heinrich, but if the women have gone to the police, we'll never be safe. The law will always be after us."

"Face it, Max, the law has always been after us. I'm going to call our young friends and ask them to help us find a new safe house quickly."

"In the meantime, if we could find the women maybe we could take care of them before they cause us more trouble."

Heinrich smiled. "I thought you were a bit reluctant to do this. Now you seem rather eager."

"After all these years, where's the loyalty to us? As soon as things get a little uncomfortable, they bolt. After decades of providing for them and caring for them, we get this. I'm afraid I'm past caring."

"And here all these years I thought you and I were different. I guess we're not so different after all. You have to look after number one. Nobody else really cares. Oh, they pretend to care, but they really don't. I'm afraid we can't take care of them now as we'd both like to. For one thing, we can't afford to take the chance. We need to find a new safe home and fast. Of course, the other reason we can't take care of them is we don't know where they are. Once we get ourselves a new place we can look into it. I'm sure they're at one of the many hotels and motels in this area, but I have no idea where to even begin looking. That's a lot of hotels and motels. Okay, enough talk. Let me call Robert or William so they can get us a place to stay. All these hotels and motels and I don't feel safe going to any of them."

"William, glad I got you. Max and I have a problem. We can't stay in the safe house anymore."

"What happened?"

"It's complicated. I'll explain later. Right now we need a new place to sleep. Can you find something fast?"

"Robert handles that. He's not here now. It's a good thing you called today because we were going back to the city in a few hours. As soon as we hang up I'll call Robert and tell him you need a new safe house. He's not gonna like it."

"We don't like it either, but we need that new safe place, and we need it tonight. Don't fail us."

"Where are you now?"

"We're driving from the miniature golf course just north of Lake George village. We're heading toward our place on Assembly Point, but when we get there we won't stay long. Can't afford to. Just need to get our luggage and other things. I don't think we can be there very long because law enforcement may now know about the place."

"How would they know about it?"

"I said it's complicated. We'll explain when you get us another place, but we don't want the police or FBI to find us at Assembly Point. Now I expect you to help us today. We only have a few hours. You and Robert need to work this out quickly. Meet us at the Assembly Point house in less than an hour with all the information we need about our new safe house. As I said, we can't afford to be there long."

When he ended the call Schmidt said, "You were awfully demanding of that guy. He's doing us the favor."

"That's true, but what's also true is he's dedicated his life to helping people like us. He can't afford to fail because it's a cause he's proud of. He looks up to us. We're heroes to him. He doesn't want to let his heroes down."

"How do you know this, Heinrich?"

"Don't you read body language? It's all over their faces and in their voices. Besides, I know enough about the movement these guys belong to. to know they idolize what the Western world calls war criminals and believers of National Socialism consider heroes. These two guys and their little organization believe in National Socialism. It's like a cult and these guys are hooked. They want us to be happy because we're the last of a vanishing breed of their superheroes."

"So you think William will call Robert, and Robert will find us a place to stay tonight? Even with such short notice?"

"Yes I do. We're dealing with zealots, and zealots will do amazing things. Not always good things, but in this case it will be good for us."

"Fine, if they really do come through. If they don't, we have a serious problem. No place to go and the law on our case. Heinrich, at this stage of our lives do you ever think maybe it's best that we just give ourselves up? Don't you ever get tired of running?"

"Of course I do, but so far we've been winning. Here we are in our mid-nineties and they still haven't caught up with us. We're winning once again. It's like a game of chess and we're winning. Don't you find that gratifying? Us against the finest law enforcement agencies in America, and we're winning."

"This is not a game, Heinrich."

"Oh but it is, my friend. It definitely is a game that we're winning. We have to keep winning or we'll find ourselves spending the remaining few years of our lives in a prison cell. We of all people know what that's like."

"A prison cell might not be wonderful, but the stress would finally be gone. They'll treat us better than we treated our prisoners. Not great, but we wouldn't be running. Aren't you tired of running, Heinrich?"

"It's physically tiring at my age, but psychologically it's challenging and even kind of fun. What else do we have at our age? We can't play golf or tennis. We can't have sex."

"We can read, listen to music, watch TV."

"These are all things you do sitting down. I need to be more active. And if we're in a prison cell you won't have your music or your TV. So you better focus your attention on winning the game. *Say*, you're not thinking of throwing in the towel, are you?"

41

"There it is," said Doreen excitedly. "That's the house. And there's somebody there." As she said this a young man came out of the house. She recognized him immediately. "That young man is one of the men who helped us exchange cars and find this safe house." I slowed down and parked a hundred yards away from the house.

I said, "I wonder if his partner is there too. I want to get these guys. Lopez should be here any second. Mrs. Zweig, you and Liam need to wait in the car when Special Agent Lopez and I confront these two men. Assuming they're both here. As I said that Lopez pulled in behind me. She got out and came to my door. "What's up? Is that the place?"

"Yes, and that young man is one of the men who helped Zweig and Schmidt switch cars. They also provided this safe house for them. We need to bring these guys in."

"What if Zweig and Schmidt come here when we're bringing these guys in? We'll lose them. If Zweig and Schmidt are running scared, they'll want to come here, get their stuff and move on. These two guys will probably help them. If we take these guys in, the two Nazis will probably panic. They won't know where to go, but they won't come here.

"I know," I said. "We have to do this so we don't lose them. I'll call BCI Melillo at the state police barracks. He and BCI Steele need to get here ASAP. We'll hang back here and try not to move in until the two BCI people get here. Maybe we should back the car up a bit more. This guy keeps looking at us. Don't want to scare him or his buddy away. Assuming his buddy is there."

"He is," said Lopez. "Just came out of the house. They look like they're just killing time."

"Let's hope that's all they're killing. Must be waiting for our two guys. No other reason they'd be hanging around here.

42

William said, "Who you calling?"

Robert said, "We can't let Zweig and Schmidt come here. At least not now. I don't like the looks of that car. If they're here to see someone they would have gotten out of the car. It's either cops or the Feds keeping an eye on us. Probably hoping Zweig and Schmidt will show up so they can make a collar."

"They can still collar us," said William nervously.

"Yeah, they can, but then they would lose the two Germans. That's who they really want. Hold it for a minute so I can call our guys before it's too late."

Robert's call was answered on the second ring. It was Heinrich Zweig.

"Yes, Robert. What's up?"

"William and I are at your cottage. Unfortunately, there's a car parked nearby. People in it. We're guessing they're either police or federal agents. They seem to be watching the cottage, so I don't think you should come here now. Wait, a second car just pulled in behind them. Now I'm sure it's cops or FBI. There's a state park just south of the miniature golf course. If you go there and pull in a hundred yards or so we'll meet you there in twenty-five or so minutes. Assuming law enforcement doesn't take us in. We'll get your stuff out of the cottage, so don't worry about that."

"Excellent. What if they do take you in? You won't be able to meet us in the park."

"If we don't show up in about 35 minutes, figure they have us. Don't worry about that. They'll have a hard time proving we've been helping you."

"What if law enforcement follows you?"

"Then we'll return to our hotel. I have some disguises there. I'll disguise myself and drive to the state park. That'll take more time, and if I have to do that, I'll call you."

"I was getting tired of waiting for the two Nazis to show up at the house on Assembly Point. Now that Lopez had just arrived, we debated the merits of arresting the two men there or waiting until they made a move. Fortunately, we didn't have to wait much longer. The two young men were loading what appeared to be suitcases into a Chevy Equinox. Then they got into the SUV and slowly drove past us toward Rte. 9L. I told Lopez if she hurried she could catch up and follow Robert and William. I'd be a quarter mile behind. She immediately turned the car around and headed out of the Point in pursuit of our two young men.

Lopez and I followed the two men into Lake George village until they reached the northern side of the village and pulled into the Water View Motel. We drove on past the motel and turned around a hundred yards beyond the place. Then we slowly approached the motel noting where the two men had parked. It was a large parking area so we pulled into spots as far from the Equinox as we could. We then waited five minutes. Then I went over to the Equinox and attached a GPS tracking device to the undercarriage. I then went into the motel leaving Lopez with our three family members.

I approached the front desk cautiously wanting to be sure our two young men were not there. They weren't so I approached the desk. The desk clerk was an attractive young woman.

"What can I do for you today, sir?"

I flashed my credentials and said, "I'm with the FBI. Just a few minutes ago two men came in here. Did you notice them?"

"Yes. I believe they went to their rooms."

"Can you tell me their names and what rooms they're in?"

"I don't think I'm supposed to give out that information. I'm sorry."

"Did you see my badge? I'm with the FBI. These two men may be killers. Do you feel comfortable with someone like that staying here?"

The clerk was clearly struggling with what to do. After what seemed like forever, she said they're in rooms 212 and 213."

"Their names?"

"Robert Ocasio and William Horan."

"Thank you. Please don't call their rooms."

I was about to go to the elevator when two older men entered the lobby from the hall that led to the rooms. The two men moved slowly, one of them shuffling with a walker, nodding to the desk clerk on their way out the front door. Then I proceeded down the hall toward rooms 212 and 213. I hadn't gone more than a hundred feet when it hit me. I jogged back to the front desk and said to the clerk, "Do you remember ever checking in two older men? One with a walker?"

"Now that you mention it, I don't. Maybe the night clerk, though."

I then ran to the front door and noticed the Equinox leaving the motel. It turned left out of the parking area. I sprinted back to where my car was parked and Lopez's was idling. I went to the driver's side of Lopez's car and said, "I'm almost certain the two old men who just left in the Equinox are our Robert and William in disguise. See if you can catch up to them. They went left out of here. I'll be right behind you. I have a feeling they're gonna lead us to our two Nazis."

About a minute later we had caught up with the Equinox. The road north along the lake snaked around a lot of curves so you couldn't go very fast. Fortunately, the traffic was light and when the SUV came into view it was easy to follow. Wisely Lopez held back so as not to make it obvious she was following. A couple of minutes later we passed the miniature golf course on our left. Two minutes past the golf course I noticed Lopez slowing because the Equinox was slowing. Then it took a slow turn to the right. I could see now that it was some kind of a park. As we eased closer a sign told me it was a New York State park. We hadn't been needing the GPS because we were able to stay in sight of the Equinox most of the time. Lopez was wisely holding back so as not to scare the occupants of the vehicle. Then she pulled into the park entrance. I followed her. She pulled in a few feet and stopped. We got out of our vehicles and considered our next move.

Lopez said, "The Equinox took that dirt road off to the right. That building we're parked in front of is the park rangers' base. It's where the park rangers assign camping spots. They must have a map of the park. Let's take a look before we go looking for the car."

I realized that we had the two wives of our fugitives and the son Liam. I said, "We need to get the two wives and Liam back to the hotel." I called Melillo of the BCI and asked him to send a car to take the three people to the hotel in Glens Falls. I added that they should probably keep a plain clothes cop in the hotel to ensure that the three didn't take off. I then explained to our three guests that they should remain calm in the two cars until a state police car came for them. It would be within the next 20 minutes.

In the meantime one of the park rangers showed us a map on the wall showing the layout of the park. A dirt road in the form of a loop went through the park. The dirt road allowed us to enter both ends of the loop so as not to lose the car or its riders.

"What's up?" asked the park ranger nervously. "Why is the FBI so interested in this car?"

"It's not the car," I explained. "It's the two male passengers. They're fugitives from downstate. Could be quite dangerous. If you see them, don't confront them. Just make a note of where they're going and anything else that you think could be helpful."

"How will I know them if I see them?"

"They're disguised to look quite elderly. They don't look dangerous, but we believe they've killed someone recently. We think they're meeting two other men who really are elderly. In their 90s. We think these two really older men have also killed a couple people downstate recently and maybe killed many more years ago. Don't underestimate them just because they look old. You probably won't see them anyway. I'm hoping my partner and I will collar them when we find them here in the park. You should probably stay right here until we tell you that we've got all four men in custody. The state police may also be joining us soon. Now you'll know why. If anyone else wants to enter the park, ask them to stay away for the next hour or so. And make sure campers stay away from these guys if you can."

"There's only me and one other ranger. She's out in the park now."

"Can you reach her?"

"Yes. She has a phone. I'll call her and tell her what you told me about these guys. I'll tell her to stay away from them and warn any campers she sees to avoid them too."

As I left the office I wasn't entirely comfortable with things. There was no way two park rangers could warn every camper and everyone entering the park in the next few minutes. Lopez and I had to check out our fugitives now and if they were here we had to summon the BCI cavalry ASAP.

Lopez and I needed to confirm that the two Equinox passengers were visiting our Nazi fugitives. I called BCI Detective Melillo and told him we needed him and one or two other detectives or state troopers to help collar our four bad guys. Lopez and I were not going to apprehend four desperate killers by ourselves unless we had no alternative. If the fugitives made a move to leave before the state police back-up got here, we'd have to take our chances. I was hoping that wasn't going to happen. It's not that I didn't have confidence in Lopez's and my ability, but two trained law enforcement people against four desperate, panicky killers was bad odds.

Lopez and I spoke briefly about our plan. The plan was for one car, mine, to drive down the dirt road that went off to the right. According to the map in the ranger's office that road circled back to the park entrance, so Lopez started down the other end of the loop. Theoretically this way our guys couldn't get away without our knowing it. As soon as one of us spotted the fugitives we were to stop and quietly notify the other. I would then place the call to state police BCI detectives. Hopefully the fugitives would remain in place until the reinforcements showed up. This was reason enough to be concerned, but I worried about something else, too. I worried that as we got closer one of the fugitives' relatives riding with us might try to warn the bad guys by shouting out a warning.

I started down the dirt road. I warned my two passengers to remain quiet when we approached our quarry. We passed campsite after campsite with no sign of our guys. Then I saw the Equinox. It was a good hundred yards away and I immediately pulled to a stop. I had been in touch with BCI Detective Melillo and kept him aware of where we were. He now said they were about three minutes from the state park. I then called Lopez to let her know. We were so close to capturing these guys now we couldn't afford to screw up.

As we waited for the state police backup and a car to take the two wives and Liam, I noticed one of the two younger men we'd been following walking over to a neighboring campsite with something in his arms. He placed it right next to the tent at that campsite and jogged back to his campsite. As he bent down I saw that it was the one called Robert. What the hell was that all about? Just as he returned two state police cars rolled in behind us. BCI Melillo and BCI Steele emerged from the two cars followed by a couple of troopers. Now we had a total of six officers ready to bring in the bad guys. The odds were looking a lot better now. I exchanged hellos with Melillo and Steele. Melillo suggested to Steele that he and his trooper take the other end of the loop so we would have the bad guys trapped if they tried to escape.

Melillo and I agreed that this was as good a time as any to move in. We contacted Lopez on the other end so she could coordinate with Steele and the other trooper. I turned to Melillo and his trooper and said, "Let's do it." We then drove closer to the bad guys' campsite. So far they hadn't noticed us. We continued to inch closer, wanting to get as close as possible before the fugitives saw us. We were now maybe 30 yards away. I could see past the campsite. Lopez and the troopers were about the same distance away on the other side. We continued to close in on the criminals' campsite. Then one of the young men, I think it was Robert, came out of the tent and saw us. He yelled something back toward the tent and then ran over to something and put his hand on it. A blast lifted the neighboring tent 15 feet into the air. The explosion was followed by screaming. From our vantage point all we could see were bodies flailing on the ground where the tent had been seconds ago. The four fugitives were piling into the Chevy Equinox and burning rubber up the other side of the loop. They left their old Ford behind at the campsite. I yelled to Lopez to send Steele and his trooper after the Chevy Equinox. She said she would and that she would follow them. We couldn't let these vicious bastards get away. The Equinox was past Lopez and Steele before they could get shots at them.

    There were several people in the tent when it blew. Most likely a family. I ran toward the blasted campsite hoping to help the survivors. Melillo and his trooper also ran to the scene. A young girl, maybe 10 or so lay motionless on the ground. A boy of maybe 12 or 13 was struggling to get up. Two middle-aged adults, a man and a woman seemed stunned.

They slowly shook away the cobwebs. Suddenly the woman became aware of what had happened and began screaming as she stared at her motionless daughter only feet away. I ran to the girl and felt for a pulse. Nothing. The boy was now aware of his situation. He stared at his sister in disbelief as his mother worked her way painfully to her daughter's side, screaming at the horror she was beholding. The father slowly got up and held his wife as her screams now turned to tears and sobbing. I looked into the mother's eyes and felt her pain. All I could think of was the evil that had deliberately caused this family tragedy.

The husband breathlessly asked, "Who did this?"

I said, "Vicious criminals. They're not going to get away with this." As I said this I saw that Melillo was already on his phone calling a couple ambulances. While we waited for the ambulances, Melillo, the trooper and I did our best to console the survivors. It wasn't much, but we couldn't just leave them alone after what they'd just gone through. I got the names of the victims and as soon as the first ambulance came, Melillo, the trooper and I tore off in our vehicles hoping to catch up to the fleeing killers. I immediately called Lopez to see how the pursuit was going.

She said, "They're about a half-mile ahead of us. It's dangerous on this narrow road to pass cars because of the curves. They can't go too fast either, but they're maintaining a half-mile lead right now. I don't think we'll lose them, though."

"We're right behind you."

43

Heinrich Zweig was not happy. "They're right behind us, Robert. It's only a matter of time before they catch us. Do something other than this. They can go as fast as we can. They'll catch us in the next mile or two."

Robert said, "Hold on. Right after this next turn I'll take care of it."

"What do you mean, take care of it?"

"Watch." As he said this he turned the car sharply to the right and into a dirt road that took them deep into the heavily treed area leading down to the lake.

Zweig was shaken by the sudden move and said, "Where the hell are you taking us?"

"When William and I first started working up here in the north country I scouted out possible escape routes that could bail us out in just such a situation as this. After checking Google Maps I found this one and came over and did a dry run just to be sure it was doable in an emergency. Hopefully the law following us didn't see us turn off. We can just hang out down this side road and wait until they're long past."

"Sounds good, Robert, if they didn't see us. What if they did see us?"

"If they did, we'll know in a matter of minutes. We'll then have to move on to Plan B."

"And Plan B is?"

"We'll have no choice but to fight it out. If we do, we'll shoot first. Element of surprise."

"I don't like those odds. Us against two cars of law enforcement people with the latest weapons."

"We've got good weapons. We'll give them a good fight."

"I don't want a fight. I want to get out of here in one piece."

"Don't worry, Mr. Zweig. You will."

"Let's hope it doesn't come to that. So far there's no trace of their two cars. If we do manage to shake them, what plans do you have for us?"

"We have another place you can stay near Pilot Knob. It's on the eastern side of the lake. Not as populated as the western side and southern end. You're still going to have to get out of there in the next few days, though. We're going to have to get you into Canada so you can then fly to Europe. Sooner the better"

"Europe?"

"You know you can't stay in the States? They kind of lost track of you in recent years, but now, after the killings down at your senior citizen place, they're after you. All of them. And after we bombed that tent, who knows who got hurt in that? You'll be the subject of a national manhunt. We just have to get you to Canada. Even there there'll probably be pressure to extradite you. You guys are hot and so are we now. We may all have to go to Canada. I'm not even sure how safe that'll be now. I have to say, Heinrich, you and Max have not handled things well. Most guys from Germany who fought for Hitler kept a low profile when they came to the United States. You guys have done just the opposite. You've been waving a red flag saying look at us. Come and get us."

Zweig was not used to being talked to like this. In the old days he was the one who talked this directly. Who the hell did this Robert kid think he was? He, Heinrich Zweig and Max Schmidt, were the ones who did everything they could to advance the Third Reich. Robert and William weren't even born when he and Max were doing their part for the Reich. He was about to let his temper control his response, when he realized he still needed these young men, no matter how uppity they were.

"Yes, we have made a few mistakes. We have not handled things as well as we should have. We do appreciate your help and regret it if we have made things difficult for you two. Can we now put our four heads together and come up with a plan to get us all out of this predicament?"

"Well," said Robert, "So far nobody has followed us down this road. Looks like we've lost them for the moment. Let's wait a couple more minutes and if they still don't show up, I think we can sneak out of here and go back the way we came in. Instead of heading the way we were, though, we'll retrace our steps and head eastward and up the road past Pilot Knob and plunk ourselves down in our other safe house. We'll only be there a short time, though. We're going to get the two of you out one at a time and we'll need disguises and new passports for each of you. That will take some time. We just have to hope we can get the passports before law enforcement finds this safe house."

"If it's truly a safe house," said Max, "then they shouldn't find us."

"I don't think you guys give law enforcement in this country enough credit. They will eventually find it. Just a matter of time. Let's hope it takes them a while, though. I certainly hope so because now they're after William and me as well as you two old guys."

Zweig asked out of curiosity more than concern, "How will you and William evade the law? Will you leave the country too?"

"We may be able to change our identity. We look and sound American, so that's an advantage. You guys sound and look just like what the law is looking for. Sorry, Mr. Zweig, but that's the truth. You two may be the last World War II survivors we help. There aren't many of you left anyway. This is probably a good time for William and me to try something new."

"Right now Max and I need your help. Think we can get out of this road safely now?"

"Looks pretty good. Let's give it a shot."

As the Equinox slowly made its way up the road they'd come in on, things looked more promising. They didn't encounter any other vehicles. Obviously law enforcement had missed this little escape route. As Rte. 9L came into view Robert turned left and headed east toward the eastern side of the lake. On the way they passed the little hamlet of Cleverdale. The Cleverdale area was fairly well populated, but as they drove a few miles beyond it the houses were few and far between.

44

The eastern side of the lake was markedly less populated than the west side. A few minutes later Robert took the Equinox deep into the woods. Up ahead was a fairly sizable log cabin.

"Okay, gentlemen," said Robert, "This is your new safe house. As you can see, it's in a very remote location, though it's only about a 15-minute drive from Pilot Knob, which is pretty small, but does have a store and a post office. You should be safe here for a few days, at least as long as you don't do anything to draw attention to yourselves."

"And in the meantime you'll have someone preparing fake passports and other IDs we'll need to get into Canada?"

"Exactly. To do this I'm going to need some money from you guys. Our organization only provides so much for each case and you guys are costing us a lot more than the usual case."

"Now wait a minute," said Zweig. "This wasn't part of the deal."

Robert smiled. "This deal is a pretty good bargain for you guys. Face it, we're the only game in town. You think you can get yourself safely into Canada and then on to Europe without our help, then hop to it. William and I have our own problems. We don't need to help two ungrateful bastards if that's the way you want to play it."

Zweig looked toward Schmidt, who pursed his lips and held his hands palms up helplessly. Zweig shook his head in frustration and said, "How much will you need?"

"Forty grand each."

"Forty thousand dollars! Where do you think we can get that kind of money?"

"You guys have been stashing it away all your lives. You've got plenty more than that or you wouldn't have been accepted by us in the first place. Our organization does a deep dive into your finances or we wouldn't take a chance on you. So don't give me that poverty crap. You can afford it. I know you understand how much it takes to buy the help of others who are willing to risk their necks for you. Now do you want our help or not? If not, you're on your own. As I said before, William and I have our own necks to worry about, so don't whine to us. You're the reason for our problem now so don't expect any sympathy. We'll help, but you have to pay. It's as simple as that."

"Then you leave us no choice. We'll agree to your terms."

"I'm glad to hear that. We're going to need to see the money before we help you."

"You'll get your money. I don't have it with me and my bank is in New Jersey."

"That's okay, just show me your account online so I can see that you have the funds. If you do have sufficient funds you can write both of us checks made out to cash."

"That's very risky carrying around checks for $40,000 made out to cash. Are you sure you want to take that chance?"

"You let us worry about that. We can take care of ourselves. You obviously can't. Now show me your account on your phone."

"I'm not too good at this," said Heinrich Zweig.

"I'll bet you're not. Stop dragging your feet, Heinrich. Show me your account. I need to see yours, too, Max." Robert had lost all patience with his ungrateful charges. He had no desire to call either of them 'mister'.

"I'm trying to think of the name of the bank," said Zweig. "I think it's the Bank of South Jersey. It's something like that."

"This is getting annoying, Heinrich. Just go to the web site."

"I'm trying. I'm trying." As Zweig said this he typed awkwardly on the keyboard of his iPhone. The Food Bank of South Jersey came up.

"Obviously that's not the name of the bank. What kind of game do you think you're playing, Heinrich. We're not fools and you're running out of time."

"I'm not playing any game, William. I just went to this bank recently knowing I might need to move some assets quickly. Believe me, it's something like Bank of South Jersey. Maybe it's Bank of Southern Jersey. Here, let me try it." He started typing and came up with nothing. He was clearly feeling the pressure of his dire situation. He had long ago sensed that William was as callous as he was and that it made no sense to try to put something over on him. And yet that was exactly what he was trying to do. What he didn't want to do was show William his real bank account. If the young man saw that account, there was a good chance he'd demand more than $40,000.

"Heinrich, you're starting to piss me off. I can't believe you don't know how to access the bank account where you keep your money."

Zweig realized he had no choice now. "All right, I think I remember it. He quickly typed in the URL for the bank and then logged in to his account. He then went to his account and Robert's face formed a jaw-dropping expression.

"Holy Shit! You're loaded. I think you can afford a lot more than forty grand for a safe exit from North America."

"No, Robert, we have an agreement. I hope you will keep your word."

"Don't go all morality on me, Heinrich. We both know who you are. I think we're going to need sixty grand to make sure you get out of here safely. Take it or leave it."

"If we leave it, you get nothing. How can you pass up that money?"

"I only get part of it. Besides, helping two men who are on law enforcement's radar in every state makes it a lot riskier for William and me. They're already looking for us. If we help you guys, our chances are worse. We'd probably be smarter to just leave you here to fend for yourselves."

"All right. All right. You'll get your $60,000. Just get us out of here. By the way, I don't think you noticed that the account was in a different name. Both Max and I used different names in our new bank accounts. For obvious reasons. That works to your advantage as the checks we give you won't connect you to us."

"I just hope they're cashable. Tomorrow we're gonna deposit them and we won't do anything for you until they clear our bank, so I ask you now, will they clear?"

"Yes, they will. They certainly should."

"They better or you're up shit creek."

"As far as I know they will. As you can see, that's where I put my money."

"We're counting on it. Okay, let's assume you're not conning us. You're gonna need a car. Can't go back to the state park for yours. William will get you another one."

"Where do you get these cars?" asked Max.

"Steal 'em," said William. "We don't steal fancy cars. They draw too much attention. We'll get you something reliable, but fairly common."

Robert then said, "We take risks all the time for you guys. I hope you appreciate it. Oh, just a suggestion, but when we get you the car and you go into Pilot Knob for food, maybe just one of you should go. I'm sure the cops are looking for two elderly gentlemen. Less risk if only one of you goes."

"We're going to need the car soon," said Zweig, "as I see there's no food here now." He'd already done a quick walk around the rustic cabin and found that the cupboards were bare and the refrigerator, while cold, was empty. The place had that musty, mildewy smell that abandoned cabins often have. He didn't like it, but was in no position to complain.

"You'll have it later today. We're going to leave you now as it will take William some time to find a suitable car in a neighborhood that lends itself to car theft. He can't just grab a car in front of people. I'm sure you guys understand."

"Yes, yes," said Zweig. "We understand perfectly. Now you'd best be on your way so you have time to pull this heist off successfully. Max and I are going to need some food before this day is over."

"As soon as we bring you the car you can go for something to eat. Remember, only one of you should go to a store at a time."

"Yes, of course. We haven't made it into our 90s by being stupid."

"I wonder," said Robert, "just how smart you were when you killed those people downstate in the same place you were living. Not too smart in my opinion. If you have to kill someone, don't do it near your home."

"You weren't there, Robert. If you were, maybe you'd understand. That's where they were living too. I had to kill them there or they might have caused trouble.'

"The worse they could do was say you reminded them of their guards. They couldn't have proved anything. It might have been uncomfortable for you, but you wouldn't have been on the run as you are now."

"No, they already had the FBI on the case. It would have been a lot more than uncomfortable."

"We'd better get going if you're going to have your car today. Oh by the way, we'll need those checks when we get back."

"You'll get $30,000 checks today and the rest when you finish the job."

45

Back in their hotel room in Glens Falls, Doreen, Heidi and her son Liam tried to relax. It wasn't easy because of what they had been through. What they had known about Heinrich and Max just a few days ago was enough to weigh on anyone's conscience, but after witnessing the explosion of the tent in the state park and knowing that a young girl was killed by the blast a new level of horror was added to an already terrible day.

"I just called Madison," said Liam. "Brought her up to date. Told her I wasn't sure when I'd be home, but not to worry. Said I was pretty sure I would be allowed to go home."

"You are sure of that?" asked his mother. "You haven't done anything wrong. What do you think will happen to Doreen and me?"

"They can't charge you with anything, Ma. Not your fault for what Dad did in the past."

"Well there's a state cop downstairs to make sure we don't run off. They must want us for something, Liam."

"They're going to want to interview all of us before they let us go. They want to build a solid case against Dad and Heinrich. You can understand that I'm sure. Even after they let us go I'm sure they're going to want to keep track of us because they'll probably want us to testify when all this goes to trial. When that'll be is anyone's guess."

"Oh my God," said Heidi, "How will we be able to live in Liberty Village now. What will our friends say? How will people treat us?"

"It won't be easy Ma, but hopefully most people will see you and Doreen as victims, not criminals."

"I'm not so sure about that, but even if they do, I don't want to live the rest of my life as victim, Liam. I don't want people's pity for the rest of my life."

"It'll get better with time. Time heals everything eventually."

"Maybe, but it won't be easy at first."

"I know it won't, Ma, but your really good friends will understand. It'll take longer with your acquaintances. Frankly, it's not going to be easy for Madison and me, either."

"No, it won't be easy for any of us," said Doreen. "If possible it'll probably be even harder for me because of what Heinrich has done, not just in the past, but recently, too. People are going wonder why I would live with such a monster. I could tell them I was frightened to death most of our married life, but nobody is going to ask me about that. They're just going to think the worst." She looked at her friend Heidi and her son and added, "I hate to say it but people are going to wonder why any of us stayed with such a man."

"Wait a minute, Doreen," said Heidi. "You're not going to compare my Max to your Heinrich?"

Liam could see where this was heading and interrupted quickly. "Let's not go there Mom. We have to stay together on this. We need each other's support. All of us are victims. Let's not get into who's the greater victim. That'll get us nowhere.

46

Robert and William did not return to the log cabin until 9:00 that night.

Robert said, "Sorry gentlemen it took so long, but we decided to go into Glens Falls to heist the car. It's a bigger town, but a lot sleepier than Lake George village. Easier to find a car on a side street without anyone nearby. Even then you have to scout around in a quiet neighborhood for a car that won't attract attention. Not as easy as you might think. Got you a nice blue Kia. Suggest you don't drive it in the Glens Falls area, though. They'll be looking for it."

"Yes, yes," said Zweig. "I understand. Good. We were afraid you wouldn't have any luck."

"It's not luck. If you do this right, you'll get a car. Just have to know what you're doing."

"I suppose so," said Heinrich. "I'm afraid the local general store may not be open at this hour. Max and I are starving. Now we must wait till morning just to get a bite to eat."

"William and I anticipated that. Brought you a couple ham and cheese sandwiches with a couple Cokes and two bottles of water. Should be enough to get you through till morning."

Zweig was about to say that he wasn't that fond of ham and cheese, but kept quiet, knowing it wouldn't take much to lose the help of the two young men.

"Thank you for that. Appreciate the thought. I suppose you're expecting your checks?"

"Damned right we are, Heinrich." Zweig and Schmidt reluctantly handed over their $30,000 checks.

Zweig then said, "When will we have our passports and other papers?"

"Have to talk to my guy tomorrow. Had no time today, as I'm sure you know. He can usually deliver in about a week. I'll tell him we need these ASAP, but I'm sure that's what everybody tells him. Now if you want to ante up some more dollars, maybe he'll make an extra special effort for you two."

"After you talk to him tomorrow call me and tell me what his earliest delivery time is. And what that fastest time will cost us."

"I don't know how much but I'm sure it'll cost you. You have to weigh it against serving the remaining years of your life behind bars. Your call my friends. Your call."

"We have no leverage in this do we? You guys can just demand anything you want and we have no choice but to pay."

"That's about it. What the hell did you expect: A national charity for war criminals? I don't think so. In case you don't know it you guys are not the most popular people on the planet. Be glad you have money to pay for our services. Some of you guys don't even have that.

47

Dantry's phone rang. It was BCI Melillo

"Dantry, we might have a lead. The little general store in Pilot Knob, on the east side of the lake says a customer claims to have seen one of your guys."

"I hope that's true. Have to wonder how someone up here in the boondocks would even know about our guys."

"Amazingly enough, that someone happens to be a resident at this Liberty Village place down in Putnam County. He's up here on vacation with his kids. They have a place on the lake. This guy claims he knew of our guys back at the senior-living place. He's almost certain this is one of the guys."

"Does this guy know where Zweig and Schmidt are?"

"Says he saw Zweig head north on Pilot Knob Road in a blue Kia. Described the car and even got the plate number."

"Okay," I said. "Gives us something to go on. Do you know what's north of Pilot Knob? Is it heavily populated?"

"Just the opposite. A few houses, but very sparsely populated. Can't go too far north or it's all undeveloped state land. We have a fairly good chance of eyeballing the car if they didn't hide it somewhere. And because it's sparsely populated if we talk to someone, we might get lucky. Zweig has to stand out as new and much older than most of the residents in that area. The other guy has to stand out too."

"Okay, Lopez and I are going to head north on Pilot Knob Road. If we spot the Kia I'll call you so you can come and help us make the arrest. You might want to bring some uniforms too." After Lopez and the others had lost the quarry, she had rejoined me.

* * *

I hadn't been in touch with Joanna in a while and I liked to keep her up-to-date. I could only imagine how frustrating and worrisome it could be when someone doing what I do isn't heard from for a long time. I excused myself and called Joanna. She was at work so we couldn't talk long.

She sounded concerned when she answered. "Everything okay?"

"Yes. Just wanted to let you know we're still in pursuit of these two guys. We think we're getting closer, but you never know. Just didn't want you to worry."

"These are bad guys so of course I worry, but I know you don't take reckless chances. I'd be happier if you were out on your boat, but I know you need to play detective from time to time. Keeps your brain healthy. I do understand. I've got a couple minutes so tell me what it's like up there?"

"If I wasn't chasing bad guys I could really enjoy this place. One of the most beautiful lakes you'll ever see. Maybe *the* most beautiful. Easily as beautiful as Tahoe. The water is crystal clear. You can see the bottom when it's ten or twelve feet deep. A good part of the east side of the lake is state land so there's no development there. It's just like it was when the Europeans first discovered it 400 years ago."

"What are the chances you'll land these two guys?"

"Well there's the two Nazis and two young white supremacists who've been helping them. I think we've got a decent chance, but these guys are not stupid. They don't make it easy. We've got the state police, the state police BCI and an FBI special agent from the Albany field office all after these guys, so I'd say our chances are good. But you never know."

"Sounds like you've got the manpower."

"We do, but this is a big lake and everything is spread out. By the way, it's not all manpower. I'm working with a woman special agent. Seems pretty sharp."

"You have a way of ending up with sharp women," said Joanna with a wry tone in her voice.

"Yes I do, don't I? Only one of them matters though."

* * *

When I rejoined Lopez I said, "Shall we head north? If we spot the Kia we'll call BCI Melillo and BCI Steele to join us for backup. Hopefully they'll bring some uniforms too."

Lopez locked her car and came with me. As we made our way northward up the Pilot Knob Road it soon became clear how underpopulated this side of the lake was. Lake George was not a small lake. It was 32 miles long with over a hundred miles of shoreline, but most of the populated shoreline was on the southern end and western side of the lake.

We passed through the little hamlet of Pilot Knob and continued on up the lake on the narrow road. I was taken by the beauty of this gem of American lakes. I turned to Lopez and said, "You're out of the Albany field office. Where you from originally?"

"Saratoga Springs. My folks have a place on Lake George, so I'm familiar with the area. Don't know this side of the lake too well though. How about you? I gather you're not from around here?"

I told her about City Island and she actually seemed interested. "Originally I'm from this area. Lived in Glens Falls and parents had a place here on the lake. After college I worked for the CIA overseas, but City Island always fascinated me. Finally moved there. A few years ago my partner moved in with me."

"I was going to ask if you were married. I take it you like your present arrangement?"

"Joanna and I do. We've thought about marriage, but never found a pressing need for it. Who knows, maybe someday. I know our parents would like it." There was a pause and I then asked, "How about you?" She was clearly a lot younger than me.

"I just met a guy I like a lot. Who knows? This job doesn't make it easy for relationships. I'm away a lot."

"I understand. And you're right, but you can make it work. Sometimes I'm away for a week or more, but we stay in touch every day and the reunions are great." I grinned as I said this. "Joanna has a very responsible job and sometimes she has to travel. If it can be done, I'll go along, but that doesn't always work. Again, we talk on the phone every day and when she returns we appreciate our relationship all the more."

"Hey," she said. "Do you think a war criminal can ever be forgiven if he's led a good life all these years since World War II? Should he still have to pay for his crimes that took place in the 1940s?"

"We're pretty sure these guys recently committed murder, and more than once, so I'd say our guys should pay. But if they've been good guys ever since the war, should they still be punished? That's an interesting question. I think in Germany they still prosecute these people because they feel it's a deterrent to others. While anyone convicted now will obviously not face many years in prison, he or she will face humiliation and the loss of freedom that they denied others years ago. Most important, though, is the deterrence. Hopefully it will keep others from ever committing such crimes in the future."

"Nice thought," she said, "but I'm not so sure it will do that. Prison sentences don't seem to deter modern day criminals."

"Not all of them. That's true. Still, you can't reward these criminals just because they've survived this long without committing more crimes. If somebody commits murder today and gets away with it for 50 years, do you just forget about it?"

"No, of course not," said Lopez. "Still, what if they've done more than just keep a low profile for 50 years? What if they've led exemplary lives? Actually done good? Helped people? That's certainly not the case here, but what if it was?"

"I suppose a prosecutor and jury might lighten up on them. I imagine it would depend on how exemplary. I doubt that many people who had committed terrible war crimes are likely to become saints in later life. I guess anything's possible, but I'd be skeptical. I know war criminals are not all the same. Some of them actually killed people. Others typed lists and followed orders either because they believed in what the Nazis were doing or because they felt they had no choice. I suppose I'd be lenient with the latter ones. From what I've read the SS didn't take kindly to anyone under them who didn't follow orders or who went so far as to treat prisoners with kindness. Looks like our two guys plus their young helpers are not in the lenience category." I concentrated on the road and then said, "How long have you been with the bureau?"

"Four years."

"Ever fired your gun?"

"Not on the job. Think I might have to today?"

"I don't think the two older guys will want to get into a gunfight, but the two younger guys are apparently fanatics, or they wouldn't be risking their lives for two old Nazis. You never know what to expect from someone like that."

48

As we drove north we saw a couple Kias, but they weren't blue. Most of the cars we saw were clearly in sight in driveways, but occasionally cars must have been parked behind the cottages. Fortunately there weren't many parked this way because there weren't many houses, but obviously we had to check when we came to them. Our guys would certainly want to hide their car if they could. Every time we came to a house or cottage where the driveway seemed to run behind the building we stopped, got out and took a quick look behind the structure. Occasionally a person would come out of their house and ask us what we were doing. We had to explain that we were with the FBI and that we were looking for a certain car and its occupants. We would also describe the men we were looking for and say they were desperate men who should be avoided. I left my card and said, "If you see any of these four men give me a call, but don't confront them." Went through a lot of cards.

It was turning out to be more labor-intensive than I thought it would be. There were enough places where it looked as if a car might be behind a structure to slow us down quite a bit. We had to check every one of them. We couldn't let these guys get away again.

"How long do these guys think they can hide out here?" wondered Lopez openly. "They must realize that sooner or later somebody's going to spot them."

"It's almost certainly a temporary safe house where they're waiting for someone to take them somewhere where they think they'll be safer than they are right now. Maybe these young guys who've been helping them have a plan. Maybe there's a remote retreat further up in the Adirondacks. A place where there aren't many police, and you can live without seeing anyone if you stay hunkered down. Or maybe they're planning on slipping into Canada, though I can't imagine them being much safer up there. The Canadians don't take kindly to war criminals any more than we do.

49

When Robert and William were gone, Heinrich and Max wolfed down their sandwiches. It had been a long and tiring day.

Zweig took a sip of his Coke and winced. "Never liked this stuff. Never liked any carbonated drinks."

"Well you better drink it," said Schmidt. "You need fluids. You're probably already a bit dehydrated."

"We're in a helluva situation, Max. At this point in our lives we should not have to worry about such things. We should be able to relax and enjoy life—
not concern ourselves with the law."

Schmidt just stared at his friend.

"All right, come out with it, Max. You want to say something. Spit it out."

Schmidt allowed a stress-filled moment to pass, then said, "You really believe God owes you comfort in your old age?"

"Maybe not God. You know how I feel about such things. But yes, I think near the end of our lives we deserve some comfort. Not grief."

"You really don't get it, do you?"

"What?"

"What we did back in the camp. Do you think that entitles us to comfort in our old age?"

"That was a long time ago. And it was war time. You do a lot of things in war time you don't do in times of peace."

"We did a lot of things we shouldn't have done even in war time. Much of what we did was unnecessary. Much of what you did was particularly unnecessary and I'm sure you know it."

"I didn't do enough. We didn't do enough. If we'd been more effective Germany would have won the war and the Aryan race would now rule the world. We made a good start on ethnic cleansing, but the Americans and the Russians intervened too soon. We never had a chance to finish the job."

"I believed in ethnic cleansing then, but I don't now. Too simple an answer and far too cruel. Besides, who knows how many diseases might have been cured if we hadn't killed the smart ones?"

"What's happened to you, Max? Are you swallowing all this liberal garbage that the media is all awash in? I thought that in you, at least, I had an ally."

"I think we started growing apart a long time ago. You only see things one way. I know what it's like because I was that way when I was younger. But you've never evolved. You depend too much on violence. Violence begets violence. Besides, if there is a God, I'm sure he created all of us for a reason. Even the Jews. Sure, there were Jews who were not perfect, but so were a lot of us Aryans. We lumped all the Jews together because of the failings of a few of them. We got caught up in the Zeitgeist promoted by Hitler. It was a terrible time, and we were part of it, Heinrich. Come on, you must see that."

"Here is what I see: The Third Reich was the last chance to create an Aryan world. It's gone now. Now the left is in control everywhere in the world. Diversity is the new buzz word. Everybody is supposed to love everybody. Even the Jews. Things are worse than ever. You and I are lucky we don't have to face a lifetime of this kind of thinking. What I don't understand is how you've changed so much, my friend. What happened to you?"

"Maybe I grew up. Maybe I evolved. Maybe I learned from the world around me. My only regret is that I evolved too late. I can't undo the bad things I did. The only thing I can do now is act like a human being and treat my fellow human beings decently. However, thanks to what happened back in Liberty Village I'm not sure I can even do that from this point on."

"Right now, my friend, we have to concentrate on getting into Canada and then on to the continent."

"I'm afraid that's out of our hands, Heinrich. Can we trust Robert and William?"

"Money talks. I'm sure they'll want the rest of their money."

"I'm sure they're going to up the ante, too, and we'll have no choice but to fork over whatever they ask for." Schmidt pursed his lips as he considered the plight they were in. "We wouldn't be in this mess if it weren't for your paranoia, you know."

"Paranoia? What the hell are you talking about?"

"As soon as someone even suggests that you were a guard in the camp, you think they have to be silenced. You think anyone who even hints at your past is after you. Hell, there's a very good chance that we could have weathered those accusations, because they weren't really accusations. They were questions. They were faint memories. Some old dame thought you looked like her camp guard at Buchenwald. She could never have proved it. Even she wasn't certain. If you were calm and not paranoid, you could have just ignored her. If she didn't stop, you could have quieted her up by demanding she prove it or shut up. You could have made her look like a foolish old woman. And if she still continued her accusations, you could have sued her. It would all be bluff on your part, but where is her proof? No prosecutor would even try to prosecute you without proof. Her word against yours is hardly proof. Especially since even she wasn't sure. The point is you didn't have to overreact and kill her. That's what brought the law's attention on us."

"Where is this coming from, Max? You have never turned on me like this in the past. I can't believe you would turn on me at a time like this. We need to stand united."

"We will stand united because we have no other choice now. I'm accusing you now because you've done some reckless things lately. Instead of remaining calm, you've overreacted. I thought you got the violence out of your system back at Buchenwald, but apparently it never left you. What I'm saying is that you haven't left the past behind you. I've at least tried to do that. Now, because you overreacted and killed those two people, admittedly they were annoying, we're on the run. I don't know about you, Heinrich, but now in my mid-nineties I don't have much energy to run. I'm tired. I'll give this a try, but if it doesn't work, so be it."

"So you're giving up on me, just when we need to stick together?"

"I didn't say that. I'm just saying we can't expect to have a problem-free life considering what we did back in the camp. Nobody owes us anything. Don't you see that?"

"I just see that my best friend has changed. Let's just focus our attention on getting across the border and then on to the continent. We can discuss philosophy when things settle down."

50

It was decided that Schmidt would drive to the little general store in Pilot Knob. While both he and Zweig were wanted, it was felt that Heinrich Zweig's face was the one that was circulated more frequently than that of Max Schmidt because Zweig was the one wanted for two murders down in Putnam County. As soon as Schmidt entered the rustic store his eye caught sight of the newspaper rack. The *Adirondack Journal*, the local weekly, was hard to miss. The headline popped out at him.

Nazi War Criminals Hiding in Lake George

This week local residents in Lake George village and Assembly Point have reported sightings of two alleged Nazi war criminals. Customers at the Blue Moon sandwich shop in Lake George village believed they saw two men who looked well into their 90s with two elderly women. Most likely their wives.

The local man who claimed to have seen the war criminals said he had just come up from the metro New York area where he heard about the two Nazi criminals on the TV news. A woman from Rye, New York, who owns a cottage on Assembly Point claims she, too, saw two men walking on Assembly Point Road who resembled two men she'd seen on New York TV.

An officer at the local state police barracks confirmed that two war criminals were believed to be in the area. He advised anyone who sees these men to report it to their local police or to the state police.

Schmidt bought the paper and enough food to get them through a few days if they weren't too fussy about what they ate. *God knows, we're in no position to be fussy*, thought Max. Still, Heinrich would quibble about what he bought for them. Heinrich was rarely satisfied. Max was beginning to wish he'd taken his leave from Heinrich a long time ago. They didn't have much in common. The main thing was their camp experience and even with that, they viewed their experience dramatically differently. Heinrich was proud of it, and he, Max, was ashamed of it. They should have gone their separate ways a long time ago. However, their kids were married to each other so they were probably inseparably bound together whether he, Max, wanted it or not. Now, of course, it was too late. There was no turning back at this point.

Because Heinrich had overreacted to that Miller woman's comments, they were now on the run. At his age, Max didn't feel like running. He'd done enough of that in his younger years. Finally, at Liberty Village, he'd been able to relax and put the ugly past behind him. But Heinrich wouldn't leave things alone. He could've just waited things out when someone thought he was their former camp guard. It would have blown over, because the old woman had nothing but her vague memory. Half the people at Liberty had faulty memories and most of them knew it. If Heinrich had just laughed it off, the whole thing would have gone away in a few weeks and they wouldn't be stuck here in the wilderness waiting to be bailed out by two greedy young white supremacists who might not even return with the fake passports.

Out of ideas and lacking enough energy to implement them if he had them, Schmidt headed back to the cabin. He pulled the old car in behind the rustic structure where it couldn't be seen from the road. Before he could enter the cabin, Heinrich Zweig had come out and was standing with arms akimbo, glaring at Schmidt.

"Where the hell have you been?"

"Excuse me!"

"Where have you been? I've been waiting here patiently. You've been gone a long time. You knew I was here waiting."

"With that attitude, you should be glad I came back at all. I'm not your slave, Heinrich."

"I thought you were my friend, yet you take forever to bring me something to eat."

"I went as fast as I could," said Max. "Now let's eat and figure out what we're going to do next."

"We're going to wait for Robert and William to bring us our documents. What else can we do?"

"How do we know they're coming back? They're not very happy with us and they know the heat is after us. We could be caught at any time and I doubt that these young men want to be with us when we're taken in. Maybe Robert and William will take the money and run."

"You could be right. All right, we need a Plan B."

"I wish we had a Plan B. We don't have much to work with."

"Well, we have this car. Not much of a car, but it obviously works. And we have two handguns."

"What are we going to do with two pistols? Rob a bank?"

"This is no time for sarcasm, Max. No, if Robert and William don't come back by a certain agreed upon day, we take our junkheap of a car and head north."

"How do we get across the border without the new passports we're paying big money to Robert and William for?"

"We still have our old passports. I know, it'll be a big risk using them, but if we get a stupid or lazy immigration official at the border, we might get lucky."

"I doubt if they're that stupid. Besides, won't they be looking for us?"

"Yes, of course. What I'm counting on is some back road across the border that isn't an official border crossing. I've heard there are such roads. I think I read that there's about a dozen unguarded back roads between Vermont and Quebec. We should be able to find one. If we do, we won't need passports."

"If we're lucky enough to make it across the border safely, then what do we do?"

"We find an inn or motel and rest. Then we can consider our options. Do we buy plane tickets to some place in Europe or do we find a place to live in Quebec or elsewhere in Canada.

This isn't going to be easy, Max, but at least we do have options."

"I'm hoping Robert and William decide to come back. If they do, that means they have a way into Canada and on to Europe that's apparently been tested. Hopefully a fairly safe way. I'm also assuming that they will be our guides and do the schlepping for us. I get tired easily now. I'm willing to pay these guys to be our travel guides."

"So am I, I'm just not sure they're going to come back. If they don't, we're going to have to confront Dantry and his fellow FBI agent or the state police or whatever law enforcement gets here first. Sooner or later they're going to find us. If we do as I suggest, we won't have to confront Dantry or any other U.S. law-enforcement person. Here's what I suggest. We call Robert and get him to agree to be here on a certain day. It has to be fairly soon or law enforcement will beat them to us. Let's say three days from now. If he agrees to that, we wait for him. If he doesn't come, then we head out on our own."

"What if he says he can't make it in three days?"

"Then I think we have to move out anyway. We may not even be safe for three days."

"You're probably right. Dantry or some cops could be here any time now. What do we do if they get here before the three days are up?"

"We just might have to give up," conceded Zweig. "But we might still have one last option," he added mysteriously.

51

The log cabin somehow seemed out of place. It's not that log cabins couldn't be found in remote places, but they were not as common as they once were. In recent decades people who built in rural and remote touristy areas tended to use more standardized materials. For a lot of reasons. Log cabins were hard to modernize. Electrifying them was awkward, as was adding plumbing. Insulating them was not easy either. The quaintness no longer had the appeal it did in days gone by. Still, the ones that remained obviously appealed to some. This one was clearly quite old.

While log cabins don't appeal to me, I suppose I can understand how some people might like them. This one looked well-built and seemed in good repair at first glance. I noticed car tracks leading to the rear of the structure, so I got out of the car to take a look. I followed the tracks behind the cabin. Less than a minute later I reappeared motioning for Lopez to join me. As she met me I said *sotto voce*, "Go back to the car and call Gary Melillo or Mac Steele at BCI for reinforcements. Give 'em the GPS coordinates. As soon as you do that, join me. I want to look around here for a couple minutes. Then I'll wait with you in the CRV until the state police reinforcements arrive. Don't want to lose these guys."

Two minutes later she emerged from the CRV. "Melillo and Steele are on their way with two uniforms. We should probably get back in the car and wait for them."

I agreed. "Hopefully they didn't see me casing the joint. I'd rather face them when the odds are in our favor."

She grinned confidently, "Well, they are in their nineties. I'd say the odds are already in our favor."

"Don't underestimate these guys. They've avoided capture for almost 80 years. They obviously can handle themselves. Still, I think we could handle them if we had to, but this is too important to rush things. We'll have help in a few minutes."

These words had not left my lips when an elderly man came out of the cabin walking unsteadily toward his car. As he got within ten feet of the vehicle he fell to the ground. Apparently no one in the cabin saw this and the man on the ground was now helpless. "Okay," I said, "Guess we better help this guy. Looks like the odds just tipped farther in our favor. I'll go see what the problem is. You hang back a bit. Keep out of sight till we see how serious this is, or if it's a ruse. You never know. Have your phone ready. We may have to call for a bus if this guy is unable to get up."

I approached the man cautiously. As I had mentioned to Special Agent Lopez, you never know. I yelled to the fallen man and got no response. When I reached him I kneeled and again asked him to tell me how he was. No answer so I felt for a pulse. There was one. Fairly strong, too. Again I tried to get a response from him. "Can you talk sir? If you can, just say something so I know you can hear me."

There was a muffled response. The man tried to get up. I could see he was struggling so I tried to help him up. For a man this old it wasn't easy but he slowly was able to get up with my help. I had already identified him as Heinrich Zweig. He could tell that I recognized him and said in a low voice, "I see that you know who I am. If you'll help me into the cabin for a moment, I'll get my phone and wallet and then surrender. I think you'll find that my friend Max is ready to surrender too."

My inclination was to put him in cuffs and lock him in the back of my CRV now, but since he was being cooperative, what did it matter if he got his things and eased the arresting process with Schmidt. It was only a few more minutes. This was going to go a lot easier than I thought. These guys must be tired of running. Why wouldn't they be? They were in their mid-nineties. They might be bad guys, but bad guys when they're this old must get tired when expending the least little effort.

I let him walk slowly ahead of me toward the cabin. I had my Glock out and he knew it. I don't think he was aware that Lopez was near my Honda CRV and coming up to the rear of us. As we entered the door to the cabin Zweig grabbed a gun from a shelf near the door and held it on me. Admittedly I had let my hand holding the gun hang by my side, knowing Zweig didn't have a gun when I went to him.

"Now Agent Dantry I would appreciate it if you would drop the Glock and turn around with your hands behind you. I see that you have handcuffs at your hip. My friend Max is going to take those and cuff you. Then we shall decide what to do with you."

"This isn't a very smart move, Zweig. State police are already on their way here. You would help yourself by letting me take you in."

"That would help you. I don't see how it would help me."

"Where are you going to go from here? Every law-enforcement agency in the country is looking for you."

"You leave that concern to me."

"Seriously, you're already hiding out. I'm sure you've run out of places to go. I see that your young friends have deserted you, so you and Schmidt, both in your nineties, are on your own. You can't stay here because the state police will be here soon. If you leave, you won't dare show yourselves in public. You'll soon get hungry and tired. You'll need sleep and where will you get it?" I could see that this was registering on him and his friend, too.

But Zweig wasn't inclined to give in. "Shut up or I will silence you permanently. I need to think."

Max Schmidt had been digesting everything I said and now spoke up. "Heinrich. Listen to him. He makes sense. What will we do next? We have no plan. Robert and William didn't come back—"

"Shut the fuck up, Max! Give me a minute to think. I'll figure this out. We're not surrendering. If we surrender it'll mean the rest of our lives behind bars. Is that what you want?"

"No, but we can't run forever. And we have no idea where we can go next."

"That's not exactly true, and you know that. There's still Canada," he said quietly, and then bellowed, "but you have to shut up. If you even mention it, I'll have to kill Dantry. Is that what you want?"

"Good Lord no! Enough killing."

"You've got a big mouth, Max. Keep it shut or you'll be the end of us."

I said, "You should listen to your friend. You're running out of time and if you kill me or anybody else you could end up dead yourself. My colleagues don't look kindly at someone killing one of their own. Give it up now, Zweig, and you'll be treated fairly." As I said this I wondered what Lopez was doing. Was she coming to help me, or was she waiting for the state cops to back her up? I was hoping it was the latter and that Zweig and Schmidt wouldn't look outside.

"All right," said Zweig to Max Schmidt, "here's what we're going to do. You tie Agent Dantry here to a chair. Then we take the food you just got and put it back in the car. We're leaving here now. If Dantry isn't lying, the state police will be here soon. Even if he is lying, they'll be here soon enough. Oh, after you've tied Dantry up, stuff a rag in his mouth. If he resists you when you're tying him up, shoot him—or I will. I'm running out of patience. Do you hear me, Mr. Dantry?"

"I hear you. You're making the wrong decision though. Too bad."

Zweig sneered, "I'm not the one who's in cuffs."

52

Maria Lopez was on the phone with BCI Detective Melillo. "Dantry has been inside the cabin a few minutes now. I haven't heard anything from inside and I have no idea how he's doing. I'm starting to get worried. If you can't get here in a minute or two, I'm going inside. I'd prefer to wait for you though."

"We should be there in three minutes," said Melillo. "Don't do anything unless you hear something from inside that suggests Dantry's in trouble. Odds are against you. These guys may be old, but if they have guns they'll probably use them if they think they have no choice." He went silent for a moment, then said, "Can't imagine why Dantry went into the building alone."

"One of the old guys fell in the driveway. Dantry went to help him. When the guy finally made it up off the ground, Dantry followed him into the cabin. He was behind the old guy and careful. He had his gun drawn and I'm sure the old man knew it. Once they disappeared in the cabin, I don't know what happened, but there's been no yelling, screaming or gunfire. Wait, one of the old guys is coming out with two bags of stuff. Looks like grocery bags. He's putting those in their car. Looks like they're moving out. Hope you get here soon. The old guy is going back into the cabin. Now he's coming out again with two more bags. This time they look like soft suitcases. Yes, they're moving out. I don't like the looks of this. Where are you now?"

"Less than a minute away. If they get in the car draw their attention. Keep them occupied till we get there."

"Looks like they're taking Dantry with them. I think he's cuffed from behind. Yes, that's it. They've forced him into the back seat of their car. One of the old guys is now in the back seat with him. The other just went back into the cabin. Like he's checking to see that they didn't forget anything. Now he's coming out. He's scanning the area. Turning his body in a 360. Now he's getting into the driver's seat. Okay, I'm gonna yell now and get their attention."

"Hold on a sec. Don't say anything yet. We took a wrong turn. We might not be there for another few minutes."

"We can't let these guys get away—especially now that they have Dantry." There was a short pause, then she said, "Wait a minute. Another car just pulled in and stopped next to these old guys. Two younger men got out. They've both got guns. What the hell do I do now? I can't take on all four of these guys."

"We should be there in a couple of minutes. Can you see the plate number? If they leave that will help."

"Wait a minute. Yes. Got it. The two old guys are now in the back seat of the new car. A silver-gray Ford Explorer. They left Dantry in the back seat of the other car. I hope he's okay. He seemed okay when they forced him into the car. I haven't heard any shots, so I assume he's still okay. Still, who knows what they might have done to him in the car?"

* * *

I was humiliated. I'd underestimated these old guys, thinking they were ready to throw in the towel, when they were just play-acting to get me to lower my guard. If Robert and William hadn't come, I feel certain Zweig would have killed me and tossed me into the woods for the wildlife to feast on. Fortunately, Robert talked him out of it. Said they didn't need to run from another murder. Said if Zweig killed me, all bets were off, and Zweig and Schmidt would be on their own.

Zweig and Schmidt had gotten careless around me though. They'd been talking about sneaking into Canada by way of one of the many back roads that crossed the border into the country to the north. I guess at the time they figured they'd be disposing of me so it wouldn't matter if I heard their plans. I still didn't know what road they'd be taking, but just knowing they intended to enter Canada was going to be helpful if I ever got free of these cuffs. I was fairly confident I would get free now because I could pick locks. Years ago, when I first worked for the CIA I learned to pick cuff locks. They're usually not too difficult if you can find a paperclip, hairpin or other thin sharp object. Zweig had taken my Glock, but was in such a hurry that he didn't search me carefully or he would have found my Swiss Army Knife which has a small tweezer. Perfect for picking the locks on cuffs.

53

I had just freed myself from the cuffs when the BCI guys and two uniforms pulled in. They were as relieved to see me as I was to see them. We had the license number of the vehicle we were pursuing. That was a good start. I took just a minute to explain what I'd heard Heinrich Zweig say they were going to do. He'd thought he had spoken in such a quiet tone that I wouldn't hear him, but it wasn't too quiet for me to hear. I have good hearing. I told the BCI guys and the uniforms what I was fairly sure the two Nazis and their young pals were going to try to do: Head for Canada. The odds were against them succeeding, but we all agreed these guys were desperate so to them it probably seemed like their best bet. Now we had to alert the American and Canadian border patrols to be on the lookout for these guys. What we obviously didn't know was which of the several roads crossing into Canada our guys were going to take. We didn't even know if they themselves knew at this point.

One thing we figured was that going north our fugitives would want to be in Vermont, not New York. If they headed north in New York State they would have to cross over into Canada in a fairly well-marked location on the New York-Canada border. In Vermont, apparently, the crossing points were more remote and infrequently traveled. Zweig and his pals would have a much better chance of making it safely into Canada crossing from Vermont. If they headed north in New York State just a few miles and then decided to go east into Vermont, 30-mile-long Lake George would be in their way. Immediately to the north of Lake George is Lake Champlain, well over 100 miles in length from north to south. No, the logical and safest way for our fugitives to go from here would be east into Vermont.

We'd alerted the border patrol in New York as well as Vermont, but it was likely the crossing would be attempted somewhere from Vermont.

BCI Melillo called the Vermont state police and asked them to be on the lookout for our fugitives on all the north-south roads leading to the border. This took a lot of manpower, but Melillo convinced them it was important. Lopez and I were now heading east toward Whitehall, New York. From there we would continue eastward toward Fair Haven, Vermont. At that point we had to decide whether to head north toward Vergennes, which is Vermont's smallest city, or go a little farther east and then head north toward Middlebury.

There were at least three other roads leading north, but we had a feeling our guys would choose one of the first ones they came to. They were in hurry to get across the border. Not that that being in Canada in itself would mean they were safe. It wouldn't. The Canadians didn't love war criminals any more than Americans did. Their chances of making it to Canada were not good, but I had to admit, we still didn't know which road they had taken. With the help of the Vermont state police I had a feeling we'd be closing in on our guys fairly soon. With police looking for them on every road leading north and with border patrol personnel alerted up north, their chances of slipping through were not good. Still, they hadn't been seen yet, despite all this law enforcement looking for them.

Lopez, who was in the passenger seat, said, "How long do you think before someone spots them?"

"Has to be soon. Unless— Unless they pull over someplace and wait a couple hours figuring we expect them to head directly to the border. This could throw a monkey wrench into our search. They can't afford to linger too long though." I pursed my lips and thought for a moment. Lopez was expecting something from me. I finally said, "One thing we know about our guys is that they're not acting like nonagenarians. These guys are full of surprises just when you think you've got them pegged. Don't be shocked if they pull something we would least expect."

54

Robert Ocasio was now driving the Explorer. As they headed north on State Highway 30, Zweig barked, "Pull over here. Just behind that jogger. The jogger was a fit-looking young woman with her blonde hair tied in a ponytail.

Ocasio was taken by surprise. "What in the Devil are you up to now, Heinrich?"

"Just do as I say. Pull in behind her." Robert shook his head in disbelief. What the hell was Zweig up to now?

Robert pulled off the road and slowly approached the jogging woman from behind. The woman turned to see what was behind her and then continued jogging.

"She's not stopping," said Zweig. "Continue following her slowly at her pace. See if she stops." Robert moved the car forward slowly, keeping pace with the woman. The woman looked back again. She looked annoyed.

Robert said, "What the hell are we doing, Heinrich? Don't we have enough trouble?"

"Just do as I say." Robert rolled his eyes and continued to drive slowly behind the jogging woman. They continued in this way for perhaps 100 yards, at which point the woman stopped, turned and faced the slowly moving car with her arms akimbo. Anger was written all over her face. She shook her head in disgust and slowly resumed jogging. As she went forward, Zweig told Ocasio to continue ahead slowly. Now both the woman and Ocasio were annoyed. After going forward a few hundred feet, the woman turned around again and stared at the vehicle behind her. When no one in the car said or did anything, she walked to within ten feet of the car and yelled, "Why are you following me?"

Heinrich Zweig rolled down his window, stuck his head out and said in a weak voice, "We need help."

"What kind of help do you need?"

"Come closer and I'll explain."

She moved a few feet closer—tentatively. "What's your problem?"

"I can barely talk. Come closer and I'll explain. Don't be afraid. I can hardly move."

"You should probably call 911."

"My phone is dead. Forgot to charge it. I'm in bad shape."

The young woman was torn. While she sensed that something was not right, her instinct to help would not allow her to turn away without seeing what she could do to help this obviously enfeebled old man. The man could barely speak. He needed help, yet he had a driver who could probably take him somewhere where he could get help. Why didn't the driver just take him somewhere quickly so he could get help? Only one way to find out. Go closer and see for herself if the driver looked competent. She cautiously approached the passenger-side window. The closer she got, the weaker the man on the passenger side appeared to be. He could barely hold his head up. The young driver seemed at a loss as to what to do.

When she was only about two feet away from the passenger his head snapped up and he aimed a gun at her. At the same instant he said, "Please don't move or I shall have to shoot you." Then he said to the driver, "Robert, get out and take some of our rope and tie this young lady's hands behind her back. Then you and I are going to take her into the woods."

"Oh my God," said the woman frantically. Who are you people?"

"You don't want to know," said Zweig. "Just keep your mouth shut and you might live."

As the two Nazis led the woman into the woods she struggled spiritedly and was almost too much for the two elderly men to handle. Zweig barked, "Stop fighting or I'll end it right here." As he said this he stuck the end of the pistol three inches from her face. He then added, "We don't want to kill you. We just want the police to look for you, so if you know what's good for you, you'll stop struggling and do what I say. You might be a little uncomfortable, but you'll be alive. If you don't like those terms, I'm not going to waste time trying to persuade you."

The woman stopped struggling and said, "Why are you doing this to me? You don't even know me?"

Heinrich Zweig sneered. "I suppose this is just your lucky day. We need a distraction, and you came along at just the right time. Now stop talking and keep walking." They continued on deeper into the woods until they got to a very secluded spot. Zweig then instructed Robert to tie her to a tree. "Make sure it's secure."

The woman then asked desperately, "How will anyone even know I'm missing? Why would anyone even look for me in here?"

"Oh they'll know you're missing. It's important that they know about you because then you become their priority, not us. We'll tell the police about you, but we won't tell them where to look. Then he forced a smile and said, "We'll be taking your phone I'm afraid. Can't make it too easy for them."

At this the young woman's spirits sank. She was hoping the searchers would find her by way of the GPS in her phone. She reluctantly pulled out her iPhone and handed it over.

Then Zweig did something that surprised even himself. He went over to Robert Ocasio and said, "You're tying her to the tree standing up. She seems like a nice young lady. Let her sit on the ground and then tie her to the tree. Do a good job, but there's no reason she should be too uncomfortable." He allowed another smile and added, "I must be getting soft in my old age."

The woman could think of a hundred things to say at this, but realizing she was in the hands of two desperate, perhaps even insane, old men, she decided to remain quiet.

At this, Zweig couldn't restrain himself. "Aren't you going to thank me for my consideration?"

"You've kidnapped me and tied me to a tree. Do you really expect a thank you?"

He grinned and said, "I suppose you have a point."

55

My phone rang. I listened for more than a minute. Then said to Lopez, "Gary Melillo. Says the state police just got a call from Heinrich Zweig. You're not going to believe this."

"Try me."

"Apparently our lovely Nazis have just kidnapped a jogger. A young woman."

"They're taking her with them?"

"No. They've taken her into the woods and tied her to a tree. Took her iPhone, so she can't call for help."

"What the hell kind of kidnapping is that? They don't even have her in their control."

"Actually it's a fairly smart move. By telling us about the kidnapping it will divert some of the already limited law enforcement efforts to finding this woman. She has no food or water, so she can't last too long. Then there's animals to worry about, too. She has to be found soon."

"How do we even know they kidnapped a woman?" asked Lopez. "It's just their word that they did."

"Apparently Zweig gave the state police her name and the name of her husband. They tracked the husband down and he confirmed that she was out for a run. Said they would divert some of their cruisers to looking for her. All they know now is that she's tied to a tree about 150 feet off one of the northbound roads. Most likely U.S. 7 or Vermont 100."

"Good Lord, it's going to take a lot of manpower to find her. Even then it could take a long time."

We continued north for another 15 minutes when my phone rang again. It was Melillo again. He said that the husband had called him back to tell him that his wife had an iPhone and they used the Find my Friend app on both of their iPhones. That meant that he could locate within a few yards where his wife was. Assuming she still had her phone. Melillo pointed out that the kidnappers had taken her phone. Still, if they kept it the police should be able to find the kidnappers. Melillo then told me that the phone had apparently been thrown away and a cruiser was on its way to look for it. Hopefully it had been thrown away not far from where the kidnapped woman was located. I asked that I be notified the minute they find the phone. Lopez and I would go there immediately.

Less than an hour later Melillo got back to me to say they'd found the phone. It was definitely an iPhone. He gave me the GPS location and an approximate physical location on Vermont 100 that ran north and south parallel to the road we were on: U.S. 7. Another 40 minutes and we were there. One of the state police officers, a woman, showed us the iPhone and said they'd been looking in the area for the kidnapped woman, but so far had had no results. I ask her where she and her partner had looked so far so we could check out places they hadn't yet looked.

As I said this Lopez asked for the iPhone. Less than a minute later she said "I think I know where the woman is. Or at least I think we can narrow it down."

"What did you do?" I asked.

"IPhones have a *Find My Device* function. I guessed that this woman might have an Apple Watch. Sure enough she does and the phone found it. Looks like the kidnappers overlooked it. Maybe at their age they're unaware of the *Find My Device* function or the fact that an Apple watch can be located that way.

The screen on the iPhone indicated a wooded location about a mile behind our present location. Looks as if the kidnappers tossed the phone soon after leaving her to the elements. I did a U-turn and headed back toward where the iPhone indicated the woman was. As we headed slowly south we gained confidence that we'd soon find her. I stopped the car on the side of the road where the map on the phone screen showed she was located. The Vermont state police cruiser had followed us and they pulled over just behind my car. We all set off into the thick woods stumbling over dead branches and hidden rocks. The *Find My Device* app led us directly to the woman, who I had learned was named Michelle Gilman. She was clearly terrified, but otherwise unharmed.

When we reached her I introduced Lopez and myself and the state troopers who accompanied us.

"Thank God you found me. I was afraid nobody would. Does my husband know?"

I said, "We'll notify him right away. First, how are you?"

"I'm thirsty and itchy because of the bugs, but otherwise I'm okay. Have you caught those bastards?"

"Not yet, but we will. What can you tell us about them?"

"Two of them are old. Real old. German accents. They're running from something. Can't be everyday criminals. Too old. All I can think of is maybe they're former Nazis. But that's just a guess. If they aren't, they could've been. They said they were using me to distract law enforcement from them. I hope they didn't. What I mean is I hope you still get these old guys. I'd normally want two old men to be treated decently, but these guys didn't worry about me. Oh, one of them said I could be tied up sitting down at the base of the tree instead of standing. That was his way of being considerate. However, when they first grabbed me, they said I should not resist. If I did, they made it clear that they wouldn't waste time trying to persuade me. They'd just kill me because they weren't going to let me get in their way. I took them at their word. They were clearly desperate men."

"Did they say anything about where they were going?"

"One of them mentioned Canada and the other one told him to shut up. The one who mentioned Canada then said, 'What does it matter? If they find this woman it'll be too late to matter.'"

56

Max Schmidt seemed confused. "Why are we heading east? Shouldn't we be heading north? The sooner we get to Canada the better."

"Jesus, Max, sometimes you can be so dense. If they find the girl they'll assume we're north of her on the same road. They'll concentrate on that road. Ergo we don't stay on that road. We have to go east a bit in order to find another road going north to Canada. Got that?"

Schmidt glared at Zweig, his one-time friend. Now regrettably just a fellow fugitive.

"Yes, I got it."

"Interstate 89 is coming up, but we can't take that either. They'll expect us to take an interstate because it's faster. We'll take either state road 12 or 12A. Probably 12A."

Schmidt couldn't resist. "You think the authorities won't figure this out? Maybe they'll outthink you on this."

An exasperated look transfigured Zweig's craggy face. "Who's side are you on, Max? Of course I know the authorities could figure it the same way. We have one advantage, though. We *know* which way we're going to take. They, however, have to consider the possibility that we might choose any of several roads. They might guess right, but they won't know they're right so they'll have to spread their efforts over those several roads. They don't have that many cruisers so maybe they won't get lucky and we will."

A voice from the back of the car said, "You want to knock it off. The only reason we're letting you guys work this out is that so far you haven't screwed it up." It was Robert and his bold voice startled the two old Nazis in the front seat. Robert and William had been fairly silent so far. Zweig had almost forgotten that they were there.

Robert went on. So far you've made the right decisions. But keep in mind that as we get closer to the border, William and I will be making the decisions. Any problem with that?"

"Yes," said Zweig. These are decisions that affect Max and me. I think we should have some say in what's decided."

"Do you want to get out of North America and into Europe safely or not?"

"Of course we do," said Zweig somewhat deflated.

"Then either you do as we say or you're on your own. William and I are the ones with contacts in Canada and we're the ones who are getting your papers. Don't forget that."

About two minutes passed. Then Robert said, "By the way, we'd like the final payment now."

"Why should we give you your payments now? You haven't finished the job. We'll pay you just before we get on the plane to Europe."

"No, it has to be now or in the next hour at the latest. Our contacts in Canada cannot know that you're paying us.

They think we do this out of respect for you guys and what you did back in the day."

Max Schmidt spoke for the first time. "I thought that *was* why you were helping us."

"Originally that was why, but as we've gotten to know you guys, especially Herr Zweig, we've lost a lot of that respect and now believe you should pay for our help."

"What the hell are you talking about?" barked Zweig. "We are the same people you started helping. Why the change in attitude?"

"It's quite clear that you don't appreciate our help. We risk our lives for you and you show no appreciation. When we started, you were people we admired. Now you're just a job. As such we want to be paid now, or maybe we'll just dump the two of you here in the Vermont woods. Do to you what you did to that innocent girl. She didn't deserve it. You do. Now are you going to give us those checks or not?"

"How do we know you won't dump us as soon as we give you our checks?"

"You don't. All you have to go by is our word. So far we've done everything we said we would. We've kept our word. You're going to have count on that."

"Yes, but once you have our money you have nothing to gain by still helping us. You just admitted that you don't like us, so why will you continue to help us?"

"Because it's a job that we would like to finish. Helps our resumé. Frankly, it's kind of a challenge. Getting you two old birds out of Canada safely, while you don't deserve it, would be quite a feather in our cap."

"And this person we're meeting will have our new passports and other papers?"

"That's the plan."

"What are these other papers?"

"Drivers licenses. Canadian."

"Are we meeting this guy in Vermont or Canada?"

"Canada. At an intersection of two main roads in Quebec. Not in some town where we could be spotted, but out in the country. Just off the highway."

Zweig pressed for more information. "How will this person know when we'll be there?"

"As soon as I think we can be there within a couple hours I'll call him and tell him. I'll describe our car and ask him to describe his."

"What's this intersection? What two roads?"

"I don't see why you need to know, but if it satisfies your curiosity, it's the intersection of Chemin de St-Armand and Quebec 235. About two miles over the border. There, are you happy?"

"Who is this guy?"

"Works in the art department of an insurance company. Very good with Photoshop. Has access to the kinds of paper and card stock needed to do all kinds of credentials. Very creative guy. You know, if you use the wrong paper in a passport, the people who check them can tell immediately that they're fake. You can't tell with the passports this guy makes. A real professional."

Max smiled weakly as he said, "A real professional counterfeiter."

"Well yes. We're not dealing with the U.S. government here."

"What's his name?" demanded Heinrich.

"You're not going to know his name. Even if he gave you a name it wouldn't be his real name."

Heinrich bit his lip, but said nothing. He wasn't happy about the arrangement, but there was nothing he could do about it and hoped that what Robert and William had set up was viable. Hell, he didn't even know if they were bullshitting about the whole setup. He said nothing as he slowly shook his head from side to side, getting tenser by the minute.

They were on Route 100 just north of Waitsfield when Robert's phone rang. "Yes," he said. He listened for a little more than a minute. When he closed the phone he said, "That's our guy. He's down here in Vermont. Wants to meet us just south of Stowe. That's about two miles from here. He's got your passports and licenses. He feels safer making the transfer here in Vermont. He'll do that and give you explicit instructions on how to handle yourselves at Montreal-Trudeau Airport."

Heinrich started thinking. "Will we go to the airport in his car or this one?"

"His car. It has Quebec plates. Attracts less attention. Not to mention that this one is stolen. Okay guys, just relax for a while till we get to the meeting point. Not much longer."

Zweig said, "Assuming Dantry or some cops don't find us first. This is going too smoothly. I don't like it."

"Unbelievable," said William. "You're not even happy when things are going your way. You should be glad they haven't found us. I didn't think so at the time, but maybe grabbing that jogger was the right move."

"So far, so good. I won't feel safe till we're on that plane. How much longer till we pull over and meet this guy?"

"Just a few minutes," said Robert. "Not long."

Five minutes later Robert said, "There. That red Toyota that's pulled over. Okay, gentlemen, this is where it gets interesting. I'll pull in behind him." He pulled in about three car lengths behind the Toyota and said, "William you and I will go up and take care of our business. Herr Zweig, you and Herr Schmidt wait here. We'll let you know when we're ready."

Zweig said, "I think we should go with you now."

"No, not yet. This guy is very difficult and very exacting in how he operates. Don't mess things up when you're so close to getting what you want. Wait here in the car until I come over for you. It'll only be a minute."

"Okay, but make it quick."

William, Robert and the stranger standing behind the Toyota seemed to be nodding their heads in agreement. Heinrich Zweig didn't think the new guy looked that exacting or difficult. He looked like he could have been a brother of Robert. He seemed to be enjoying his conversation with Robert and William. After what seemed a prolonged moment Robert motioned for Zweig and Schmidt to join the group. Heinrich and Max got out of the Explorer and made their way toward the three men. As they approached the three young men, Robert walked toward the explorer with William close behind. The as-yet-unidentified third young man remained near the driver's side of the Toyota. As Zweig and Schmidt neared him he offered a friendly, "Hi" and opened the door to the Toyota.

Zweig yelled, "Hold on. Where are our passports? Our drivers licenses?"

"You'll have to take that up with Robert and William. Have to leave now. Sorry we didn't get to know each other better."

Zweig and Schmidt stood confused halfway between the two vehicles. The unnamed young man was now in the driver's seat of the Toyota. The engine turned over and the car started to drive away. Heinrich Zweig and Max Schmidt raised their arms in frustration. They then turned and headed toward the Ford Explorer. Robert and William had already reached the vehicle and were in the process of taking their seats. Zweig, now realizing what was happening, was apoplectic. He still had his handgun. He pulled it out of his waistband and fired at the disappearing Explorer. He had no idea whether he hit anyone or not as the car disappeared down the road.

Max said, "What's going on, Heinrich? Why are they doing that?"

"For God's sake, Max, what do you think they're doing? They're robbing us blind. But that's not the worst of it. We're defenseless. We're helpless. We're at the mercy of the elements. We're at the mercy of the law when they find us."

"What do we do, Heinrich?"

"We don't give up. We'll stop some car and get ourselves a ride."

"You're not going to shoot some innocent driver, are you?"

"Not if I don't have to. Hopefully we can use charm or just sympathy for two old codgers. We may not need to kill anyone."

"But if we get a ride, where are we going to go? We don't have the fake passports that guy was going to give us. We don't even have fake drivers licenses."

"Yes, but we do have our real driver's licenses and we still have access to our money, though not as easily as before. It won't be easy, but if we get lucky, Max, we can still make it. Come to think of it, we still have some of the old passports we've used in the past. Under different names of course."

"Two of those old passports have expired. I still have one that's valid. You need a U.S. passport just to enter Canada. You must have an old passport that's still good. Our luck better change quickly, Heinrich."

"Yes, we do need some good luck. We're not giving up yet."

"Even if some kind soul does give us a ride, Heinrich, where do we go?"

"Stop pestering me with questions. Let me think. Let me think."

"For all we know Dantry or the state police will find us before we even get started."

Zweig glared at his friend. "Aren't you the cheerful one. Yes, it may happen, but it hasn't happened yet. Now let's get away from the road, so if your friends in law enforcement come looking, we don't make it easy for them."

"We can't flag anyone down if we're in the woods."

Zweig shook his head in disbelief. "We're not going deep into the woods, Max. Just off the road enough so we can see what's coming. If it's not the cops, we go out and hitch a ride. Got it?"

Mortified, Schmidt uttered a quiet, "Yes, I've got it," to his unfeeling friend. After a period of silence, Schmidt worked up the courage to say, "If we get a ride, where do we go? What do we tell the people?"

"We tell them . . ."

"I can't go on like this much longer, Heinrich. I'm tired. Right now I wouldn't care if Dantry, or the cops came. I'm just so tired."

"I know, Max. I'm tired, too. We have to hang in there a little longer. We'll figure something out. You know if the law finds us, it's all over.'"

"I know, but I'm so tired now I really don't care."

"Hold on. A car is coming. It's not the state cops or Dantry. Hang in there just a little longer."

"What will you tell them?"

"I'll think of something. Let me do the talking. Okay, they're slowing down. I'll take a few steps toward them and motion with my thumb that I need a ride. You be in sight, but back a couple of steps so we don't appear threatening. Okay, they're pulling over."

A middle-aged man rolled down the driver's side window and said, "What's the problem? I can see you need a ride, but why is that?"

Zweig said, "We were driving along in our Explorer when someone waved us down. Very much like this. When we stopped they took our car at gunpoint. With all our luggage, too."

"I have to say you don't look too dangerous. Where do you want to go?"

"Just take us to the nearest hotel or inn. If you're going through Stowe, we'll find a hotel there. We need to eat and rest before we start looking at summer cottages. We live in Virginia, but we want a place up here where the summers are cooler and where we'll be near the mountains. We have some places to look at lined up, but they'll have to wait until we've had a good night's sleep. At our age we tire easily. Anyway, that was what we were in the process of doing when these people took our car and our possessions. We're both very tired now so any hotel will be welcome." Max Schmidt stared at his friend in awe. Where did this come from?

Actually it was good news for Max who couldn't imagine how they were going to convince anyone in Canada that they were citizens of the U.S. or Canada without valid passports or drivers licenses. Even in Vermont there was a huge risk, as it was possible, even likely, that word had gotten out that there were two elderly men on the loose. Still, elderly men were not uncommon in modern America, and if the staff at a Stowe hotel was more interested in texting, video games or Facebook than they were in the latest news, he and Heinrich might just be able to register and finally get some food and rest. It wasn't risk free, but not as risky as struggling in the remote Vermont woods without food, drink or a bed.

57

We were heading north on Route 100 just above Waterbury Center when Lopez's phone rang. She listened attentively and then closed the phone.

"A man just called the Vermont state police. They notified us. This man was heading north on Route 100 just north of us. He saw an elderly man who appeared to be close to falling down from exhaustion. There was another elderly man with him. They told the driver that someone had stolen their car. Said they were in Vermont looking at summer cottages. Claimed to be from Virginia and wanted a cooler place for their summers. Something didn't seem right to the driver, though. He played along with the two old guys until he dropped them off. Then called the state police to report the two suspicious-looking men. The driver said he'd read something about two old war criminals. Wasn't sure these were the guys, but it didn't make sense that anyone this old would be looking for summer cottages."

Sounded like an alert driver to me. "Where did this man drop these guys off?"

"A place called the Pewter Inn in Stowe. That can't be far from here, Tony."

"No, shouldn't take too long. Why don't you let Melillo or Steele know so they can meet us there. Don't want to lose these guys again."

"I thought these guys were heading for Canada. They started out with those two younger guys who were helping them. What do you think happened?"

That was a good question. I said, "Looks like their young friends left them. Why? We don't know. I can only guess. Maybe the young guys made off with some money they got from the two Nazis. Maybe they didn't want to take the risk of taking these guys to Canada. Maybe it was all a scam and they never intended to help the Nazis. Or maybe the two Nazis dumped them. Didn't want to pay them. Who knows? We're dealing with criminals. Doing the honorable thing is not usually their priority. I have a feeling we'll find out soon, though."

"Don't you wonder how these guys survived all these years without getting caught? They had to have been awfully smart."

"Or awfully lucky. But yes, I do wonder. They're obviously not stupid to have avoided capture in three or four countries over a period of almost eighty years. They got out of Germany at the end of the war. They went to Argentina or Uruguay. Or was it the reverse? Uruguay and Argentina. Then they finally made it to the U.S. They still haven't been caught. They even had a career during those years. Zweig was an auto worker. Retired from it with a pension. I think Schmidt was, too, though I can't confirm it. I don't respect these guys, but in a way you have to give them credit for eluding capture for more than eight decades. After an early career as heartless camp guards, they apparently lived a relatively normal life. Remarkable. That normal life doesn't erase the evil of what they did in the camp, but it is an indication of how clever they are. We shouldn't underestimate them now.

58

Max was exhausted. "Thank God we can relax. Nice hotel. I'm glad you decided not to try to get into Canada. This is much safer. Maybe life in Vermont was not in our plans, but it's very pleasant up here."

"Let's not get too comfortable. Dantry, the FBI and the state police aren't going to quit looking for us."

"Don't you think they would have found us by now if they had even a clue?"

"Jesus, Max. As naïve as you are, I don't know how you made it this far. They're not going to quit. If we're smart, we'll get out of this hotel in a day or two. I know Stowe is a small town, but it's one of the most active towns in Vermont and heavy with tourists. Someone will notice us. Hell, maybe even the desk clerk did, but didn't let on to us that he recognized us. We can't be too careful, my friend or it'll be over in a flash. Let's get some badly needed rest. Then a good meal. After that we can make plans for our next move. Has to be soon, though. I don't feel too secure here, even though things seem peaceful right now."

"Oh, God, Heinrich. Do we have to rush? I'm so tired. Can't we just stay here a few days before we move again? Let's just take our time. We've been so rushed we haven't taken the time to consider our future. Now we know it's not going to be someplace in Europe. Vermont or maybe New Hampshire seem nice. But let's do some exploring before we make that decision."

"You do realize, Max, that we don't have a car? How are we going to explore anything without wheels? For Christ's sake, Max, I often wonder if your head is on straight. As much as I need sleep, I think you need it more. Why do I have to do all the thinking?" He paused, then said, "It's because you're a fucking moron, Max. Just go to your room and get some rest. Leave the thinking and planning to me."

Max gave Heinrich a withering look and dejectedly left Heinrich's hotel room. Max had been thinking a lot lately about his relationship with his friend Heinrich. Heinrich had never been a tactful man. He'd never been a considerate man. Certainly he'd never been a kind-hearted man, but lately he had taken a turn for the worse, if a former Nazi camp guard could get worse. As far as Max was concerned, Heinrich had become insufferable. Five minutes after entering his own room he picked up the hotel telephone receiver.

59

We were only a few minutes away from the Pewter Inn when my phone rang again. This time it was the state police saying they'd just received a call from a man named Max Schmidt. Said he was traveling with Heinrich Zweig. This Schmidt said he assumed we wanted to take this Zweig into custody. Right now, said Schmidt, Zweig was in room 211 in the Pewter Inn in Stowe. Schmidt added that he himself was in room 214. He warned the state police officer that Zweig had a handgun in his possession. He added that they were registered under the names of Henry Wilson and Walter Eiger.

The officer told me that he'd already alerted BCI Melillo, who was on his way to the inn to join up with Lopez and me.

I told Maria what the state cop had just told me. All she could say was, "Wow! This has gotten interesting."

I agreed. "Yeah. Sounds as if one of our war criminals is turning on the other. Especially interesting, since these guys have known each other for 80 years and apparently stood by each other for all those years. What could have happened?"

"Either Schmidt is getting panicky and decided to rat on Zweig, or Zweig did something that really pissed off Schmidt. If it's the latter, it had to be bad because these guys are used to doing bad things. If Schmidt is ratting on Zweig it's probably because he thinks he can work a deal by turning on his friend. No matter what it is, we're not dealing with upstanding honorable gentlemen here. What do you think it is, Tony?"

"Just a guess, but I wouldn't be surprised if Schmidt got really pissed at his old friend. From what we know, unlike Schmidt, Zweig hasn't mellowed after all these years. The guy is just rotten to the core. Maybe with the pressure of running from the law one more time, Zweig did something that Schmidt just couldn't overlook. As I said, this is just a guess. We'll find out soon enough. Looks like that's the Pewter Inn just up ahead. Let's pull in and park out of the way. Wait for state police backup.

Less than 15 minutes later a state police cruiser pulled in and four officers got out. Two of them were BCI Melillo and BCI Steele. Lopez and I met with Melillo and Steele and agreed on how we wanted to proceed. Hopefully both Zweig and Schmidt were in their rooms now. That would be ideal for making the arrests. If both of them were in the same room, that would be okay too. We didn't want them to be in any of the public rooms of the inn. Too many innocent people could be in danger if our two guys acted violently.

We had already circumvented the building, noting that there was both a side door and rear door in addition to the main entrance. Two of the state troopers covered the rear and side door. Lopez and I entered the lobby of the inn and went up to the front desk. Melillo and Steele stood a few feet behind us. The desk clerk said, "Can I help you?" She looked like she might still be in high school.

I said, "We're with the FBI. The two men behind us are state police. We need to see two of your guests. I think they're registered under the names Henry Wilson and Walter Eiger. They're quite elderly. Do you know if they're in their rooms now?"

"Yes, we do have two elderly gentlemen registered. Under those names. They're the only elderly men here now."

"I have a feeling they're the two men we're looking for."

"I haven't seen them since they registered earlier. Why do you want to see them? My God, they're so old. I can't imagine why the FBI and the state police would be interested in them."

"Weren't you curious when two men their age registered to stay at your inn? Do they look like typical tourists?"

"People have all kinds of reasons to visit Stowe. They don't have to be tourists. We don't ask people why they stay with us. Why are you interested in them?"

"They might be more dangerous than they look. I'm going to need their room numbers." I already knew the room numbers, but I wanted to see if the info we got from Max Schmidt could be counted on.

"I'm not sure I'm supposed to give out room numbers without first calling the guests."

"You're not going to call them first. We don't want them alerted that we're coming. If you care for the safety of your other guests, you'll give me the room numbers and stay out of the way. If you see any other guests going toward the guest rooms, tell them to wait in the lobby until you've heard from us that it's safe for them to go their room."

"They're in room 211 and 214. Mr. Wilson is in 211. There's not going to be any shooting is there?"

"I certainly hope not, but these are dangerous men, so you never know. That's why you need to keep people in the lobby until this is over. Hopefully it won't be long."

The young clerk was now clearly concerned about what might happen next.

I went directly to the stairs with Lopez, Melillo and Steele following close behind. It wasn't hard to find the two rooms. It wasn't a big inn. Room 214 was just across the hall from 211. I knocked on the door of 211. Melillo and Steele kept an eye on 214. No one came to the door right away, but I could hear what sounded like footsteps. Lopez and I stood aside a step in case Zweig greeted us with gun blazing. I rapped again. This time louder and yelled, "FBI."

Finally, after what seemed like a long minute, the door handle turned and the door slowly opened revealing a tired-looking Heinrich Zweig. Finally, after our long search, we had him.

"Ah, Special Agent Dantry. I can't say it's a pleasant surprise. I suppose I should ask you in."

"We'll come in, Zweig, but we won't be staying long.'

Lopez and I entered his hotel room. I would say he was literally living out of a suitcase, except that there was no suitcase in the room. I later learned that it was in the car Robert and William drove away in. Zweig was ready to move at the slightest need. Well it was too late for him to bolt now.

He said, "How's this going to go? I assume you're going to arrest me and take me in?"

"For once in your life Herr Zweig, You're right. I'm going to need your handgun."

As Zweig took a step toward a side table, Dantry said, "Stop right there. Special Agent Lopez will get the gun. While she's doing it, I'll cuff you and then frisk you. See if you have any other weapons on your person."

"I can assure you, I don't. Just what are you arresting me for?"

"For one thing, suspicion of murder. For another, war crimes."

"Ha! That'll never stick."

"We're not here to debate you. Is your friend, Max Schmidt in his room?"

Zweig answered with a sneer, "Am I my brother's keeper? How do I know?"

"Okay, so you're gonna be the tough guy right to the end. Play it your way. Special Agent Lopez, tell the BCI folks they can arrest Schmidt across the hall. We need to bring these two lowlifes back to the city."

Zweig asked, "Where are you taking us?"

"You're going to 26 Federal Plaza in Manhattan. Where you'll stand trial for murder will be determined by the prosecutors. My guess is Putnam County where the alleged homicides took place. If you're still alive after your incarceration for murder, you'll probably be extradited to Germany to stand trial for war crimes. That's my prediction. However, since you're quite advanced in years, you may never get the opportunity to pay for your war crimes. That in itself would be a crime in my opinion. Any way you look at it the legal system is going to keep you off the street for the rest of your godforsaken life."

There was a knock on the door. Lopez opened it to see Melillo, Steele and a sullen Max Schmidt in handcuffs between them. Upon seeing Schmidt, Zweig said nothing. Apparently he had no idea that his friend of many decades had turned him in. I wasn't going to mention it. At least not now. Maybe I could use it during interrogation.

"Okay gentlemen. Why don't you each use the toilet. We're going for a long ride. I'll be just be outside the door, so don't try anything funny."

BCI Melillo said, "I'll be outside the door for you Mr. Schmidt. Let's make this fast. We have a long trip ahead of us."

I suggested that Lopez and I would take Zweig with us, and Melillo and Steele would take Schmidt. Better chance to get revealing info this way since they'd be more inclined to cut a deal and rat on the other if they were traveling alone.

We'd been in our cars less than ten minutes when BCI Steele called me saying, "Schmidt wants to say goodbye to his wife where she's staying in Glens Falls at a hotel. I agreed to give him ten minutes. Thought you should know."

Max Schmidt was escorted into his wife's hotel room by Melillo and Steele. They stood to one side while Schmidt and his wife Heidi spoke in low tones. She almost refused to see him, but agreed grudgingly because she had a feeling it would be the last time the two of them would see each other. As Max approached her he was about to speak when Heidi said, "You want to see me—after you had agreed to let Heinrich kill me? Why do you even care?"

"You know what kind of a man he is. He would have killed me if I'd disagreed with him at that moment. Knowing him, I figured he'd change his mind when he settled down. Good Lord, Heidi, I've agonized about this so much. Some nights I couldn't even sleep."

"You're quite the man, aren't you, Max. What happened to the knight in shining armor I married all those years ago? You agonized, but you would have let him do it."

"No, I would have talked him out of it at the last minute. I'm sure I would have."

"Okay, Max. I guess I was wrong all those years when I thought that you'd truly regretted being a camp guard. I guess I was wrong when I thought you were ashamed of what you said you were forced to do to those helpless victims. I see you now as a blade of grass that bends with the slightest breeze.

You have no standards. You only do what's right when it's easy. Now I guess it's time for you and your heartless friend to pay the price for your callous disregard for the lives of innocent adults and children."

"I never hurt a child."

"Did you ever hurt the parent of a child?"

"That's not fair."

"Oh my God, I've deluded myself all these years. You better go now before I say something I'll regret. I'll try to remember our good years, but your weakness now will probably erase those memories. You'd better go, Max."

"Dear God, Heidi, please tell me you still love me."

"Don't ask me that, Max. Now go."

Max realized that Melillo and Steele had heard their entire conversation. He asked himself whether he cared or whether he was embarrassed that they had heard Heidi reject him. He wasn't sure.

60

Back in the police cruiser heading south on Interstate 87 toward Albany and ultimately toward New York City, Max settled in for the long drive to his incarceration in the Manhattan FBI headquarters. Max looked grim-faced. Melillo and Steele accompanied him on this unpleasant trip. Both Melillo and Steele lived in the Glens Falls area, but they were going to see this through till their prisoner was safely behind bars.

"Didn't go so well, did it Max?" said Steele. "Did you really expect her to forgive you for agreeing to a death threat against her?"

"I didn't exactly agree to it."

That's not what you said to your wife. You said he would have killed you if you didn't go along with it. What kind of man are you, Max? Were you that afraid of this man? Even if you were, you could have reported his threat to the authorities."

"Yes, and if I'd done that what was to stop him from coming after me? The police would have told him to stay away from Heidi. You know how effective that is. We lived in the same retirement community. He was very good at making his assaults look like accidents."

"So you just went along with it?

"What choice did I have?"

"You're serious?"

"Yes. If he was arrested because I turned him in, they'd learn that he was a camp guard. If that came out, he'd tell them I was too. You see, I had no choice."

"How about doing the right thing? That's a choice many people would make."

"That's easy for you to say. You didn't have to make it."

Steele rolled his eyes and said, "Don't think I would have allowed my friend to kill my wife. Wouldn't even have agreed to consider it."

Melillo then said, "How did your marriage last so long? If this is an example of how you were willing to see her treated, how did you treat her in all those years you were married?"

"I treated her very well. Bought her the best of everything. I treated her very well. She did everything I ever asked her to do. We never had a problem."

Melillo snorted. "Sounds like a great relationship. Sounds as if she was a docile prisoner who never gave you any trouble. Just like in the old days, huh?"

"No, no, no. It was not the way you're making it sound. It was a good marriage."

"Yet you were willing to let your friend end it?"

"I was not happy about that. I've already explained the situation."

"Yeah, Max. Hell of an explanation."

61

As I drove into Manhattan with Lopez and my prisoner, Heinrich Zweig, I said, "Well, Heinrich enjoy your last few minutes of freedom. Pretty soon you'll be the guest of the FBI at 26 Federal Plaza."

Zweig glared at me, but said nothing.

I had called ahead to alert Marco Polo that we had our two Nazi fugitives in hand, and that we were bringing them to 26 Federal Plaza for lockup and interrogation. Marco said, "Good work," and added that he would call the Putnam County DA and ask him or one of his ADAs to join us on the following day when we interrogated the two Nazis.

The next day Lopez and I were in the interrogation room with Heinrich Zweig. Marco Polo, who didn't take part in a lot of routine interrogations, had joined us. He brought another special agent with him. Bringing in two World War II war criminal suspects who were also accused of homicide took this interrogation well out of the routine category. Polo wasn't going to miss the interrogation of one of the few remaining Nazi war criminals. Since Zweig was also being accused of as many as four recent murders, this meant headline news for the New York field office. This was more than local headlines. Probably national and very likely international. Polo wanted to be on top of this, not just because it was likely to be a big news event, but because he felt it was his responsibility to be informed of the cases the New York field office was involved in. Polo wasn't going to get this second hand from one of his field agents.

Even though New York State BCI investigators Melillo and Steele were based 200 miles north of Manhattan, they were directed by their superior to attend the interrogation too, since they'd played a major role in apprehending the two prisoners. Of course, the Putnam County DA, and his ADA were also present for the interrogation of Zweig, since two of the alleged murders took place in their county and both war criminals lived there.

All told the interrogation room was occupied by nine law enforcement officials plus a trained office assistant to Polo who was there to record the proceedings and take notes on the body language of the suspect.

When everyone was seated Polo began the proceedings with a question. "Heinrich Zweig, do you know why you're here?"

"Because Mr. Dantry here couldn't track down any real criminals. He makes up this story about my being some kind of war criminal. Me, an old man. Do I look like a criminal to you?"

"Mr. Zweig, I've been going at criminals for 30 years. One thing I've learned is that criminals can look like anybody. I can tell from your response that you're not going to be reasonable, so I'll remind you why you're here. Count number one, you've been accused of being a camp guard at Buchenwald, a Nazi concentration camp. Count number two you've been accused of murdering two of your fellow residents at Liberty Village, a senior living center in Putnam County in New York State. Count number three you've been accused of two homicides near Lake George, New York, in Warren County. Do you deny any of these charges?"

"Of course I do. All of them. They're ridiculous."

"Where were you born, Mr. Zweig?"

"I was born in Germany."

"During the war, World War II to be specific, did you serve in the German military?"

"Yes I did. Most young men did at the time."

"What branch of the service?"

"The army."

"Were you a National Socialist?"

Zweig hesitated, clearly realizing that what he said now would have a serious effect on his future. "Yes, but in name only. I was told that I would receive better treatment in the army if I joined the National Socialists. I didn't join because I was ideologically committed to the Nazis. It was a pragmatic decision only."

"I see. So what kind of benefits did you receive when you became a Nazi?"

"See you make it sound bad when you say I became a Nazi. I didn't become one of those committed Nazis. I was a Nazi in name only. You have to see the difference."

I felt I had to speak up. "That's not what one of your victims told me. She told me you killed her sister right in front of her. I'd say you were quite committed to the Nazi belief that all Jews were your enemies. I don't see how a teenage girl could be your enemy, but apparently you did."

"Who told you this lie?"

"One of your fellow residents at Liberty Village. Gisela Miller."

"She never liked me. She made up that whole story. Wicked woman."

"Then, as if killing her sister back in the camp wasn't enough, you killed her too—just recently. No doubt because she was going to reveal what you did in the past. I guess you can't take the Nazi out of a Nazi. Even after eight decades."

"I understand the woman is now dead, so we only have her word against mine. Or should I say your word? There is no proof that the Miller woman even said such terrible things."

"Oh but we do know that she did. She told me to my face. She told her friends. Hell, Heinrich, you even told your wife about some of the terrible things you did in the camp."

"I've heard about you, Dantry. You like to make a name for yourself. It would be a real feather in your cap if you brought in a real World War II war criminal. You can make up all these accusations against me, but where are these so-called victims. You'll never get anybody to testify against me because you've made all this up."

"I wouldn't be too comfortable if I were you," said Polo. "As I said, your wife can testify against you."

"Assuming there is anything to say, I believe in this country a spouse cannot be compelled to testify against her spouse." Zweig looked smug as he said this.

Polo forced a grin, "You're right about that. She can't be compelled, but she can testify if she chooses to. She's already told us she wants to testify about what you've told her you did at Buchenwald." At this, Zweig fell silent.

"As if the evil you committed during the war was not enough, you're now being accused of committing at least four homicides in the last few weeks. You've been a busy man, Heinrich Zweig. Very busy."

Zweig looked genuinely surprised at this. "Four murders? Where do you get such things? Do I look like I'm capable of murdering anyone?"

I said, "I wouldn't put anything past you, Heinrich. With your experience, killing must be easy."

Polo then said, "Two at Liberty Village and two more in Lake George.
First a groundskeeper and then a young girl. A young girl you and your two young associates blew up in a state campground. You did it as a distraction when you were fleeing from Agent Dantry and Special Agent Lopez. Surely you remember that?"

"I remember hearing an explosion when we drove out of a campground, but I have no idea what caused it."

Polo continued. "By the way, Zweig, your two young friends have been apprehended in Vermont and will be joining you here at 26 Federal Plaza soon. Do you still maintain you don't know what caused the explosion?"

"Of course I do."

"Your two young friends may disagree." Zweig showed no emotion on hearing this.

"Why were you fleeing from Agent Dantry and Special Agent Lopez in the first place? Why did you up and leave the Liberty Village senior living center without telling the front desk, which is the standard practice at Liberty Village?"

"We weren't fleeing Agent Dantry or that woman agent. My wife and I just needed a vacation. Needed to get away because some of the residents were treating us like lepers. We did tell our neighbors we were taking a vacation."

"Yes, and you gave them the wrong information. No doubt deliberately. But back to why you left Liberty Village. You were treated like lepers because of what you did at Buchenwald?"

"Because of what people were saying I did at Buchenwald. Because this crazy Miller woman said I reminded her of some camp guard at Buchenwald. People at Liberty who used to be my friends started avoiding me. Then someone else said I reminded them of a camp guard. Then, the Miller woman fell into the pond on the grounds of Liberty Village and people said I must have done it. It was too much for my dear Doreen to take. We had to leave."

"And you thought Vermont was the place where you would live? Or was it Canada?"

"We just had to get out of Liberty Village."

"Where did you plan to live then?"

"We weren't sure. We just knew we couldn't live at Liberty Village any longer."

"So you left with no destination? I find that hard to believe. You're an intelligent man. You plan everything you do. You wouldn't just take off without a destination. You didn't even have a reservation at a hotel?"

"No. As I said, we just felt we had to get away. Things were so unpleasant at Liberty it was intolerable."

"So why did you then go to a cottage near Lake George? If you had no reservation at a hotel, how did you find this cottage?"

"I was contacted by the two young men you've referred to. Robert Ocasio and a William Horan, who said they liked to help former German soldiers in distress. I thought this was strange, but we were desperate. When they told us they could put us in a pleasant, but rustic cottage on Lake George it was appealing. I wanted to know what the catch was. What they got out of it. They said they admired the Nazis in particular and wanted to help former Nazis who were being persecuted in their declining years. I told them I wasn't a Nazi, but they assumed I was just saying that. I could tell, these young men viewed former German military as heroic, and they treated us like heroes. They said they had helped a few others. Not many, though. There aren't that many living German veterans from World War II. Anyway, I discussed this with my friend, Max

Schmidt, who is also a veteran and we said, 'What have we got to lose? We can't stay at Liberty Village.'

As I said, Robert and William belong to an organization that helps German World War II veterans. They have these safe houses for people like us who feel pressured by a biased society—a society that treats us like criminals instead of men who served their country in time of war."

Polo sneered. "You make your service sound so noble. From what I've learned it was far from noble. You abused and killed defenseless innocent civilians. What's more, you worked for a camp whose sole purpose was to exterminate thousands of innocent civilians, mostly Jews. Are you saying you're proud of this?"

"I had no control over the extermination. In the military you do what you're told to do. My job was to see to see that the detainees didn't abuse each other." I noted that Zweig was no longer denying he worked at Buchenwald.

"That may have been your job," I said, "but according to people who were there, that's not what you did. They say you were the abuser."

"I feel so defenseless. Where are these accusers? Let them say these things to my face. I am confident that you will not find anyone who will make such accusations to my face."

I was surprised that Marco was pursuing this. Especially since two of the accusers were dead. Besides, the U.S. has not prosecuted many war crimes cases. Usually we extradite such cases to Germany where they prosecute.

It seemed to me we had some pretty strong homicide cases we could prosecute. If we could convict on any one of them Zweig would probably die in prison before any extradition took place. I was surprised that Marco hadn't followed up on Zweig's statement about Gisela Miller's death in the pond. He just went on without even accusing Heinrich of pushing her. I knew Zweig would deny it, but he had to be asked. Why was Marco avoiding this? Why was he focused on Zweig's activities in the camp when we had so little evidence, when we were more likely to convict Heinrich and Schmidt for the killings at Liberty Village and Lake George? The room went silent for a minute and I wondered where we were headed.

Then Marco said, "You mentioned the Miller woman dying in a pond at Liberty Village. Did you push her?"

Zweig's eyes looked like they were going to pop out of his head. He apparently thought he'd dodged this bullet. "Good Lord, why would you ask that?"

"Because she had accused you of being her camp guard at Buchenwald. I can see why you'd want to shut her up. You didn't answer my question. Did you push her or in some way make her fall into the pond?"

"No. Of course not. Yes, she mistook me for her guard at Buchenwald, but I knew it was a case of mistaken identity and just ignored her."

"Come now, Mr. Zweig. You've no longer denied being a guard at Buchenwald. Don't play games with us. Don't say it was a case of mistaken identity."

"Well perhaps it wasn't. Perhaps she did remember me, although I find that hard to believe after eight decades. I certainly don't look like I did then. How could she be sure?"

"It is a long time. However, as surprising as it may be, she did recognize you and you weren't happy about it. You had to do something about it, and you did."

"That's not true."

"Someone thinks she saw you hit her and then push her into the pond."

"I don't think so. No one could have seen me push her because—"

"Because it was early in the morning and as far you could tell, there was no one else around."

A hint of doubt crossed Zweig's face. He then said, "Because I didn't push her. Nobody could have seen me push her because I was not even near the pond that morning."

"If we ask your wife, will she verify that you never left your apartment that morning?"

"She should, though now she's probably annoyed with me. Who knows what she'll say?"

"Why would she be annoyed with you?"

"Because these accusations against me about being a guard during the war have forced us to move out of our comfortable lifestyle at Liberty Village. I suppose I can understand. I'm not happy about it either."

"If we ask your friend, Max Schmidt, if you killed Gisela Miller, what do you think he'll say?" Zweig closed his eyes for a few seconds before responding.

"We're old friends. I'm sure he'll say he knows I didn't kill that woman. Hey, this is getting out of hand. You're treating me as if I'm a killer. I'm an old man who just wants to enjoy his final years in peace. I'm not a killer."

"Oh please, Heinrich, don't play the naïve victim card. You killed people at Buchenwald and we're going to prove that you've killed people since then. You're old, but you're not this cuddly grandfather type you're pretending to be."

62

Max Schmidt was alone with his thoughts in his cell on the 23rd floor of the Federal Building in Manhattan at 26 Federal Plaza. The cell was not comfortable, but it was clean and a lot better than the barracks that had housed his charges at Buchenwald. He'd already had some food and drink and was not suffering. Heinrich Zweig was housed in a nearby cell. Half an hour ago Heinrich had been ushered out of his cell and taken away. Max didn't know where, but he suspected it was to be interrogated. Obviously, the FBI wanted to get testimony from each of them independently. Now Max was worried about what Heinrich would say. Would it contradict what he'd say when he was interrogated? Could he trust Heinrich? Probably not. But what would he say?

Would the FBI interrogators delve into what the two of them did as camp guards during the war? Or would the interrogators be more interested in the recent killings: two at Liberty Village and two at Lake George? If those recent killings were the law's primary concern, he, Max Schmidt would have less to worry about. Zweig was responsible for three of the killings. Robert and William killed the little girl with their bomb in the tent. Even that was on behalf of Heinrich. He, Max

Schmidt, wasn't home free, but he was in better shape than Heinrich was. Sure, as Heinrich's collaborator, he might bear some responsibility, but far less than Heinrich did as the primary perpetrator.

Why had he remained so close to Heinrich for all those years? They weren't at all similar. They didn't share the same interests. The only thing they had in common was the work they did back at Buchenwald. But even that experience was viewed differently by the two of them. He was ashamed of it now. Admittedly he wasn't then, but he had evolved. Heinrich hadn't. Heinrich was still proud of it. What the hell had kept them together? It wasn't even that he liked Zweig, because when he thought about it he didn't like Heinrich very much at all. Yes, they could share memories, but to Heinrich they were fond memories and to him they were memories he wished he could forget. The more he thought about Heinrich, the more he rued remaining friends with him. No doubt that superficial friendship was going to cause him the loss of his freedom. It had already resulted in the loss of his wife.

Good God. What an ass he had been. He'd never had much self-confidence. When he was younger, he'd always been a follower. He'd never been the one to step forward. He'd always left that to others. He'd been comfortable with that until now. And look where it got him. Probably a prison cell for the rest of his life.

Why had he taken Heidi for granted? Why had he always taken the easy way? The sad thing is, he'd taken the easy way even when he knew it was the wrong thing to do. If doing the right thing meant exerting himself, he always took the easy way. Face it, he was a lazy, spineless excuse for a man.

They were bringing Heinrich back to his cell. What had he told them? After the guard locked Heinrich back in his cell, Max saw that his 'friend' was looking at him. Their cells were only about 15 feet apart. Heinrich just stared, so he, Max, felt the need to say something. "How did it go?"

"They did some initial probing. Hoping I'd confess to being a war criminal and killing those people in Liberty Village and Lake George. Of course I gave them nothing. I'm sure they'll try to break you. They'll want to use what you say against me. Stay firm. They don't have that much. If we don't concede anything they may have to let us go or just give us a very light sentence. I'm not impressed with American law enforcement. Oh, I'm sure they'll take another crack at me after they talk to you, so don't give them anything. Remember, Max, whatever you give them affects both of us."

63

"Mr. Schmidt," said Polo, "Do you consider yourself a war criminal?"

"Of course not. Why do you ask such a question?"

"Because, we have reason to believe that when you were a guard at Buchenwald, you abused some of your prisoners."

Max felt fairly confident he could deflect this. As far as he knew there was no one around who could testify against him. "You say you have reason to believe this. Where does this come from? Why do you make such accusations?"

"Because you are a known affiliate of Heinrich Zweig and we have good reason to believe he abused his prisoners. We have statements to that effect from his victims. Since you and he worked together, it is logical that you would do many of the things he did. Are you denying this?"

"I knew Mr. Zweig at Buchenwald but I did not abuse the people under my care."

"Come now, Mr. Schmidt. Under your care? These were prisoners destined to be executed. They were not under your care. You were not a physician or a nurse. You were a prison guard. We all know what happened to many of your prisoners. You were not some caring individual concerned with their wellbeing."

"Yes, I suppose I knew how many of them would end up. Still, I tried not to make it too difficult for them when I could. I did not enjoy seeing them suffer. I did not enjoy knowing what was likely going to happen to them."

"But didn't you believe that you were at war and that Jews and other non-Aryans were your enemies?"

"Well, yes, I suppose I did at the time. We all did. Many Germans did at the time."

"But you killed elderly Jews. You killed women and children. How could you believe they were your enemies?"

"We believed that the elderly ones had conspired against us. We believed that the women brought more Jews into the world to be our enemies in the future. We believed that the children would soon become our enemies. It was better to deal with all of them before they could cause more trouble. But as much as I felt this way, I didn't have the heart to harm them, to cause them pain. I could see that they were human beings who themselves were suffering."

"Are you saying you were kind to them?"

"No, I was not exactly kind to them, but I didn't enjoy abusing them."

"Then you did abuse them?"

"I wouldn't put it that way. I did what had to be done. I did what was expected of a guard. It was sometimes a bit harsh, but I didn't go out of my way to make them suffer. I could see that they were suffering enough."

"So," said Marco, "You were cruel, but not as cruel as you could have been."

"That's not what I'm saying."

"That's exactly what it sounds like you're saying. Okay, let's leave that for a moment. Let's move to the present. Did you and Heinrich Zweig conspire to kill Gisela Miller?"

"Absolutely not. Why would you even say such a thing?"

"Because there is evidence that your friend Heinrich Zweig may have done this and, as I said, you are friends—going back a long way.

"I don't believe he did this, and I had nothing to do with it no matter who did it."

"You don't think your friend could have done this?"

"No. He was harsh back in the camp, but that was during the war. This is peacetime. I would hope that he wouldn't kill someone just because she said he reminded her of a bad experience in the camp. This is peacetime. Still, I'm so conflicted by all this. Heinrich is different. Often in the wrong way."

"But you don't think he could have killed Joe Avila?"

"My God, this is terrible. You can't accuse a man of murder just because he was a German soldier eighty years ago."

"He wasn't a German infantryman," clarified Polo. "He was Nazi SS at Buchenwald. You were, too. So let's not make him out to be the innocent World War II veteran. Let's not make you out to be a saint either."

"I'm not a saint, but I didn't conspire to kill Gisela Miller. I didn't kill Avila, either."

"But you knew Zweig was going to kill Avila, didn't you?"

Schmidt drew in a deep breath. It was important that he offer up a good answer here. "I knew that Avila had a big mouth and that Heinrich felt that he talked too much. That's not saying I thought he'd kill the guy. A lot of people with big mouths can be annoying. You don't kill them because they annoy you."

"That's really not an answer to my question. Did you know that Heinrich Zweig was going to kill Joe Avila?"

"I knew he *wanted* to kill him."

"And you didn't warn Avila or call the police?"

"People say they could kill people all the time. Or they say they'd like to kill someone. It's not the same as saying *'I am going to kill so and so.'* Most of the time people are not serious."

"But you knew that your friend Heinrich Zweig was capable of killing. You knew that he'd killed before. Why didn't you take him seriously?"

"Because he says things like that all the time. He's got a helluva temper and I didn't want to provoke him if he wasn't serious. Then he'd kill me."

I decided to take a different approach with Schmidt. "Much of what you've said makes your friend Heinrich Zweig look bad. How does that make you feel? He's a friend of eight decades and you're saying things about him that could hurt him."

"We've known each other for eight decades, but to say that we're friends is a stretch."

"But you've done a lot of things together. Isn't that true?"

"Yes. I suppose we have."

"You, Heinrich, and your wives have done things together. Your children are married to each other. This is what friends and close families do, so you must be friends."

"On some level I suppose. Much of it comes from our having similar backgrounds and knowing each other for such long time. We were really forced to spend a lot of time together because of our backgrounds. But it's a stretch to say that we're close friends."

"But haven't you exchanged innermost secrets?"

"I suppose we have."

"Superficial friends don't do that."

"We have a very unusual friendship. Because we were both camp guards we've always had to stick together because we knew we weren't always going to be accepted."

"What you're saying then is that you have a friendship built on adversity?"

"I suppose you could say that."

"Then it must bother you that you've said things here that make your friend look bad. Things that might even help convict him. Does that bother you?"

"Not too much, frankly. I've put up with him for far too long."

"Aren't you afraid he'll say things against you?"

"I'm not afraid he will. I know he will. He doesn't have a loyal bone in his body. He wanted to kill my wife."

"He wanted to kill your wife? Why did he want to do that?"

"Because recently she had behaved erratically and unpredictably. Out of character. She knew of our background in the war and Heinrich was afraid she'd get so nervous she would begin blabbing to the authorities. At one point, when we were at the cabin, she secretly took the car, and we had no idea where she went. She eventually came back saying she just needed some air, but that kind of unpredictable behavior was too much for Heinrich. His way of dealing with difficult people was to eliminate them."

"Even his long-time friend's wife?"

"He never liked her anyway. You see, I'm fairly certain Heinrich is a sociopath. He only likes people for what they can do for him. He's incapable of true caring or compassion. He's admitted to me that empathy to him is only a word."

"Even if he didn't really like your wife, she was, after all, your wife. Didn't it bother him that he was planning to kill his friend's wife?"

"As I said, he didn't feel about people the way normal people do. People were only chess pieces to be moved around the chessboard of life. If they benefitted him, he would tolerate them. Hell, he was such a good actor that he'd even make it sound like he cared for them when he really didn't. By the way, I was never going to let him kill my wife."

"But you let it get so far. When were you going to stop him?"

"Very soon. I had to play it carefully, though because he's such a loose cannon. I had to be sure I *could* stop him. Frankly, I was hoping I could stop him and not bring attention to my wife and me. I am not the person I was during the war, but Nazi hunters don't care. I was hoping I could stop Heinrich without the law knowing it."

"When you say you hoped to stop him. What do you mean? You couldn't just tell him 'no' because you wouldn't expect that to stop him. What did you think you'd have to do to stop him from killing your wife?"

"That was the problem. I probably would have had to resort to some form of violence, and if I did, it would almost certainly bring in the law. The last thing I needed was to be in trouble with the law at this point in my life. I've avoided it since the end of the war, partly because of Heinrich's help, I suppose I should admit. That's what makes all of this so difficult. It's complicated. In many ways I owe Heinrich. I couldn't disrespect him, yet I didn't want him to kill Heidi. Believe me, this was not easy."

"In other words, while you disagreed with Heinrich in this instance, you still respected him and even felt you owed him something. Is that about right?"

"Yes. Yes. You do understand. You see why it was so difficult for me to give Heinrich a hard time when I owed so much to him."

"Let's see if I've got this correctly. Give us some examples of what you feel you owed Heinrich?"

"Over the years he helped us negotiate our entrance into Argentina and Uruguay. He helped us avoid detection by local authorities when we otherwise would have been sent back to Germany. Oh, I'm forgetting a very important thing. He helped us get into the United States."

"Why do you think he did these things?"

"Not because he cared about us. Not because we were friends. Of course on one level my being a friend helped because he knew me and frankly knew that I didn't like confrontation. In other words, I would do what he asked. He knew I would be useful to him—then and in the future. That was the way he thought. Still does." Schmidt went silent for a few seconds, then added, "There's no question that because I was so amenable to his demands, I helped him. Looking back now I regret that because I helped create a—"

I couldn't help but interrupt. "Create a monster."

"No," he said. "The more I think about, he already was a monster. I just made him worse."

"And yet," resumed Marco, "you helped him for decades, knowing this. Why did you continue helping him, knowing what a monster he was?"

"Because, despite that, our two families lived fairly comfortable lives. Face it, we were prisoners of our own past. When we were together, the four of us could be ourselves. Whenever we let others into our circle we had to be on our guard. That in itself was stressful. Knowing our past, I'm sure you understand that. Knowing how people in Europe and America viewed that past, it was always stressful and tiring to be on guard with people who didn't share our background."

"Okay," said Marco Polo, "Let's take a break."

64

When Max Schmidt had been taken back to his cell, Marco convened us without either prisoner being present.

"So folks, what do we know now that we didn't know before interrogating these two men? Are we any closer to a conviction?"

Marty Cohen, the Putnam County District Attorney spoke first.

"I don't know how much evidence we have against these guys as war criminals, but I think if we push, there's a good chance we can nail them for some of these recent homicides. If not Schmidt, almost certainly Zweig. Schmidt is obviously the weak link here. No doubt because he has at least a semblance of a conscience. I think if we push him he'll give us Zweig."

I said, "We can use what Jean Fullbright thinks she saw." Everyone turned to me when they heard this. I then went on, "She saw a man near Gisela Miller when Gisela was walking near the pond. The man had something in his hand. As if he were going to throw it. Then a vehicle passed in front of her. When the vehicle was gone Gisela was in the pond and the man was walking away. He made no attempt to help Gisela. Jean Fullbright thinks that the man must have pushed Gisela and that he may have first hit her with whatever it was he was holding. Here's where it gets more interesting. She recognized the guy. Thinks it may have been Heinrich Zweig, though she won't swear to it."

"It would be helpful if she could or would swear to it," said Cohen.

"By the way," said Marco, "Didn't Jean Fullbright at least attempt to help her friend?"

"She doesn't swim. She immediately called 911 and Liberty Village security, but by the time they arrived it was too late."

"Now that's too bad. In other words, if she could swim, her friend might still be alive."

"Maybe. The Miller woman might have already been dead by the time Jean Fullbright could have gotten to her, but maybe. Another good reason everyone should learn to swim."

"Okay then," said Cohen, "this could give us some leverage against Zweig. We can tell him that someone saw him push Gisela Miller into the pond after hitting her on the head with a hard object. Probably a rock. Maybe this will be enough to get him to cop to the killing."

"Maybe," I said, but Zweig is no dummy. He may demand to know who his accuser is, and Jean Fullbright isn't a hundred percent sure it was him. We can't expect her to testify it was him if she's not sure. But maybe Zweig will cop. He may be tired of running. Worth a try, but I wouldn't count on it.

Frankly, I think our best bet is Max Schmidt. I think he's finally had enough of Zweig's evil ways. You can tell by the way he was talking that he's fed up with Zweig. I think we can get something solid from him. Enough to convict Zweig."

"Okay," said Polo, "Let's take a one-hour break and then come back at Zweig. If any of you have any ideas we can use on him, let me know in the next few minutes."

65

Zweig's eyes looked tired. More tired than they'd looked when we'd interviewed him earlier. This was obviously taking a toll on him. It would on anyone, but it would no doubt take a bigger toll on someone in their mid-nineties. Polo had him brought into the interrogation room before any of the rest of us. He let Zweig sit there by himself for maybe five minutes before the rest of us filed in and took our seats. Most of us brought in coffee or some other beverage. When we were all assembled Zweig said, "Could I have a cup of coffee?"

Polo waited a few seconds before responding. Then he said to his office assistant, "Okay, Jenn, would you get Mr. Zweig some coffee."

A minute later, Marco began. "Heinrich Zweig did you kill Gisela Miller?"

"Absolutely not."

"Did you kill Joseph Avila?"

"Of course not. This is ridiculous."

"Did you kill a groundskeeper up in Assembly Point, New York, on Lake George?"

"Of course not."

"Did you arrange to have him killed?"

"I don't even know who you're talking about. I don't know any groundskeepers."

"Oh I think you do. His problem was that he was too friendly. Asked too many questions. You couldn't afford to have him around. You were afraid he'd ask questions about you and your friend Max Schmidt. If you didn't kill him, your young friends Robert Ocasio and William Horan did it for you."

"You can't prove any of this." As soon as Zweig said this, I knew we'd get him.

"Oh but we can. We now have Ocasio and Horan in custody. They'll talk if we cut them a deal."

I knew that we'd get nothing from Ocasio and Horan until they were here in New York at Federal Plaza where we could interrogate them. That could be another 24 hours. But Zweig didn't know they weren't here. He knew they were in custody and probably assumed we had them here in the FBI cells. I cleared my throat to catch Marco's attention. He looked at me and nodded.

I then said, "Now if you wanted to help us clarify all this, you might get better treatment than the actual perpetrators, even though these young guys did the deed for you. You help us get them, we take that into consideration when we recommend how you get treated."

Zweig thought for a moment, then said, "Robert and William might have misunderstood me when I said, *'This guy never stops talking. He asks too many questions. I wish he'd shut up.'* Maybe Robert and William felt that they were doing me a favor by shutting the poor man up. That certainly wasn't my intention. All I meant was that he was so friendly he was becoming annoying. I certainly didn't want the unfortunate soul to be killed."

"So you didn't actually ask the two young men to kill the groundskeeper?"

"Certainly not."

"Guess we'll have to ask them about what you just said. You're sure what you just said is accurate? You're sure you didn't actually ask or order them to get rid of the groundskeeper?"

"I'm sure. I just told them that I found the man to be annoying. I didn't ask them to do anything."

"You'd better hope that they confirm that. If they do, then you have nothing to worry about as far as the groundskeeper is concerned."

"However," said Marty Cohen, the Putnam County DA, "Even if Mr. Ocasio and Mr. Horan confirm what you just told us, you'll still have to answer for two other homicides: Gisela Miller and Joseph Avila."

"I'm sure you can't prove either of them," said Zweig cockily.

Cohen responded quickly. "What makes you so sure, Mr. Zweig?"

"I didn't kill either of those people. Why do you say I did?"

"Because both of them either said you reminded them of a brutal Nazi camp guard or said something of the sort. Not long after that they ended up dead."

"That's the best you've got? You know you don't have a case for either one of these unfortunate deaths. Somebody else killed these people, not me."

Unfortunately, Cohen knew we had no case and so did Polo. I knew Zweig was guilty, but I couldn't prove it either. Here we had apprehended two former Nazi camp guards. We were holding them for war crimes and at least three recent murders but we had no solid evidence to use against them. If a prosecutor didn't come up with actual charges soon, we'd have to release them knowing that Heinrich Zweig had intended to kill his friend's wife and maybe his own, too. We'd had 72 hours to come up with the charges. They'd already been in custody 20 hours. What if we released these war criminals and Zweig carried out his threats against the two spouses? If these guys got away with their crimes, that would be a crime in itself.

There was still a chance that Zweig and Schmidt could be extradited to Germany to stand trial for war crimes, but that was not an easy procedure.

The problem, of course, was that all of the witnesses to their war crimes were long dead. The one witness who'd survived the camp, Gisela Miller, was no longer living thanks to Heinrich Zweig. But we couldn't prove that because the only possible witness to her death was Jean Fullbright, and she wasn't sure. As far as we knew there was no witness to Joe Avila's death. As far as the groundskeeper's death was concerned, we had our choice of four possible killers: Either Zweig and Schmidt or Robert Ocasio and William Horan. We were convinced it was one pair or the other. Our best chance to narrow that down was for one pair or the other to rat on the other pair. But could we get that to happen in the next 52 hours? Ocasio and Horan were still not here at 26 Federal Plaza.

To make matters worse a court-appointed defense attorney turned up and met briefly with Zweig in another room. When they returned to the interrogation room the lawyer introduced himself as Jeremy Bright. Bright reminded us in the room that if we didn't charge Zweig and Schmidt in the next few hours we'd have to release our prisoners.

"You can't keep these two elderly gentlemen locked up without charges. And frankly it's hard to believe that you could come up with any legitimate charges against these men." I shook my head at this statement. How could this guy have formed any opinion about his new clients? He'd just met Zweig and he'd only been with him a few minutes. He hadn't even met Schmidt yet.

Polo ended the interrogation in frustration. Zweig smiled, knowing that the federal war crimes case was weak and that the Putnam County DA had no evidence he could use to prosecute the homicide cases. Obviously his new attorney had given him new confidence.

Polo said we'd meet next when Robert Ocasio and William Horan were brought in. He expected they'd be in his custody by noon tomorrow. Unless he heard otherwise, we should expect to meet tomorrow afternoon at one.

66

Joanna and I were enjoying bluefish on the stern deck of my aging Chris Craft. A fellow boat owner had brought in a few bluefish and not knowing what to do with all of them, shared a couple with us. Bluefish is an acquired taste. It has a strong flavor and either you like it, or you don't. Guess I should retract that part about the acquired taste. I'm not sure you can acquire the taste if you don't like it in the first place. But if you do like it, it goes down very nicely with a tasty IPA, which Joanna and I both enjoy.

We were well into our relaxing meal when she asked, "Are you close to putting these Nazis away for good?"

"I wish I could say we were. We all know they're guilty of war crimes and at least four homicides in recent weeks, but we can't prove any of it."

"Why is that?"

"Well the war crimes went down decades ago during World War II. Not many witnesses alive to testify. The one witness we had, Gisela Miller, was just killed. She was a resident of Liberty Village. We're almost certain she was killed by Heinrich Zweig, but we have no evidence, and he won't cop to it."

"Weren't there three other homicides recently that you think this Zweig guy did?"

"Yes. One was another Liberty Village resident. Almost certainly murdered by Zweig, but no witnesses. No evidence. The third was a groundskeeper up in Lake George. We think he was either killed by Zweig and the other Nazi, Max Schmidt or two young white supremacists they had working for them. And the fourth was a young girl these bastards blew up. She and her family were camping in a state campground on the lake. To distract us from following the Nazis and their two young white supremacists, the two young guys planted a bomb and this girl died. This is the one homicide I'm fairly certain we can nail these guys for. I actually saw one of the young white supremacists place the bomb next to the tent and Mrs. Zweig did too. She was in the car with me. In fact, Mrs. Schmidt's son was with us also. So we have three witnesses to that murder. What we don't have is solid evidence against our two Nazis for any of their crimes. This is a very frustrating case because we know these guys are guilty of so many crimes, yet we can't prove it. It'll kill me if Marco or DA Cohen has to let 'em go on the murder charges."

"You'll find something."

"We're running out of time. We only have a couple days to find something. Unless one of these old Nazis tries to bargain for something, I don't like our chances."

"What about the wives? They've been with these guys for three-quarters of a century. They must know something?"

"Oh they do and I think we can get them to testify."

"Even though as spouses they don't have to?"

"They don't have to, but they can if they want to. I think they want to. If they hesitate it's because they feel they won't be able to face their friends at Liberty Village. Or they'll fear that their husbands will kill them."

Joanna then asked, "Won't it be difficult for them at Liberty Village whether they testify or not? Either way their friends will associate them with Nazis and killers."

"True, but it will be even worse if by testifying it makes them look like they knew all along how bad their husbands were. Frankly, I don't think they acquired many friends at Liberty. Their husbands discouraged socializing with others because they feared that sooner or later their past would leak out. They kept a firm hand on their wives. These were not marriages made in heaven. I'm counting on the wives finally being so fed up with their husbands that they see this as their chance to get even after all these decades."

"But won't they have to come forward in the next day or so?"

"Yes. If they don't, I think we're going to have to try to persuade them to come in and make a statement. We need them badly. This is nerve wracking as hell."

"What if you can't talk them into talking? Do you have to let these guys go?"

"Well, we still have the two white supremacists. They should be in FBI custody later today or tomorrow at the latest.

As I said, I actually saw one of them place the bomb near the tent in the campground. So we can nail one of them. Maybe both of them. If we can get them to say they were ordered to do that by Zweig and Schmidt we can nail them for one murder. So we have two chances to get these guys. Neither chance is guaranteed, but I'm optimistic.

67

Heinrich Zweig looked even more tired than the last time he was in the interrogation room. Marco Polo turned to me and said, "Agent Dantry, I believe you have something you need to say before we proceed."

"I'm sorry to say I do. Mr. Zweig we have just learned that your wife and Mrs. Schmidt, while on their way here to be interviewed, have met with an unfortunate automobile accident." Upon hearing this Zweig seemed to awaken from his state of fatigue.

"How is she? Is my wife injured? Is she alive?"

"She's alive, but apparently she has a concussion and is now in a coma. Mrs. Schmidt was also injured, but in a different way. She seems to be suffering from a stroke and can't communicate clearly. It was a serious accident. They're lucky they survived it. I'm sorry to have to tell you this."

As Zweig processed this news his face broke into a smile. He quickly erased the smile and said, "This is terrible. What is my wife's prognosis?"

I said, "They're hoping she'll come out of the coma, but they can't promise it. Her injury was so severe that they said she may remain in the coma for months or even longer." I paused for a moment to see what he was going to say. When he said nothing, I went on. "I imagine you view this as good news?"

"Why would you say that?"

"Because I have reason to believe that you intended to kill Mrs. Schmidt and your wife too."

"That's ridiculous! Where in the world did you get that idea?"

"From Max Schmidt, your friend of more than seven decades."

"Max must be confused. He's been confused lately. Old age, you know" He grinned as he said this. "It affects all of us eventually."

"We don't need Mr. Schmidt's testimony. We have yours."

"What do you mean? You couldn't have my testimony."

"When I told you about your wife's concussion you smiled. That is not the reaction of a loving husband."

"I'm sure it wasn't a smile. Probably a nervous reaction to some very bad news."

"By the way, you probably didn't know that your wife, Doreen, had just agreed to testify against you about the two murders at Liberty Village."

"How could she testify about them? I never told her—. I mean how would she know anything about them?"

"You never told her about how you killed these people. Is that what you started to say?"

"No. That's not what I'm saying. What I'm trying to say is that I never told her what I'd heard about these killings.

Doreen didn't get out much, so I had to keep her up-to-date on things. I'm sure I never told her about those awful murders. It would have upset her too much." Zweig seemed much more relaxed now than when he'd been brought into the room a few minutes ago. It was as if a great burden had been lifted from his shoulders. He now leaned back in his chair and stretched his arms out, seemingly totally relaxed.

I asked, "Are you comfortable?"

"Yes, I suppose I am, considering the fact that I'm being interrogated. How much longer are you going to hold me here? You have nothing against me. And obviously you have nobody who can testify against me."

"You mean now that your wife and Max Schmidt's wife are unable to communicate?"

"That's not what I meant. I meant that since I have done no wrong, there is no one who could testify against me because there was nothing to testify about."

"Are you saying that in the decades you and your wife have been married, you've done nothing wrong?"

"Nothing that would merit my being arrested. By the way, I intend to file a complaint against the FBI and the District Attorney of Putnam County for false arrest and defamation of my reputation or whatever the correct term is when you hurt someone's reputation."

"Now that's funny. That should be interesting since your reputation as a Nazi war criminal has been with you all your adult life. Long before the FBI or police even became aware of you. Not only do you have your history as a war criminal to contend with, you still have to contend with four recent homicides. You've been a busy man, Heinrich."

"And where is your proof? Where are your witnesses?"

"Why would an innocent man even care about witnesses?"

"Of course I don't care about them. Your accusations have got me flustered."

"Speaking of witnesses, I myself saw one of your young friends place a bomb near a tent where a young girl was killed."

"He never intended to kill anybody. He only meant it as a distraction."

"Why did he want a distraction? Why were you all trying to get away from us?"

"Why were you chasing us? You made us very nervous. We saw it as police harassment."

"That's the best you can do? You kill two innocent people and you say that the police who are coming after you are harassing you? You know perfectly well why we were after you. Those two murders at Liberty Village. If you were innocent, why did you leave in the middle of the night? Why did you tell your neighbors you were visiting relatives in Virginia and then head due north instead? This is not the behavior of an innocent person."

"As I look back I see that it was probably not the right move. Max and I knew that people were looking at us for the murders. I can understand why people might have thought we were the killers. We weren't, but Max and I have been fleeing from our background all our lives. We made some mistakes when we were young. We got caught up in the hysteria of the war. But since then we've tried to live exemplary lives. We talked to our wives and convinced them that it would be better if we left Liberty rather than face the embarrassment of being publicly investigated for two murders we didn't commit."

"That's a nice little speech," said Marty Cohen. "Not very convincing, though. We'll see how it holds up when Robert Ocasio and William Horan get here. They should be here soon. Let's see what they have to say about what you've done and what you've asked them to do."

Zweig said, "I'm sure they'll verify what I've told you." He wasn't at all sure what they'd say, as the last time he'd seen them they had taken off with his and Max's money and left them in the wilds of Vermont without even a car.

Polo then said, "Will they explain why they've been helping you? I can't wait to see why two perfect strangers would appear out of nowhere to help two Nazi war criminals get out of the country. They must be exemplary citizens."

"Well I suppose they are. Some young people play golf. Some play pickleball. Some gamble. Some chase women. These two men have dedicated their lives to helping people who are unfairly accused of crimes they didn't commit. So yes, I suppose they are exemplary citizens. Max and I are fortunate that these two young men have tried to help us." Zweig knew none of this was true, but he was playing for time, hoping

Robert and William would basically confirm what he was saying, as it would make them look a lot better than the truth did. Were they smart enough to pick up on his cues when they came together in the interrogation room? Would they even meet in the interrogation room or would Polo keep them separate? He had no idea, but he could only hope that they were half as clever as he was. Thank God he no longer had to worry about the two women. If Robert and William came through, he and Max could walk out of here as free men. He smiled at this thought, since he had never believed in God, but still referenced him in situations like this.

"If by helping, you mean they killed a young girl with explosives and they killed an innocent groundskeeper, then they are unique. I wouldn't say exemplary, though."

"They didn't intend to kill that girl. They thought nobody was in the tent. As for that groundskeeper, I have no idea who killed him, but it wasn't Robert or William. They're good young men." He had no trouble saying this with a straight face.

"We'll see what they have to say when they get here, which is any moment, I'm told."

68

William, Robert and their unnamed co-conspirator had been arrested in Vermont by the Vermont state police. They soon learned that they would be extradited to New York State—FBI headquarters in Manhattan to be precise. They knew that they were going to be linked to the two Nazi camp guards. They needed a strategy. One they could agree on.

Robert, William and their pal knew that being linked to Nazi war criminals was going to sink their boat. They had to come up with a story that made their helping of Zweig and Schmidt somewhat more tolerable or acceptable than the truth. Maybe clumsy and ill-advised, but not deliberately supportive of Naziism. They had to agree on their story before they were interrogated. If they could convince the various law enforcement agencies that they were well intentioned, but naïve young guys trying to help two innocent elderly men who were facing harassment and persecution, they might escape prosecution with slaps on the wrist. They all had to agree, though. If one of them broke ranks, they would all go down—and hard. Their problem was finding enough time together to work out such a strategy. They couldn't work out a strategy with lawmen nearby. Only Robert knew the real truth. Not only had he duped the two Nazi's, he'd also duped William and his other friend.

Since their arrest they'd been kept in separate cells. Robert knew the strategy he wanted all three of them to use, but it was difficult finding enough time together to discuss it with the other two. Only when they were being transported from Vermont to New York did a few opportunities arise where they could talk. When they stopped for food and for pit stops there were only momentary opportunities to discuss his plan, for the accompanying officers were fairly vigilant. It would have been nice to have an hour or so to go over their story, but they at least had agreed on something. Far better than going into an interrogation not knowing what the other guys were going to say. At least now Robert figured they were on the same page. Sort of anyway. Unfortunately, they hadn't had the chance to work out the details and the best language for explaining the position they'd agreed on.

Robert was not sure they could pull it off, as Zweig and Schmidt were certainly not going to support their view of what went down. It wasn't going to be easy convincing the FBI and the police that Robert, William and their friend were the victims here. Not after the three of them had taken the money from the two Nazis and then, to add insult to injury, had abandoned them in the remote reaches of Vermont. No, this was not going to be easy. Still, former Nazi camp guards were not popular, so maybe they had a chance. Heinrich Zweig in particular was hard to like. Just being in his presence made you cringe. Then again, maybe that was because Robert had his own reason for hating Zweig.

Robert was known for his baby face, even though inside he was hard as nails. His cherubic countenance attracted a lot of people. He was hoping he might win over the law enforcement people he was about to meet. It was his baby face against the faces of two known Nazi war criminals. Quite an encounter.

69

Marco Polo and Marty Cohen decided to interrogate Robert Ocasio, William Horan and their friend all at the same time. At least on the first examination. Interrogation of suspects took a lot of time, and this was not the only case Polo and Cohen had to deal with. Some would say that it made more sense to interrogate each suspect separately so that their stories could be compared later. Polo and Cohen felt confident that they could get to the truth this way and save themselves some time.

The three young men put on an air of confidence, but I sensed that they were inwardly nervous as hell. We in law enforcement were hoping that these three young suspects would turn on the two old Nazis in order to negotiate a lighter sentence for themselves. We were about to find out.

When all of us were assembled, Polo began. "The three of you belong to an organization that helps elderly Nazis and other German war criminals avoid prosecution. As I understand it, usually you help them by getting them out of the United States before law enforcement can get their hands on them. Have I got that about right?"

The room fell silent for over 30 seconds. Then Robert Ocasio said, "No, sir, that's not right. It's true that we work for an organization that helps veterans of wars achieve fair treatment, but these veterans are not war criminals. They are often persecuted as if they *were* war criminals, and that's why we help them. We help them avoid persecution and harassment."

"Are you saying that Heinrich Zweig and Max Schmidt have been persecuted and harassed for crimes they didn't commit?"

"Well yes, exactly."

"Can you tell me when and where they've been persecuted?"

"Well most recently at Liberty Village up in Putnam County. People looked at them as if they were criminals. People avoided them. People talked behind their backs. They were paying good money to be residents of this senior-living community and were treated like scum."

Polo smiled and shook his head in amazement at this defense he was hearing. "Are you telling us that the residents of Liberty Village had no legitimate grounds for shunning Mr. Zweig and Mr. Schmidt? That their records were free from all wrongdoing? That these two men lived innocent lives caring for their fellow human beings?"

"I'm not saying they were saints. Most people aren't, but they committed no crimes that warranted being shunned as you put it."

"Both of them worked as camp guards at Buchenwald, a terrible Nazi prison camp where thousands of truly innocent people were killed for no good reason. Both of the defendants have admitted they worked in that prison camp, so they are clearly not as innocent as you say they are."

"They may have worked there, but it doesn't mean they wanted to. They were ordered to work there. They had no choice."

"You don't know that. Maybe they wanted to work there. We know that they abused the prisoners. They even seemed to enjoy it."

"I don't see how you would know that they abused the detainees. Can you find anyone who will testify to that?"

"One of the victims has already told us how she and her family were abused. She even saw her sister killed by Heinrich Zweig."

"That's news to me. If she claims this, can we ask her a few questions? I find it strange that after all those years someone would suddenly make such accusations against an innocent old man."

"She can't answer any questions now because Zweig murdered her. That's the innocent old man you've been helping."

"I don't believe it. Not Heinrich. He wouldn't do such a thing."

"Oh he did it, and he's going to pay for it. That's the kindly old man you've been helping."

"I didn't say he was kindly. He's a little rough around the edges, but he's no killer."

"We're going to prove otherwise. And we're going to prove you knew exactly who he was and what he's done. If he's just rough around the edges, but no killer, why did you kill to protect him?"

"Whoa! What are you talking about? I didn't kill anybody. Where did this come from?"

"Agent Dantry here saw you plant a bomb next to a tent at a Lake George campsite. That bomb killed a little girl. If Zweig is such an innocent man, why would you plant a bomb to divert Agent Dantry and other law enforcement officers from arresting him?"

"It wasn't me. Agent Dantry must be mistaken. I've often been told I look like someone else. It definitely wasn't me."

"I've known Agent Dantry a long time and I've never known him to lie. You, however, have been helping two know war criminals. How long do you think your lies will hold up in court? If you help us nail Zweig and Schmidt I can put in a good word with the prosecution. They might go light on your sentence because of your cooperation. If, however, you want to continue to lie, take your chances. Oh, by the way, the FBI and the New York state police believe that you and your friend here also killed a groundskeeper up there in the Lake George area. Your future really doesn't look very good, so any cooperation might shorten your sentences somewhat. Every little bit helps."

Robert spoke quietly with William. After a couple minutes, Marco said what's your decision? Are you going to help us or do you want to take your chances with a jury?"

"We want a lawyer to advise us. Aren't we entitled to a lawyer?"

"You'll get a lawyer, but the offer will still stand. Cooperate or take your chances in court. If your lawyer is smart, he'll urge you to cooperate."

"You can't tell my lawyer what to do."

"No, I can't. I'm just telling you what I think. I'm giving you my advice. I've dealt with a lot of criminals and lawyers in my time. Frankly, from what we know about you, I almost hope you take your chances in court."

"Well, it's Agent Dantry's word against mine. As far as this groundskeeper thing, I think you're making it up. I don't know anything about a groundskeeper. Wouldn't know one if I saw one."

"I can't wait till you get your court-appointed lawyer. He's gonna love you."

70

The trial was being held in the Putnam County Courthouse in Carmel, New York. Putnam County is just north of Westchester County, but not nearly as wealthy as Westchester. DA Cohen decided to try Zweig and Schmidt first. After that he would try Ocasio, Horan and their co-conspirator pal.

Because of Heinrich Zweig's and Max Schmidt's records and because they were being accused of committing several homicides, they had not been granted bail. Consequently, Zweig and Schmidt had been held in jail cells in the Putnam County Courthouse building for several weeks.

When Zweig and Schmidt were ushered into the courtroom, they looked haggard and extremely pale. Jail wasn't good for the health of men in their mid-nineties.

DA Cohen's opening statement was brief and to the point.

"Ladies and gentlemen of the jury, Heinrich Zweig and Max Schmidt are accused of committing at least two homicides at the senior living facility here in Putnam County known as Liberty Village. They are also accused of aiding and abetting two other homicides

upstate in or around Lake George. When you look at them, these elderly men appear to be harmless. Certainly not killers. Ladies and gentlemen of the jury, please don't be fooled by their frail appearance. Yes, they are elderly, but certainly not too frail to kill. They do not look like they could commit violence, but violence is not new to them. Both of these men were camp guards at the Nazi concentration camp Buchenwald, one of the largest Nazi concentration camps. More than 56,000 innocent defenseless people died at Buchenwald.

Ladies and gentlemen of the jury, Heinrich Zweig and Max Schmidt have a history of violence. As this trial proceeds we shall prove that these men committed two of these murders and aided or encouraged two others."

The people in the courtroom began muttering among themselves.

Judge Henry Armstad gaveled the room to be quiet and then said, "Mr. Cohen, you may call your first witness."

Cohen said, "Thank you your honor."

Cohen surveyed the jury and then said, "The prosecution calls Robert Ocasio to the stand."

I was surprised at this. The last time we heard Ocasio he was singing the praises of Zweig and Schmidt. Why would DA Cohen want him as a witness for the prosecution? After Ocasio was sworn in, Cohen proceeded.

"Mr. Ocasio, what is your relationship to Mr. Zweig and Mr. Schmidt?"

"We're not related, sir."

I smiled. Was Robert Ocasio just being coy or was he not very smart?

Cohen didn't smile as he responded. "What I meant was how do you know these men? Are you friends or do you work for them?"

"I suppose you could say that I worked for them."

"In what capacity? What did you do for them?"

"I tried to help them get away from people who were harassing them. People who were persecuting them."

"Harassing them? Who was harassing them and what for?"

"The residents at that place where they were living. Liberty Village. Their fellow residents were accusing them of being Nazi war criminals. It was terrible."

"But," said Cohen, "weren't they?"

"No. That has not been proven. They were veterans of the second world war. Just like a lot of veterans."

"Are you saying that being a prison guard at Buchenwald was the same as being a soldier in the trenches?"

"Well yes. They were in the German army and that was their assignment. They did what they were ordered to do, like any soldier."

"You don't see a difference? A soldier in the infantry kills an armed soldier in the enemy's army. The people killed at

Buchenwald were not soldiers and they were not armed. They were defenseless civilians. Many of them were women and children. Surely you're not saying guards at Buchenwald were defending themselves from these helpless civilians?"

"First of all, who's saying that the defendants killed anybody? Secondly, it's my understanding that at the height of the war many Germans considered Jews to be the enemy."

"All Jews?"

"That's my understanding. So by killing them the Germans were killing the enemy. Not that there's any evidence that my clients killed anybody."

"Let me get this straight. You're saying that back in World War II, the German people considered all Jewish people to be their enemy?"

"Maybe not all Germans, but a great many of them. Yes, it's my understanding that they did."

"Even if the Jews weren't in some foreign military?"

"Yes. If you got rid of any of them, they couldn't join any military."

"How about the children? Are you saying that many Germans feared that the children would become enemy soldiers?"

"Objection!" barked Sean O'Reilly, attorney for Ocasio and Horan. "He's badgering the witness."

Cohen said, "Your Honor, in light of what Mr. Ocasio has told the court, I think my line of questioning is appropriate."

"I agree. Objection overruled. You may proceed."

Cohen continued. "Are you saying the German people condoned—er believed in killing Jewish children so they wouldn't become enemy soldiers?"

Ocasio seemed confused and took his time answering. "I wasn't there, obviously, but that's my understanding. Face it, it was a different time."

"So what you seem to be saying then is that when your clients killed people at Buchenwald, it was morally justified?"

"Your Honor, he's putting words in my mouth."

"I would suggest that you answer the question."

"Germany was fighting for its very survival. It was wartime and they had to do whatever would help them survive."

"It was a war they started against much of Europe. Later it was Great Britain. Then the U.S. and Russia. But while they were fighting all these countries they decided to attack some of their own citizens. Many of the Jews killed at Buchenwald were loyal German citizens. Where is the logic in that? Where is the morality? Again I ask you, was the slaughter of Jewish people at Buchenwald morally justified?"

"I'm not qualified to make that judgement. All I know is that many Germans considered the Jewish people to be a threat to them. But that doesn't matter anyway. My clients may have overseen detainees at Buchenwald, but they didn't kill anybody."

"How do you know that? You weren't even born then."

"I believe them when they tell me they didn't. Besides, there are no records that show that they did."

"As far as you know?"

"As far as I know. Besides, no one has ever accused them of killing anyone at Buchenwald."

"Now that's where you're wrong. At least one person has accused Heinrich Zweig of murder."

"Who is that?"

"Gisela Miller."

"Didn't she die recently?"

"Yes, she was killed by your client as a matter of fact."

Sean O'Reilly yelled, "Objection. Claim not in evidence."

"This has not been established," said Judge Armstad. "Please move on Mr. Cohen."

"I believe she told her husband that Mr. Zweig killed her sister at Buchenwald. I know for a fact she also told Agent Dantry. Both of these people will testify to this."

A haggard-looking Heinrich Zweig looked crestfallen on hearing this. His attorney, Sean O'Reilly, seemed taken aback. Clearly he hadn't done his homework. He'd just gotten the case and now realized that his clients hadn't told him everything he needed to know in order to present even a plausible defense.

O'Reilly faced the judge and said, "Your Honor, the defense requests a 24-hour recess. I need to confer with my clients."

"All right, but I expect this trial to move along from tomorrow on. I know you only recently acquired these clients, but the court calendar is too busy to grant many recesses of this length. I expect you to be prepared to proceed tomorrow."

"Yes, Your Honor. Thank you, Your Honor."

It seemed clear that Zweig's goose was cooked. It was only a matter of days before he would be convicted of at least one of the homicides he was accused of committing or abetting. Maybe not all four, but one would put him away for the rest of his life. The fate of Max Schmidt was a little uncertain, though. He certainly wasn't a boy scout, but as far as I knew, he had not been accused of murder. He might escape from Putnam County unscathed, though I had a feeling the federal government would either prosecute him and Zweig for war crimes or extradite them to Germany for trial there.

As these thoughts passed through my mind I watched as Zweig was ushered in handcuffs out of the courtroom and taken back to his cell. He looked terrible. He was not a happy camper. I was sure he knew what was in store for him. He'd avoided the law ever since he fled Germany near the end of the war decades ago. Now his past was finally going to catch up with him.

71

That night, relaxing with Joanna on my boat, I sipped at the only mixed drink I like, a margarita. Joanna and I hadn't seen much of each other lately, with my being in Upstate New York and Vermont for the last few days. It felt so good to be with her again. We weren't separated that much in our relationship. She worked at Hunter College during the day, and I usually worked at home or in the New York metro area. Most of the time, we were home at night. Being apart the last few days only strengthened our relationship. We really missed each other. Now, back together, we acted as if we'd been apart for a month. I got a big hug the minute I entered our apartment.

I'd taken the Chris Craft maybe a quarter of a mile out into the harbor so we could enjoy our time together without curious observers. I knew that after I'd taken a few sips of my margarita and she her chardonnay we'd end up snuggling. We didn't want to be on display when the boat was tied up to its mooring in the marina, but a quarter mile out was more than comfortable. We weren't kids, but at times we acted like two teenagers in love. I frankly hoped that that would never end.

But there was order to our teenage madness. Before we snuggled we wanted to catch up. She brought me up to date on the personnel problems that took up too much of her time managing the history department at the college. When she was finished, she said, "Enough about my last few days. You've been hunting war criminals and murders. Much more exciting. How's it been going?"

"It's kept me busy. I think we're about to convict at least one of our guys. They're both bad guys, but one of them is worse than the other. Believe it or not, even though we know he's guilty, we're having a hard time proving one of them killed anybody."

"Well if he didn't kill anybody, what did he do that makes you convinced he's a bad guy?"

"He was definitely a Nazi concentration camp guard, so it's not likely that he's a nice guy."

"That's interesting that you say that. I know virtually nothing about how these concentration guards were selected and how they were trained, but is it possible that some of them didn't want to be guards and were forced to work as guards? Maybe this man is one of them. Maybe he did nothing wrong."

"I've looked into this. I didn't know either. I've learned that when you were a member of the Waffen SS, which both of these guys were, they were pledged to loyalty to the SS and were not allowed to challenge where they were assigned. So it's possible this particular camp guard didn't want to be a guard, but had no choice. In fact that's exactly what he claims—that he had no choice, but we don't know if we believe him. He maintains that he didn't go out of his way to be tough with the prisoners but had to be fairly severe or he personally would have suffered. Said he had to be tougher on the prisoners when another guard was present because many of them were gung-ho abusers. If he didn't appear to be tough, he'd be reported and he'd be punished for being soft on the prisoners.

The gung-ho guards saw nothing morally wrong with abusing and killing Jews and other prisoners they found offensive. They, like many Germans at the time, were convinced that their economic problems were caused by the Jewish people. In short, Jews were the enemy and this enemy was like a cancer destroying their country. They had to be eliminated.

The *Weltanschauung,* or world view, of many Germans at the time led to the Nuremburg Race Laws of September 1935 that stripped Jews of their citizenship and made them merely subjects of the state. I know it's hard to believe, but this thinking at that time made it easy for camp guards to kill Jews. They saw nothing wrong with it. Maybe not all of the guards, but far too many of them."

"Sounds like you're saying that this particular guard may not have chosen to be cruel to the prisoners, but admits that he was cruel at times because he had no choice in the matter. Have I got that right?"

"Yes. That's about it. That's what he maintains anyway. We're not sure we believe him, but we have no proof that he's lying. The worst thing against him is that he's been friends with the one we know is bad. He's had chances to get away from this guy, but they still remain friends. Claims that despite his knowing the bad guy is bad, they've helped each other avoid arrest ever since they fled Germany many years ago. They've remained friends because their closeness and awareness of the past has helped them avoid law enforcement for decades.

"To be honest, he is a lot more likeable than the guy we know to be bad. The bad guy just gives you the creeps. Just emits evil. This guy is so bad that he wanted to kill his wife and his friend's wife because he was afraid they might turn him in. Would have done it, too, but we got to him first. Really nice guy."

"So," said Joanna, "are you going back up to Carmel tomorrow? I assume the trial will take a few days or even more."

"I think it'll take a few more days to get all the testimony in for the prosecution. I would guess no more than a week, but you never know. I'll be testifying for the prosecution either tomorrow or the next day as far as I can tell. Unless the defense comes up with a surprise angle, I don't see how the prosecution can lose. I don't think they can have many witnesses for the defense other than the wives and even they're hard to predict. Since they know their husbands planned to kill them, I don't see how the defense can use them as witnesses. This could wrap up fairly quickly. The more I think about it, the more I wonder what kind of a defense their attorney is going to come up with. He's going to have to be one creative lawyer."

"I'm no attorney, but I do know my history. I don't see these guys going free even if their lawyer does get them off for the murder charges. Won't they be tried separately for war crimes?"

"Yes. If not here in the States, but then overseas. If our federal government doesn't try them, they'll extradite them to Europe. Probably Germany where since the war that nation has tried to atone for what the Nazis did in World War II."

Joanna leaned closer with her glass of chardonnay in her hand and said, "Okay, enough of catching up. Give me a hug and ask Alexa to play our song."

"I knew what this meant. It meant it was time for a little intimacy. I was more than ready."

Five minutes later my cell phone rang. I shook my head from side to side, annoyed at the interruption. I slowly pulled away from Joanna. A very unwelcome interruption. Who the hell could be calling now?

72

"Agent Dantry, this is District Attorney Cohen's legal assistant, Danja Neef. The DA wanted me to let you know that there's been a surprise development in the Zweig and Schmidt case. Heinrich Zweig committed suicide in his cell less than two hours ago. Judge Armstad said he will still convene the court tomorrow at ten. Marty just wanted to give you a heads up." I was stunned.

"Thank you. Please tell the DA that I will be there." I could barely get the words out.

When I put the phone down Joanna saw the surprise on my face and said, "What happened? You look like you're in shock. Are you okay?"

"One of the two defendants just killed himself. Heinrich Zweig—the man I told you was the really bad guy. In my opinion a real psychopath or sociopath."

Joanna processed this for a minute before responding. Then she said, "If he really is a sociopath or psychopath, he's the last person you'd expect to take his own life. The thinking is that sociopaths are almost immune to suicide."

I said, "Immune to suicide? Like immune to a certain disease?"

"In a way, yes. Word is that psychopaths and sociopaths think so highly of themselves that they would never take their own life. I've read that they sometimes fake suicides to get sympathy or to make some kind of weird point, but they don't actually kill themselves. They usually think they're smarter than everyone around them and that they'll find a way to think their way out any problem they encounter."

"Well looks like this was one problem he couldn't think his way out of."

"Or maybe he's not really a sociopath or psychopath." She considered this a few seconds, then said, "Or maybe in his infinite sociopathic wisdom he saw that at this point in his life suicide was his kind of victory. You law-and-order guys didn't win."

"I suppose that could be it. If he knew there was enough evidence and testimony against him, he may have considered that killing himself was his way of beating the system once again."

Joanna thought for a moment, then asked, "Was there really enough evidence and possible testimony to convict him?"

"There wasn't a lot of evidence, but there was potential testimony that could have put him away. Both his wife and Max Schmidt's wife could have testified against him. That's why he wanted to kill them. Once they learned that Zweig intended to kill them, I doubt if any wifely loyalty still existed, if it ever had. Such a nice guy. Robert Ocasio and William

Horan could have testified against him. Especially if they thought they could bargain for lighter sentences for themselves. The very fact that they turned on him up in Vermont when Zweig thought they were leading him to safety, indicates that they had no respect for him and wanted to see him suffer. It's almost as if they had deliberately convinced him that they wanted to help him so that they could milk him for as much money as they could get and then turn on him just for the satisfaction of seeing him suffer. Zweig was not a nice guy, but Robert Ocasio and his buddy weren't so nice, either."

"Don't you wonder where Ocasio and Horan came from? Is this organization they claim to work for a real organization, or did these guys make it up so they could scam Zweig and Schmidt? It's supposedly an organization dedicated to helping former Nazis get out of the country in order to avoid arrest. It would seem to me, if this is a real organization and these guys worked for it, they would be as fanatically dedicated to the cause as they said they were when they got Zweig and Schmidt to pay for their services. They fact that Ocasio and Horan turned on the two Nazis suggests there is something we don't know about them."

"Wow!" I said. "You really do dig deep don't you? You've opened up something that never even occurred to me."

"Maybe, but if I have, what is it? If these guys are not zealous fanatics trying to help old Nazis, what is their motivation?"

73

The courtroom was deadly quiet as people filed in. The people in the room were shocked, though probably not saddened by the death of Heinrich Zweig. More likely the room was hushed because it would have been satisfying to see him convicted of at least one crime. A person that evil needed to meet justice. He needed to be convicted of homicide. He needed to be punished.

Yes, Max Schmidt was still on trial, but somehow he was not the personification of evil that Zweig was. He was a weak man who should be punished, but probably not as severely as Zweig deserved to be punished.

I was curious about Zweig's suicide. Was it really a suicide? Would the man really take his own life? If he didn't, then who killed him? And how? I needed to know exactly how it happened. And why, since it seemed obvious that he was going to be convicted of at least one murder within a matter of days? As far as I knew the only people who had access to the man were the guards and his own lawyer. Why would his lawyer kill him? Didn't make sense. The guards had access, but they were too obvious. They'd immediately be suspects. Besides, they would know that the guy was likely going to be convicted anyway.

It came down to suicide, but from what we knew, sociopaths generally didn't kill themselves, though they sometimes pretended to. Could this have been a fake suicide gone bad? I needed to know exactly how he died.

DA Cohen started the proceedings by telling us that Zweig had hanged himself from the upper crossbar of the steel bars in in his cell. He had used a bed sheet as the ligature. He'd moved a small stool into place and apparently kicked it away when he had the ligature tightly connected to the crossbar and his neck. This didn't seem like anything a killer could orchestrate. It certainly looked like suicide. Once again Zweig had eluded the law.

So the trial came down to Max Schmidt. Of course another trial would follow soon after. The trial of the three young guys who'd helped Zweig and Schmidt keep one or two steps ahead of the law.

74

The trial of Robert Ocasio and William Horan began just two weeks after the trial of Heinrich Zweig and Max Schmidt ended.

Heinrich Zweig, or course, was never convicted because he had taken his own life. The court did decide that Zweig had killed Gisela Miller when Zweig's wife, Doreen, testified in court that Heinrich had told her he did. Robert Ocasio did an about face in his testimony, saying in court that Zweig had bragged about eliminating both the Miller woman and Joe Avila. Even though Zweig was not convicted of murder and was not punished, it was important to the prosecution that a cause of death determination be made. The prosecution needed a determination that the cause of Gisela Miller's death was homicide so they could prosecute Max Schmidt. Schmidt was soon convicted of aiding and abetting Zweig even though a number of people felt that the evidence against Schmidt was rather thin.

Cohen began the Ocasio/Horan trial with his opening statement:

"Robert Ocasio and William Horan are accused of two homicides. These two men were supposedly working for Heinrich Zweig and Max Schmidt, allegedly for the purpose of helping them escape U.S. prosecution for two entirely different homicides. Ocasio and Horan convinced Zweig and Schmidt that they could flee the country and get into Canada with their help. Once Zweig and Schmidt reached Canada, Ocasio and Horan were supposedly going to arrange to fly Zweig and Schmidt to Europe under two aliases with falsified passports.

It turns out that Ocasio and Horan never intended to help the two Nazi men. Rather, they turned on their two elderly clients and left them at the very mercy of the law from which they were trying to flee.

Initially Robert Ocasio and William Horan had claimed that they worked for a secret organization that dedicated itself to helping Nazi war criminals flee the country when the law was in pursuit. They claimed that they and this secret organization had great respect for what the Nazis did during World War II.

However, it appears that all of this was not completely true. Yes, there was such secret organization—and yes, they had in the past worked for this organization. But this time these two men were not helping our two Nazis. This time they intended to hurt Heinrich Zweig.

You may wonder why? Why were these two men so keen on harming Heinrich Zweig? Well, it has come to our attention that Robert Ocasio is Heinrich Zweig's son. Robert Ocasio is the product of an infidelity on the part of Zweig some 42 years ago. It turns out that when the biological mother asked Zweig to support their child, Zweig rejected her request and avoided all contact with the woman. At first she was shocked and broken hearted because she had been led to believe, no doubt naively, that Zweig was in love with her.

Soon her shock turned to anger. She rued the day she'd ever met Heinrich Zweig. She began to live for revenge. She swore that someday she would find a way to make him pay. And not with money. She was long past money being the solution to her problems. For years she dreamed of finding some ingenious way of making him pay dearly. She wanted him to be far more inconvenienced than he would be if he shelled out money. It had to be some sort of Machiavellian punishment that would affect his lifestyle completely. It had to ruin his life.

She kept track of Zweig for four decades. Then, when she heard that he had been accused of being a Nazi war criminal at some senior-living facility in Putnam County, New York, and on top of that had recently committed two murders, she knew this was the time to strike. In a moment of weakness years ago she had confided to her son Robert that his father had never accepted him. She had never been able to control her anger and she regretted telling Robert, but it was too late now. Robert soon became zealous in keeping track of the father he'd never known. He was just as angry as his mother and just as eager to make Zweig pay.

When Robert learned that his hated father was now wanted for murder, he came up with an idea which he shared with his mother. She thought it was too dangerous and begged him not to pursue it, but he said he wanted to because he knew what she'd gone through because of this terrible man. She'd been hurt and so had he. He had no father to be proud of. He was just as eager as his mother was to teach Heinrich Zweig a lesson he'd never forget.

In short, Robert's plan was to claim that he worked for an organization that helped former Nazi soldiers get out of the country when the law was pursuing them. He said his friend William would help him. William adored Robert and would do anything for him.

Robert and William convinced Zweig and his wife Doreen to leave their apartment at Liberty Village and go north to Canada where the defendants said they could then get him to Europe so he could live free. Zweig agreed to this, but said he wanted to bring along a friend and his wife. That of course was Max and Heidi Schmidt. What the defendants didn't tell the Nazis was that they were going to abandon them in the wilds of Vermont without transportation or passports. The two Nazis in their mid-nineties would *be left in a helpless position in the middle of nowhere—15 miles from the nearest community and three miles from the nearest house.*

You could almost sympathize with Robert Ocasio and his mother, if they had just caused the two Nazis some serious inconvenience. After all, Heinrich Zweig turned out to be a terrible father and he was, after all, a Nazi war criminal. Not many people would shed a tear for Zweig if he was seriously inconvenienced. But Robert Ocasio and his friend, William Horan, clearly went too far. They went far beyond inconveniencing Heinrich Zweig. Far beyond humiliating him. To convince their Nazi victims that they would do anything to get them out of the country, they killed two people. This of course made them as bad as the two Nazis.

Ladies and gentlemen of the jury, as the trial proceeds, we will make the case for convicting Robert Ocasio and William Horan of first-degree murder."

Ocasio and Horan didn't learn from the trial of Zweig and Schmidt because they decided to keep the same defense attorney. Maybe it was because they were impressed by the way Sean O'Reilly handled the case, despite losing it, or because they had no clue as to how to choose a lawyer. In any event, O'Reilly had the case and he opened by saying, "Ladies and gentlemen of the jury, as we proceed, you will see that there is no evidence that shows in any way that my clients murdered anybody. You will also see that there are no witnesses to the murders in question, so while someone did commit these homicides, it will be clear that the killers are still at large."

When I heard this, I was shocked. Clearly O'Reilly didn't do his homework. If he had, he'd know that I had witnessed Robert Ocasio when he placed the bomb near the tent in that state campsite. The very bomb that killed that little girl. When I testify it will put a nail in Robert's coffin. I knew that DA Cohen was going to call on me. Surely O'Reilly had to know that I was going to testify. Why didn't he know what I was going to say about Robert and the bomb? Could he be so clueless? Could he be so incompetent? If he was that incompetent and clueless, he wouldn't offer a decent defense for his client, not that it bothered me because I knew Robert Ocasio was guilty. Still, I'd rarely seen such incompetence. Surely someone would have told O'Reilly that I'd witnessed the bombing. This was going to be an easy win for Cohen.

75

The shooter had accessed the roof of the three-story County Office Building without being seen. The shooter had patiently observed the comings and goings at the building and found that during the night and early in the morning the stairs to the roof were never used.

Just accessing the roof was easy. The hard part was getting the sniper rifle up there without it being seen. You obviously couldn't enter the building with a rifle. The shooter had wrapped 40 feet of sturdy wire in a tight circle under a dozen doughnuts in a Dunkin box and waited in the roof stairway until nightfall. Then the shooter had mounted the stairs, accessed the roof and unwound the wire down the outside of the building. The wire had a heavy hook that pulled the wire down to the ground.

When the shooter left the building the next morning the shooter saw that the wire was barely visible from the street or anywhere else for that matter. The next night the shooter attached the sniper rifle to the hook and hid it behind some bushes. The following day the shooter entered the building and waited for the opportunity to reach the roof unseen. So far, everything was going as planned. The shooter was coordinating the plan with the events at the trial being held in the County Courthouse next door. The shooter took pride in how well things were going. Even the sniper rifle was perfect. It was an SRS-A2 Covert sniper rifle famous because it was much shorter than any other sniper rifle. At only 27 inches, it was known for its accuracy and compactness. The shooter had chosen it because being so short in length, it was less likely that anyone would notice it behind the bushes. After the shooting, it didn't matter.

Today the shooter would pull the gun up with the wire and wait for the target to approach the courthouse. It had been a tiring, nerve-wracking few days, but if the target could be eliminated, it would all be worth it.

* * *

It was a bright, crisp day with low humidity. I had the feeling that today would clinch things in the trial of Robert Ocasio, William Horan and their buddy. Hopefully some day their missing partner in crime would be caught and face prosecution too. If Robert and William could be convicted now, it would still be a victory for justice.

I know, Robert had good reason to hate Heinrich Zweig, but he didn't have a good reason to kill that little girl or that innocent groundskeeper. His mother's feelings were hurt badly by Zweig and she seemed to have passed that hurt on rather successfully to her son. I know a lot of children have not been acknowledged by one of their parents, but you don't usually hear that they're willing to kill to get even with that deadbeat parent. Sometimes, if the missing parent has a pang of regret, the neglected offspring are even somewhat forgiving. Well, Heinrich Zweig apparently never repented, and his son never forgave.

I've encountered a lot of scumbags in my days, but seldom have I run into such a nest of bad guys as this collection.

As I strode briskly toward the courthouse, I ran into a couple people I knew. Said hello to a couple of them and nodded to a past acquaintance. I was less than ten yards from the entrance when it felt as if someone had bumped into me briskly. Almost as if it was intentional. Then a man near me said, "You're bleeding. It looks like you've been shot. Oh my God, it looks like you've been shot in the heart."

76

I knew I'd been hit. My left shoulder. He was right. I was bleeding and I felt woozy. A cop who was stationed outside the courthouse ran over and said, "Everybody step back. Get into the courthouse as quickly as you can. Someone's shooting." He then barked into his phone and said, "We need a bus at the courthouse. There's been a shooting."

The cop then turned to me and said, "Don't try to move. An ambulance is on its way. Did you see who shot you?"

I could barely make out the cop's face. I was in and out of consciousness. "No. Now that I think of it, I'm pretty sure I heard a gunshot somewhere. Whoever shot me was off in the distance."

"Well you're gonna be sore as hell for a while, but it looks to me like it missed your heart by about five or six inches. You know anybody who'd want you dead?"

I tried to concentrate on what he'd just said. "I've pissed off a lot of bad guys in my time. I work with the FBI. I was going to testify in a trial today. Looks like somebody doesn't want me to testify."

"Yeah, it does. I think the shot came from a higher elevation. Entered your shoulder at a downward angle. Only place that makes sense is the County Office Building over there." He pointed to the three-story white office building. He grabbed his phone and said, "I'm with a gunshot victim." He turned to me and asked, "What's your name?"

"Dantry. Tony Dantry" The cop said into his phone "Got that? Tony Dantry. Mr. Dantry is bleeding from the left shoulder. A bus is on the way. I think the shooter could be in the County Office Building. Probably on the roof. Can you get uniforms there ASAP?"

I was beginning to feel sleepy again. The cop yelled at me. "Hey, stay with me Dantry. Stay with me."

I woke up in a hospital bed. A nurse smiled at me and said, "You had a very close call, Mr. Dantry. Dr. Reed will be in in a minute to talk to you. Right now there's someone else waiting to see you."

Before I could ask who it was, Joanna entered the room and came to my bedside. She kissed me on the forehead and forced a smile. I could see she was concerned. For years we've kidded about the risks I take in my line of work. I've always laughed them off and she's tried not to sound as worried as she probably is.

"Now what have you gotten yourself into, Mr. White Knight?"

"Somebody didn't want me to testify, I guess. Only thing I can think of. How did you find me?"

"When you didn't come home last night I called the courthouse. Just got a security guard so I called the Carmel police and they told me what happened and that you were in the Putnam Hospital. I've been here most of the night. You were asleep. Now that you're awake we can talk, though you should probably get more sleep soon. I know this is a stupid question, but how do you feel?"

"Like crap. Shoulder's sore as hell. And I feel drained."

"Well, you are drained. Doctor says you lost a lot of blood. I see you're getting new blood now. Did you see who shot you?"

"No. Apparently it was someone on the roof of a neighboring building. I don't know how I know that, but somehow I do."

"Did you talk to anyone after you were shot?"

"I vaguely remember talking to a cop. Then things got pretty foggy. I still don't feel normal."

"You were shot, for God's sake, Tony. Thank God you're alive. The bullet only missed your heart by inches. I've already talked to the doctor."

"What did he say?"

As I said this Dr. Reed entered the room and said, "You're going to hear it from the horse's mouth. I'm Dr. Reed, Mr. Dantry. Your partner here is right. You are lucky to be alive. The bullet came from a high-powered rifle and passed clear through your shoulder. Missed your heart by about five inches. Fortunately, you should heal and be back to your normal self. It'll take some time, though. No heavy lifting or quick movements for a few months. You should be out of here later today, but only if you promise me you'll be very careful for a while. If you tear what I've done in there, it could be serious." He paused a moment, then added, "Frankly, I don't think you're going to do much for the next few days. I'd take it easy for a while. I'll give you some painkillers, but the sooner you can stop taking them the better."

"I probably won't take them. Don't want to get comfortable with them."

"You'll be fine if you take them for a day or two. You may need them. You won't get hooked that fast."

"Okay. We'll see." I didn't plan on taking them at all. I'd rather put up with a little pain than get hooked on some opioid.

When Reed had left, Joanna said, "I can tell, you'd rather suffer than take a pain killer."

"Probably. I've seen too many addicts."

"My macho man."

"No. It's not that. I just think it's too easy to rely on pain killers. A little pain reminds you that you're alive and is a good indicator of when you're healing." I smiled and said, "I wonder if the police have found the shooter. Have you seen any cops since you got here?"

"There's one in the hall. They put him here so that the shooter couldn't try to finish the job. I think he's the one who found you."

"I should talk to him."

"Do you want me to stay outside while you talk to him?"

"Definitely not. I'm a little groggy. Help me if you think I need it."

Joanna stepped out of the room. A minute later the officer came in followed by Joanna.

"Mr. Dantry, I'm officer Kelsy. We met yesterday, though you may not remember me."

"I remember your voice. I wasn't seeing too clearly. Do you know any more about the shooter?"

"I do, but are you up for another visitor?"

"It's getting a little crowded in here. Who's this other visitor?"

"FBI Special Agent Lopez. Says she knows you."

"Yes. Of course. We've worked together. Show her in, and thank you Officer Kelsy for helping me yesterday."

Maria Lopez entered the room with a big smile on her face. I introduced Officer Kelsy and Joanna to her and said, "Hey, good to see you."

"Likewise, partner. Wish it weren't for this. You had a close call." Then she turned to Joanna and said, "This really was a close one." Then she smiled and said, "This guy's a keeper."

Joanna grinned and said, "He is indeed."

Lopez then said, "We think we have a lead on the shooter. We'll know later today if things go as planned."

I said, "Who do you think it is?"

"Believe it or not we think it's Robert Ocasio's mother. If you testify, her son goes to prison."

"Wow!" I said. "Robert and his mother are one bitter, angry little family. First the mother is abandoned by Heinrich

Zweig after he knocks her up. This makes her so bitter she passes on her anger to her son. Robert then takes up the cause and plots to ruin Zweig's life, which he does rather brilliantly. He could have gotten away with it, but to convince Zweig he would do anything for him, he kills two innocent people, making him as bad as Zweig. He's not only morally bankrupt, but stupid, since he kills the little girl in front of a witness. I saw him do it. That's why he tried to kill me. What's another killing to a morally corrupt guy if he thinks it will get him off scot-free?"

"Well," said Lopez, "he's not going to get away with it. DA Cohen is asking for a delay of the trial until you're well enough to testify."

"Have they brought the mother in?"

"Not yet. She wasn't home. We're not sure the mother did it, but the fact that she hasn't been home since someone shot at you and she doesn't answer her cell phone makes her look good for this. That and the motive of getting her son off the hook. Right now the Carmel police, New York State police and the FBI are after her. She won't get far."

Joanna spoke up. "If she's as desperate as you think she is, isn't it possible she'll try again?

Officer Kelsy said, "Not as long as I'm here."

Joanna said, "I'm sure you'll handle it, but what happens after Tony leaves the hospital? What if she sneaks up on him and tries again—from close range this time. Maybe she's so frantic she's willing to risk getting caught so long as she gets Tony?"

"Hey guys," I said from my bed. "I can take care of myself."

"Right now," said Joanna, "you're not a hundred percent. Besides, if she takes you by surprise, it's hard to defend yourself. Maybe you can let the police keep an eye on you until they find her."

Officer Kelsy said, "I'll talk to my boss about that. We don't have a large force, so I can't promise he'll come up with somebody, but I'll definitely recommend it."

I said, "Thanks, but that isn't necessary."

Kelsy wasn't going to quit, "I'll see what can be done. I'm sure we can do something. By the way," he added as he nodded toward Joanna and me, "we should leave you two alone."

After everyone had cleared out, Joanna said, "You should accept help until they get this woman. You're super, but you're not Superman. If she sneaks up on you with a gun—"

"I know. If they come up with a babysitter, I won't fight it. Shouldn't be for long anyway. I'm sure they'll collar her soon." As I said this, there was a knock on the door. A nurse entered the room pulling an IV pole. She smiled at me and Joanna. "Gotta change the drip," she said. "Be just a minute. She then said to me, "You look comfortable, considering what you've been through. We'll take good care of you here."

"I won't be here much longer, but thanks for caring."

"Oh I care a lot." She then disconnected the drip I was getting and started to replace it with a new one."

I was curious. "The drip I'm getting is only half empty. Why are you replacing it with a new one?"

"Oh this is better stuff."

"That doesn't make sense to me. Better stuff? You mean you've been giving me stuff that's not very good?"

"That's not what I meant. You've had enough of that. You need this now?"

"Just what is this new stuff as you call it?"

"I have no idea. Doc ordered it, and I do what I'm told. Be patient. This'll only take a sec."

"Hold up a minute," said Joanna. "If the doctor ordered this for the drip, how did you know what to get? I'm sure he didn't go to the supplies and get it for you."

"Look, I just do what I'm told."

"You didn't answer my question. How did you know what kind of drip to use?"

"Look, you don't work here, so stay out of it."

"You should know," said Joanna, "what you're giving to Mr. Dantry. Is it antibiotics? Is it saline solution? What is it? I've never heard of a nurse who didn't know what she was administering."

"Look, we're very busy here. We just have to get things done. Now please butt out."

I said, "What's your name, nurse?"

"Angela. Now let me do my job and then I'll get out of your way."

"You're not doing anything yet," snapped Joanna. "I want to talk to the nurse who gave Tony the drip he's getting now." As she said this she came over to the bed and pulled the cord that called the nurse's station.

Angela was fuming. She was clearly annoyed that we were interfering with what she was doing. She seemed even more crazed by our interference than I would have expected. By now I had decided that she was either incompetent or was intentionally trying to hurt me. I was strongly leaning toward the latter. The woman was obviously hyped up on something. Either drugs or her own emotions. Again, I leaned toward the latter. If I hadn't been so groggy from my gunshot wound and the pain killers they were giving me I would have seen through Angela when she first came into the room.

It was now clear to me that Angela was not Angela. Angela was Robert Ocasio's mother, the woman who'd shot me yesterday. She was here now to finish the job. I reached over to grab her arm. Joanna got there first. She latched onto the woman's hand as she was in the process of connecting my IV to what was almost certainly a toxic drip.

"Tony," she said. "I've got it. Don't tear your stitches." Just as she said this, a real nurse entered the room.

"What's going on here?" When she saw the Ocasio woman she said, "Who are you and what are you doing here?"

The woman tried to make a dash for the door, but the nurse and Joanna blocked her way. "You're not going anywhere lady," said Joanna as the nurse went to the doorway to get Officer Kelsy. Just as she did this the door opened and Kelsy said, "There a problem in here?"

Within minutes we made it clear that the woman who was struggling to get free from Joanna was an attempted murderer.

Kelsy grabbed his phone and called for help. Then he asked us what had just happened. I explained quickly that the woman had tried to give me what I was sure was some kind of toxic IV drip. I said I was almost certain that the police would find that she was the one who'd shot me yesterday.

77

I would have preferred the deck of my Chris Craft, but the doc had told me not to stretch anything and take it easy until my stitches healed. So instead of relaxing with Joanna on my boat out in the harbor, we settled for our front porch overlooking Long Island Sound. We had a nice view of lights twinkling on Hart Island and Kings Point. The night was calm and so was I finally. The ripples in the water had a calming effect on me after what I'd gone through recently.

Joanna was enjoying a glass of Clos du Bois Chardonnay and I was happy with a can of IPA. We'd been sitting quietly for several minutes. We were comfortable in such situations. We didn't need to talk every minute. Finally, though, Joanna said, "How many Nazi war criminals do you think there are still living among us?"

"Not very many. Most of them have died out. There may be a few left, but not many. What surprised me was how Heinrich Zweig ended it. Didn't seem like the kind of man who would quit when the going got rough. He was an awful man, but he didn't seem like someone who would choose suicide."

"Maybe at his age he thought that was his best way to beat the system."

"Maybe," I said, "In any event, the world is a better place with him not in it. Unfortunately, the Nazis were not the last of the war criminals. Every generation there seems to be a new breed of evil somewhere in the world."

"Yes, just when it seems that things in the world have gotten better, some movement that seems to get its motivation from hate, rears its ugly head." She fell silent for a moment, then said, "Enough of this gloom and doom. My head isn't in the sand, but it's not healthy to focus on what's bad in the world all the time. If I could do something about it, I would, but most of the time I can't. Right now my goal is to get you better and I can't do it bemoaning all the evil in the world."

She reached over and held my hand. With my stitches, that was about all the intimacy I could handle at the moment, but it was enough to remind me what a lucky guy I was, even with the gunshot wound.

The end

Richard Scott is a retired editor, writer, and publisher, having been president and publisher of the David McKay Company and president and publisher of Fodor's Travel Publications. He's also been director of the Reader's Digest Educational Division and managing editor of *American Bookseller* and *Bookselling this Week*. In the 70s Mr. Scott was co-host with Isaac Asimov, Brendan Gill and Nat Hentoff of a nationally syndicated radio talk show called In Conversation. He lives in Peabody, Massachusetts.

Made in United States
North Haven, CT
27 April 2024